THE
COTTAGE

Lisa Stone lives in England, has 3 children, and has several books published under the pseudonym Cathy Glass, many of which have become best-sellers. This is her fifth Lisa Stone thriller.

Website: lisastonebooks.co.uk
Email: lisa@lisastonebooks.co.uk
❚ /lisastonebooks.co.uk
❚ @lisastonebooks

Books by Lisa Stone

The Darkness Within
Stalker
The Doctor
Taken

Books by Cathy Glass

True stories

Cut

The Silent Cry

Daddy's Little Princess

Nobody's Son

Cruel to Be Kind

The Night the Angels Came

A Long Way from Home

A Baby's Cry

The Saddest Girl in the World

Please Don't Take My Baby

Will You Love Me?

I Miss Mummy

Saving Danny

Girl Alone

Where Has Mummy Gone?

Damaged

Hidden

Mummy Told Me Not to Tell

Another Forgotten Child

The Child Bride

Can I Let You Go?

Finding Stevie

Innocent

Too Scared to Tell

A Terrible Secret

A Life Lost

Novels based on true stories
The Girl in the Mirror
My Dad's a Policeman
Run, Mummy, Run

Self-help guides
About Writing
Happy Kids
Happy Adults
Happy Mealtimes for Kids

THE
COTTAGE

LISA STONE

HarperCollins*Publishers*

HarperCollins*Publishers*
1 London Bridge Street,
London SE1 9GF

www.harpercollins.co.uk

HarperCollins*Publishers*
1st Floor, Watermarque Building, Ringsend Road
Dublin 4, Ireland

First published by HarperCollins*Publishers* 2021
3

A catalogue record for this book is available from the British Library

ISBN: 978-0-00-844597-3

This novel is entirely a work of fiction.
The names, characters and incidents portrayed in it are
the work of the author's imagination. Any resemblance to
actual persons, living or dead, events or localities is
entirely coincidental.

Typeset in Sabon by Palimpsest Book Production Ltd, Falkirk, Stirlingshire

Printed and bound in the UK by CPI Group (UK) Ltd, Croydon CR0 4YY

MIX
Paper from
responsible sources
FSC C007454
FSC
www.fsc.org

This book is produced from independently certified FSC™ paper to ensure
responsible forest management.
For more information visit: www.harpercollins.co.uk/green

A big thank you to my readers for all your wonderful comments and reviews. They are much appreciated. Thank you to my editors, Kathryn and Holly, my literary agent, Andrew, and all the team at HarperCollins.

Although this book is a work of fiction,
incredibly the basis of the story is true

ONE

There was something outside.

Jan was sure of it. Just as she'd been sure the evening before.

The living-room curtains were closed against the night sky, but on the other side of the window lay a small patio, and there was something lurking out there. She hadn't seen or heard it, but the dog on her lap certainly had. Tinder had been asleep, then his ears had pricked up as he'd raised his head. He was now staring at the curtain and growling, his pupils enlarged to black orbs. His behaviour was unsettling her even more.

Jan knew a dog's heightened sense of smell and hearing gave it an advantage over humans, so Tinder could smell and hear things she could not. There was something out there and the dog knew – something alive, ominous and threatening.

It had begun four nights ago. Jan had been sitting on the sofa in front of the television with Tinder on her lap, as they'd got into the habit of doing most nights. She stroked his soft, wavy fur and he slept peacefully. Then suddenly he was awake, on guard, making her start and a little bit afraid. Now it was happening again. There was just her and Tinder in the cottage, which was situated on the edge of Coleshaw Woods.

With her senses tingling and not taking her eyes from Tinder, Jan picked up the remote control and muted the television. She listened, straining into the silence. But there was nothing: no noise in or outside the cottage. Outside the air was still; it was a chilly but calm autumn night. Tinder was still on guard, staring menacingly at the curtains, ready to attack if necessary.

'It's OK,' Jan said quietly, stroking his back. 'There's nothing to be afraid of.' She felt she'd said it more for her own benefit than the dog's, although she wasn't reassured any more than Tinder appeared to be.

She continued to stroke his velvety fur, hoping he would return to sleep – he was only small, a lapdog, and if he settled then so would she, for it would mean that whatever was out there had gone and the danger had passed.

She'd never thought of herself as a dog-lover before moving into Ivy Cottage, but Tinder had come with the cottage and she found him rather cute. He was a Bichon Frise cross and looked like a little teddy bear with his button nose and light-brown fur. He was part of the tenancy agreement, a welcome one as it had turned out, or Jan would have been lonely. She'd taken a six-month let on the cottage at a very low rent in exchange for looking after the cottage and Tinder while the owner, Camile, worked abroad.

Jan had scarcely believed her good luck when the offer had arrived. It had come at exactly the right time and was just what she needed. She'd been made redundant from her job in retail management after a restructuring programme to save the company money. She'd started with them as a trainee on leaving college and had assumed it was a job for life, but she'd received one month's notice with the other employees they were letting go. Then two days later her long-term boyfriend, Danny, whom she'd been living with for five years, had announced he wasn't ready for commitment yet and asked her to move out.

2

'It's not your fault. I just need my own space,' he'd said.

'It took you long enough to figure that out!' she'd snapped, fighting back tears.

Devastated, and with her life in ruins, Jan had packed and moved in temporarily with her parents, storing the boxes of her belongings in their garage. Thirty years old next year, with no job and having been heartlessly dumped, Jan was at an all-time low. But then, while searching jobs and accommodation on the Internet, she'd come across the advertisement for Ivy Cottage. It seemed like fate. As if it was meant to be. A ridiculously low rent and a complete change of scene. It would give her time to recharge her batteries and think about what she wanted to do next and with the rest of her life. She might even find the inspiration to start that book she'd been meaning to write.

'Are you sure it's what you want?' her mother had asked anxiously when she'd told her of her plans. 'The cottage sounds very isolated and you'll be living there all alone.'

'I'm sure, and I'll have the dog to keep me company,' Jan had replied with a reassuring smile.

But it was at moments like this when she had doubts and thought her mother may have been right. Living on the edge of Coleshaw Woods was very different to living on the edge of a town or city. Here there were noises at night she wasn't accustomed to, and then deafening silence – the like of which you never got in the town. The cottage creaked with its own sounds and sometimes the wind whistled through the woods as though the trees were talking, whispering between themselves.

But she'd made the decision, signed the agreement, and wouldn't let the owner down. By daylight the woods and countryside were very different – appealing. The air smelt fresher than in the town and the country walks she went on with Tinder were invigorating. She had the time alone she needed to take stock and consider her future, wherever that might be.

3

It was when darkness fell that the atmosphere dramatically changed and she would have welcomed some company. But who was going to journey out here in winter? Her parents and friends worked, and it would mean them staying the weekend as it was too far for a day trip. She appreciated they had their own lives and commitments, and she didn't want to sound needy. It was a pity the let had been for the winter months, she thought, with the nights closing in earlier and earlier. Now the end of October, it was dark by five o'clock, even earlier if it had been overcast. A summer let would have been far more attractive.

Jan glanced at her phone. It was just gone eight o'clock, the same time it had happened the previous nights. But whatever was outside must have gone, for Tinder had lost interest. As she stroked him his eyes gradually closed and his head slowly relaxed, until it was resting on her leg again. She liked Tinder very much and she'd decided that when she left the cottage in five months' time and found a place of her own to live, she would have a small dog or cat. Or was that a cliché – a singleton and her pet in a flat?

Only Tinder's ears remained alert, twitching every so often as if part of him was listening while the rest of his body slept. Jan had noticed this before – that when he was sleeping his ears seemed to stay awake. Was he actually listening, she wondered, or was it instinct left over from evolution? When dogs had been wolves, before a line had become domesticated. At a time when his ancestors had been wild and feral, catching prey, but also liable to be preyed upon by bigger predators. They'd had to remain alert even when sleeping if they weren't to be eaten.

'Tinder,' she said softly, caressing the fur on his neck.

A moment passed, then he was suddenly awake, head up and wide-eyed. Not from her voice but from whatever was outside again. A chill ran up her spine. It was back and

4

Tinder's hackles were rising. Her heart began to beat faster. He was staring at the curtain ready to attack. Without warning, he jumped from her lap onto the back of the sofa and, barking furiously, pawed the curtains to be let out.

'Get down!' Jan said, picking him up. He would damage the curtain.

He struggled to be put down, then raced to the back door in the kitchen, where he began scuffing the floor in his frenzy to be let out. The same as he had the nights before when he'd heard something.

'No. Bad boy,' Jan said, going into the kitchen.

The previous night he hadn't come back for two hours and she'd been worried sick, thinking he was lost for good and she'd have to tell Camile. When he had come back he'd looked as though he'd learnt his lesson, and had been very pleased to see her, almost as if he'd had a nasty escape. But from what? A fox? Rats? A badger? Coming from the town, she had little idea.

He was frantically pawing the door and still barking. Jan had no choice but to let him out if he wasn't to do damage. As soon as she opened the back door he shot down the garden. It was a cold night with a faint crescent moon in a clear black sky. She could see Tinder at the very bottom of the garden, having chased something into the shrubbery. Something quite large that had quickly disappeared. Then he too disappeared, following it into the bushes that separated the garden from the woods.

'Shit,' Jan cursed. 'Tinder, come back now!' she shouted. 'Tinder!' But he'd gone. 'Tinder!'

Silence. She stood at the back door for a moment, listening, and then closed and locked it, hoping Tinder would return soon. She'd caught a glimpse of what was out there, a shadowy outline, before it had disappeared through the hedge. The previous nights she hadn't seen a thing. It was bigger than a fox or badger, though, and not that shape. Perhaps there were animals living in the woods that as a townie she wasn't familiar with.

And yet . . .

She shivered and moved away from the back door. In the second before it had disappeared, she could have sworn that instead of running on all fours as an animal would have done, it had stood on two legs as if human. Surely not.

TWO

But it wasn't big enough to be a person, Jan thought as she stood by the heater in the kitchen trying to get warm. And something in the way it had moved, its agility, said it was an animal, although she hadn't had much of a look. She needed to get a grip. Of course it would be an animal living in Coleshaw Woods. Pity she didn't have Tinder's fearlessness to follow it. She hoped he came back soon.

Checking she'd locked the back door, Jan made herself a mug of tea, then fed the electricity meter that was in the cupboard under the stairs. It was an old-style coin-operated meter that required pound coins to keep the power on. Camile had left instructions on this and other matters connected with the running of the cottage, and also some coins to keep Jan going until she had her own supply, which was thoughtful. However, not in the habit of having to feed a meter and failing to realize how quickly some appliances devoured electricity, the day after she'd moved in she'd been showering when all the lights had gone off and the shower had stopped working. Naked, wet and unnerved, she had groped her way downstairs to the hall where a torch hung on a hook. She had gingerly followed the torch beam to the cupboard under

7

the stairs and fed the meter. Now she checked it regularly to make sure it didn't happen again. Being plunged into darkness had spooked her.

Reassured the meter was topped up, Jan took her mug of tea into the living room, sat on the sofa and, listening out for Tinder's return, opened her laptop. Thank goodness the cottage had Wi-Fi and a mobile signal. It came from the local village, Merryless, so named because it had once had a merry-go-round that had been removed after a tragic accident that had resulted in a child's death. Apart from its sad history, the village was pretty but small, with a single grocery shop, a pub and a church. Although it was only a mile from the cottage, it felt much further away at night.

While Jan waited anxiously for Tinder to return, she decided she should put the time to good use and try to identify what was coming into the garden at night and causing her so much unease. If it had a name it wouldn't seem so menacing, she reasoned. Taking a sip of her tea, she typed *Large animals found in UK woods* into the search engine.

Deer, badgers, beavers, foxes, wild boar in some areas was the result. And *Scottish wildcat,* but she wasn't in Scotland.

She tried again, narrowing the search, and typed in: *What large animals live in Coleshaw Woods?*

The result showed foxes and badgers and then lots of smaller animals – squirrels, mice, voles. These were far too small. What she'd seen was much bigger. Perhaps the animal wasn't indigenous to these parts but had escaped from a zoo or private collection.

She typed: *What animals can walk upright?* into the search engine. A page came up with photographs of primates walking on their back legs. Kangaroos, bears and some lizards, she also learnt, occasionally went biped. It certainly wasn't a lizard or a kangaroo. She supposed it could have been a small bear or a monkey, or was she getting carried away?

Surely they wouldn't be able to survive in the woods? Unnerved and alone, her imagination was getting the better of her. Then a picture of a fox leaping over a fence appeared on the webpage and it looked familiar. As it stretched up into its leap, it was standing on its hind legs. Yes, of course. That was the most likely explanation. The dark shadow she'd seen was a leaping fox. If it came to the cottage again tomorrow, she'd be braver and go outside for a closer look.

Jan closed the webpage and was about to reply to an email when something hard hit the window. She jumped. What the hell! With her heart thumping wildly, she scrambled off the sofa, away from the window, and stared at the curtains, petrified, waiting for another sound. Silence. Then she heard Tinder's bark at the back door. Thank goodness. He was back. Had that noise been him? She rushed to let him in, then quickly closed and relocked the door. 'Good boy,' she said, kneeling to pet him. 'You're safe.'

As on the previous night, he was very pleased to see her, although he hadn't been away for long. He rubbed against her and licked her hands.

'What was it? A fox?' she asked him.

Tinder stared back uncomprehendingly.

Then she saw it – what looked like a flake of food lodged in the fur by his mouth. She picked it off and smelt it. It was cooked meat, possibly sausage. But she hadn't given him meat to eat. He had dry dog food and only that. Camile had been most specific in her instructions that this was the only food Tinder was allowed, as it gave him a properly balanced diet. She'd left a dozen large sealed bags of the dry dog food in the cupboard under the stairs, more than enough for six months. One scoop in the morning and one at five o'clock, she'd written. No titbits or leftovers, as they were bad for him.

Jan had followed her instructions exactly, so where had Tinder got cooked meat from?

Straightening, she glanced around. Not from the kitchen. The only meat was what Camile had left in the freezer. A dustbin? But there was only her bin out here, collected once a week, and it was supposed to be animal-proof. Added to which, she hadn't eaten meat – she was mostly vegetarian, occasionally eating fish, but that was all.

It crossed her mind that Tinder might have got the meat from another bin, but she dismissed that idea. He hadn't been gone long enough to make it to the village and back, and there were no other properties between Ivy Cottage and Merryless. Also, according to Camile, he never went that far. *You can let him off the lead if you go for a walk,* Camile had written in her notes. *He won't stray far.* But he had the night before.

Could he have got the cooked meat from the woods? Jan wondered. Was someone camping there? It was possible, she supposed. A homeless person or army cadets on a training exercise? Could that be it? They'd fed him, or he'd found their leftovers, or he'd been caught stealing their meal and they'd chased him off. That would explain why he'd landed with such force against the window. She couldn't think of any other explanation, yet there'd been no sign of a camp when she'd walked in the woods in daylight. But then again, she'd kept to the paths and the woods stretched for miles. It was at its most dense behind the cottage, so someone could be living in there.

'Come on,' she said, returning to the sofa. 'No more disappearing.'

THREE

Midwife Anne Long parked her Vauxhall Corsa outside 57 Booth Lane, switched off the car's headlights and cut the engine. She sat for a moment staring straight ahead, then with a resigned sigh got out. Going to the boot of her car, she took out what she needed. The rest of the equipment for the birth was already in the house.

At 4 a.m. the air was cold and the street deserted. Virtually all the other houses were in darkness, but not so Ian and Emma Jennings's. They were up and had been all night, timing Emma's contractions and texting Anne, until the contractions were five minutes apart and Anne had said she'd come.

She walked stoically up the short path, worried and preoccupied, then pressed the doorbell. Usually a birth was a joyous occasion, but not this one.

No one answered the door on the first ring and Anne's sense of foreboding increased. She pressed the bell again. They certainly wouldn't be asleep. Had something gone wrong already? She prayed not. Ian and Emma were a lovely couple in their late twenties and were having a home birth after their dreadful experience in hospital the last time when they'd lost their first baby. Emma had readily agreed to a home birth – she didn't want to go near a hospital again – and Anne had overseen her pregnancy.

The door finally opened and Ian Jennings looked at her with weary acceptance.

'Sorry, I was with Emma,' he said, his voice flat. 'Come in.' He took the cylinder of Entonox from her.

'Thank you.'

'Emma's in bed. I've put the waterproof cover on the mattress like you said.'

'Good. How are you both?' Anne asked as she followed Ian upstairs. He shrugged dejectedly. It was a stupid question, she thought. Of course they were both scared stiff and just wanted it over with. 'Shouldn't be too long now,' she added.

She went into the main bedroom. In contrast to the landing and hall it was dimly lit, the centre light turned right down. Emma was just visible on the other side of the room, propped up on a mountain of pillows, her blonde hair recently cut short.

'How are you doing?' Anne asked gently, going over.

'I'm scared,' Emma said.

'I know, love. I'll look after you.' Then to Ian, 'I'll need the light up while I examine Emma. You can turn it down again after.' She appreciated they wouldn't want the room bright for long. The less they saw the better. But she needed some light to do her job and deliver the baby.

'Light, please, Ian,' Anne said more firmly. He was standing in a daze, staring at his wife and still holding the cylinder of Entonox. 'You can put that down there, please.'

As if in a trance, he placed the cylinder by the bed and then went to the light switch and raised the lights a little.

'Right up, please, Ian,' Anne said.

Now she could see Emma's tired, worn, anxious face more clearly. Another contraction took hold and she grimaced in pain. 'Do you want gas and air?' Anne asked.

Emma nodded.

Anne took the mask from its sealed package and attached it to the cylinder, then placed the mask in Emma's hand. She waited while she took a few breaths. Ian stood still and quiet somewhere behind her. 'I can give you a shot of pethidine if you wish,' she said to Emma. 'It will be about twenty minutes before it takes effect.'

'Yes, please,' Emma said, her voice small and strained.

Anne opened her midwife's bag, prepared the injection and then gave Emma the shot in her thigh. Normally she wouldn't have offered pethidine this close to the birth unless the mother really wasn't coping with the pain. It could cause the mother to become unresponsive and affect the baby's breathing and first feed, but that wasn't an issue here. Emma could have whatever she needed just to get through the ordeal.

Now Emma was more comfortable, Anne took her pulse, blood pressure and temperature. They were all normal for a woman in the active stage of labour. Ian was standing passively to one side, not knowing what to do for the best.

'Come and hold your wife's hand while I examine her,' Anne told him.

With over twenty years' experience as a midwife, Anne knew that the men often needed more support than the woman giving birth, even when the birth went to plan and was straightforward, which this wasn't.

Taking a pair of sterile gloves from her bag, Anne went to the end of the bed and raised the sheet. She examined Emma internally and then covered her again. 'It will be at least another two hours, if not longer,' she said, peeling off her gloves.

Ian sighed and rubbed his forehead in anguish. He wasn't doing Emma any favours, Anne thought. His nervousness was contagious.

'Perhaps you could make me a cup of coffee?' she suggested. 'I didn't have time for one before I left.'

He crossed the room towards the door and on his way out dimmed the lights.

'It's better if he's occupied,' Anne told Emma, and sat in the chair by her bed.

Emma grimaced as another contraction took hold. Anne guided her hand to the mask, and Emma breathed in the gas and air.

'You're doing well,' Anne said reassuringly, rubbing her patient's arm. 'The pethidine will take effect soon.'

'I just want it over with,' Emma cried, a tear slipping down her cheek. 'We won't try again for another child.'

'I know, love. Just stay calm and take deep breaths. I'm here with you.'

'You won't leave, will you?' Emma asked anxiously.

'No, not until it's all over.'

Ian returned with the cup of coffee, then hovered, unsure of what to do next. 'Have we got everything we need for the birth?' Anne asked him.

'I think so,' he replied, glancing around.

Anne knew they had. While the light had been raised she'd seen the pile of towels, blanket, Moses basket, maternity pads, bags for rubbish and a plastic bucket. Compared to the equipment that filled some home-birthing rooms, this was the absolute minimum. No candles, soft music, TENS machine, birthing pool or piles of first-size baby clothes. They just had what was needed to get the baby out and gone.

'It'll be a while yet,' Anne said again, looking at Ian. 'You can go if you have something you want to do and I'll call you when it's time.'

'I'll stay,' he said, and sat in the chair on the other side of the bed. He took his wife's hand and pressed it to his cheek.

Anne's heart went out to them. They didn't deserve this. Emma grimaced as another contraction took hold. Ian helped her keep the mask on her face as she breathed in the gas

14

and air. Gradually the pethidine took effect and the pain became more manageable. Now all they could do was wait and let nature take its course.

Seated in the semi-darkness, Anne looked on as Ian held his wife's hand and passed her the mask each time she needed Entonox. She wasn't making much fuss, not really. The pethidine helped. The minutes ticked by as the contractions increased, and Anne stood and checked Emma's vital signs again. They were as they should be. But a few minutes later Emma let out a piercing scream.

'Raise the lights, please,' she told Ian, standing. 'I need to examine Emma.'

She quickly put on sterile gloves and lifted the bed cover. The baby was coming faster than she'd expected. The cervix was fully dilated. Emma screamed again.

'Bring a towel quickly,' Anne called to Ian. 'It's on its way.'

Ian rushed from his wife's side, brought back a towel and watched as Anne placed it beneath Emma. Just in time. The baby's head appeared. Emma screamed again, her cry so chilling and intense it seemed to come from the depths of her being, as if she were being torn apart.

'Push, love,' Anne said. 'Take a deep breath and push.'

Emma gulped in the air, gave a long, hard push and screamed as the baby tumbled out.

'Well done.'

'Don't look, Ian,' Anne said.

But it was too late. He was still by her side, now staring at the baby, his expression a mixture of awe and horror.

'Ian, go to your wife,' Anne instructed.

He remained where he was.

'Ian, now,' she said more firmly. 'Emma needs you.'

He turned, dazed, and went to her side. Enfolding her in his arms, they both wept openly.

Anne wiped the baby's face free of mucus, cut and clamped the umbilical cord, then carried it to where the towels were. Wiping its body, she wrapped it in a fresh towel and placed the bundle on its side in the Moses basket facing away from them.

'Is it alive?' Ian asked.

'No,' Anne said.

'Boy or girl?' Emma asked between sobs.

'Boy,' Anne replied. 'But you don't want to see it.'

Emma's sobs grew.

Anne returned to her patient and concentrated on delivering the placenta as Ian and Emma comforted each other. She checked the placenta was all there and then disposed of it in one of the rubbish bags, firmly tying the top. She checked Emma's vital signs again. They were normal. Neither of them looked at the Moses basket on the far side of the room where the infant remained quiet and motionless. Anne gathered together her equipment and returned it to her bag.

'I'll come back for these later,' she said to Ian, placing the cylinder and her midwife bag to one side. 'I expect Emma would like something to eat and drink now.'

Ian nodded dumbly.

'I'll be as quick as I can.'

Leaving the couple to their grief, Anne crossed the room to the Moses basket. She covered the baby with a blanket and then picked up the basket. She looked at Ian and Emma clinging tightly to each other, consumed by grief. Her heart clenched, but there was nothing more she could do here and she needed to go now. She dared not leave it any longer. She began towards the door.

'Anne,' Emma called through her tears.

She paused. Don't change your mind about seeing the baby, she thought. Just let me go. 'Yes?' she asked tentatively, keeping her back to the couple.

'We called him David,' Emma said. 'It means loved.'

'I'll remember,' Anne said, and continued out of the room, then carefully downstairs, the Moses basket at her side.

She quietly let herself out of the front door. It was nearly eight o'clock and households were on the move – dog-walkers, people beginning to leave the house for work. She pulled the blanket right up over the baby's face and hurried to her car.

Opening the rear door, she carefully placed the Moses basket on the back seat, uncovered the baby's face a little and secured the basket with the seatbelts. It wasn't ideal, but it would have to do.

She closed the rear door and got into the driver's seat, then started the engine. As she did a woman appeared at the upstairs window of the house next door. Anne went cold. Had she seen her leave with the Moses basket? It was possible, although she wouldn't have seen what was in it. When she returned to Ian and Emma's later she'd make sure they had their story straight. One slip of the tongue, one small inconsistency, could be their undoing.

FOUR

What the hell!

Jan's eyes shot open. Panic gripped her. She stared across the room. Where was she? A small crack of light showed between the gap in the curtains. Those weren't her curtains. This wasn't her bedroom. She sat bolt upright in bed and stared around.

Then she remembered. Of course this wasn't her bedroom. It was the bedroom in the cottage she was renting. Relief flooded through her.

She rested her head back on the pillows and waited for her pulse to settle. Judging from the light outside, it was morning. But what time was it? She reached for her phone. It was 9.10, later than she normally woke, but she hadn't gone to sleep until very late. And then she'd been plagued by nightmares in which someone or something had been chasing her through Coleshaw Woods. Even now she was awake she could remember the terror she'd felt as she'd run from the inescapable horror. She guessed it was hardly surprising she was sleeping badly after what had been happening all week. Tinder was downstairs, shut in the kitchen, now waiting for his breakfast. Camile didn't allow him on her bed, but if Jan was honest, she would have found his company reassuring.

A loud knock sounded on the front door, making her start. Someone was here at this time? It could have been the sound of the door knocker that had woken her with a start in the first place.

Getting out of bed, Jan pushed her feet into her slippers – all the floors in the cottage were stripped wood, making going barefoot uncomfortable and cold. She put on her dressing gown and went to the small casement window that overlooked the front. Parting the curtains, she looked out. How much braver she felt now it was daylight.

The autumn sun flickered between the trees. Looking down, she could see her car parked to the right of the cottage, but not the person at the front door, which was immediately beneath the window. She opened the window a little and called down, 'Hello! Who's there?'

The visitor stepped back into her line of vision. 'Oh Chris, it's you. You gave me a shock. I was asleep.'

'Sorry. I thought you'd be awake by now on a glorious day like this.'

'I should be, but I had a bad night,' Jan admitted.

'Sorry to hear that. I brought you some eggs,' Chris said, holding up a box of eggs. He lived in Merryless and kept chickens. 'Shall I leave them on the doorstep?'

'If you can wait while I put on some clothes, I'll make you a coffee,' Jan offered. Chris usually came in for a coffee when he visited.

'Sounds good, thanks.'

Jan closed the window and began dressing. She had met Christopher – or Chris, as he liked to be known – a few times since she'd moved in. A friend of Camile's, he called on her from time to time, ostensibly to check she had everything she needed. Jan suspected there was also an element of making

19

sure she was looking after the cottage and Tinder, which she didn't have a problem with. After all, Camile had entrusted her home and dog to a complete stranger.

Running a brush through her hair, Jan checked her face in the mirror. It would have to do. She liked Chris, but suspected he was more than just friends with Camile. Although he'd never said as much, she'd noticed a warmth creep into his voice whenever he spoke of her. But Jan liked his company and was grateful for it, especially now after the worries of the last few nights.

She went down the narrow cottage stairs, thinking she might ask him about the animals that inhabited the woods. He had lived in the village most of his life so knew the area well. He was an electrician by trade.

'Come in,' she said, smiling, as she opened the front door. The sunlight flooded into the small hall. 'It *is* a nice day. Are you not working?'

'It's Saturday,' he reminded her.

'Oh yes.' She laughed. 'I'm losing track of the days here.'

'Camile says the same when she's home for more than a week,' he said, following her to the living room. 'She usually goes into the village each day to buy a paper or something as part of her routine.'

'I get news alerts on my phone,' Jan said, and opened the living-room curtains.

'But you don't get the local gossip,' Chris pointed out with a smile.

'That's true.'

Chris opened the door to the kitchen and Tinder rushed to greet him, tail wagging.

'He'll be wanting his breakfast,' Jan said, joining Chris in the small kitchen.

She picked up Tinder's food bowl and scooped in a measure of dry dog food. Chris placed the box of eggs in the fridge.

He was at home here and knew where most things were from all the years he'd known Camile. Jan refreshed Tinder's water bowl and then filled the coffee machine. One thing she, Chris and Camile all had in common was their love of decent coffee.

'So, is everything OK here?' Chris asked, as he always did when he visited.

'Yes, fine, thanks.'

'You've got plenty of coins for the meter?'

She'd told him about her scare when she'd first moved in.

'Yes. I won't do that again. I keep plenty.'

'You can always phone me if you have a problem. You've got my mobile number.'

'Yes, thanks.' Camile had included Chris's contact details in her instructions, saying she should call him if she needed help with any matter in the cottage.

As Jan waited for the coffee to brew, Chris wandered into the living room, thrust his hands in his trouser pockets and gazed thoughtfully through the patio windows. 'The grass will need its final cut before winter,' he said. 'I can do it if you like.'

'That's kind of you, but Camile left instructions on how to work the lawn mower. I'll give it a go. The exercise will do me good.'

'OK, call me if the mower won't start. It can be temperamental in damp weather.'

'I will, thanks.'

Jan poured their coffees and added milk – just a splash for Chris, the way he liked it – then carried the mugs into the living room. The cottage was compact, quaint, and Camile's Royal Doulton mugs suited the décor perfectly.

'Thank you,' Chris said as Jan passed him his coffee.

Leaving the window, he settled in his usual armchair while Jan took the sofa. The living room, like the rest of the cottage, was furnished in the style of a country cottage with oak-wood furniture, white-emulsion walls and floral fabrics, giving it a tasteful but homely rustic feel in keeping with its age.

There was a few moments' silence as they sipped their coffees, then they both spoke together.

'You go first,' Jan said, with a laugh.

'I was just going to say, Camile sends her best wishes and hopes you have been able to do some writing.'

'Tell her I'm fine,' Jan said, slightly embarrassed. She'd confided in Camile in an email that she was hoping to write a novel during her stay at the cottage, but now wished she hadn't told her. It seemed a bit of a cliché and she hadn't produced anything except a few scribbled notes. Chris often passed on short messages from Camile, although he knew they had each other's mobile numbers and email addresses. Jan wondered if it was an excuse to visit her.

Tinder, having eaten half his breakfast now, barked to be let out. It was his routine to eat a little, go for a run, then return and finish his food. Jan went to the back door and let him out.

'I'll walk into the village later,' she said to Chris as she returned, making conversation. 'While the weather's good. I need some more milk.'

'Don't forget the store closes at six in winter,' Chris reminded her.

'I won't. I always make sure I'm back before it gets dark anyway.'

He smiled indulgently. 'It's fine. I've walked along Wood Lane plenty of times in the dark.'

'I know, but I take the car if there's any chance of it getting dark before I'm back.'

He smiled again. 'Nice coffee.'

'It's the same one Camile buys from the village store.' She paused. 'Chris, what animals live in the woods behind the cottage? Do you know?'

He stopped drinking his coffee and lowered his mug. 'The usual. Why?'

'I've never lived in the country before, so I don't really know what is usual.'

He was looking at her carefully. 'Grey squirrels, rats, mice, voles, birds.'

'No, I mean larger animals.'

'Why, have you seen something?' he asked.

'Not exactly. But Tinder hears something outside this window.' Without realizing it, she'd cupped her hands around her mug as if drawing warmth from it, although the cottage was heated.

'Like what?' Chris asked.

'I don't know, but something has been coming up to this window at night, after dark when the curtains are closed. Tinder hears it and gets very agitated to be let out. Last night I saw something disappear through the hedge at the bottom of the garden and into the woods. I don't know what it was, but it seemed quite large.' She stopped. She'd decided not to mention that she'd thought it could have walked on two legs because she'd more or less discounted that after seeing the picture of the leaping fox. Neither was she going to say that Tinder had arrived back with cooked meat on his fur. Sitting here with Chris in daylight, it sounded weird, as if she was becoming paranoid being alone in the cottage after dark.

'Perhaps it was a fox or badger,' Chris suggested, taking another sip of his coffee. 'Or it could be a dog or cat from the village. Occasionally they get lost and stray this far, but not often.'

'Has Camile ever mentioned anything to you?' Jan asked.

'She might have done, I really can't remember,' Chris replied easily. 'But it's nothing to worry about. Forest animals are hungry at this time of year. They get brave and approach houses looking for food when they wouldn't

23

normally, especially foxes. I have to keep my chickens cooped because of them.'

Jan nodded. 'Yes. We have foxes in the town. They've lost their fear of humans and can be seen in daylight foraging in bins. Some even go into people's homes.'

'But you didn't see whatever it was that came here?' Chris asked.

'No. It's a pity that motion-sensor light outside isn't working. It would light the patio.' She nodded to the window behind her.

'It stopped working some time ago,' Chris said. 'I don't think Camile used it, otherwise I would have taken a look at it for her.' He drank the last of his coffee.

'Would you like a refill?' Jan offered.

'No, I'd better be going. I've got a few jobs to do.' He stood and took his mug to the kitchen, placing it in the sink as he always did.

'I might email Camile and ask her if I can replace the light,' Jan said as she walked with Chris to the front door. 'Would you be able to do it if she agrees?'

'Yes, but speak to her first. As I said, she wasn't keen before.'

'OK.'

She watched him go and then closed the front door.

It seemed slightly odd that Camile wouldn't want the sensor light working, Jan thought as she returned to the living room. If nothing else, it would show the way to the dustbin in the dark. Having tripped over a couple of times, she now waited until daylight to take out the rubbish. She wasn't sure if she should contact Camile about replacing the light. Chris hadn't been very encouraging. But it would be useful to have it working.

Perhaps she could repair it herself, Jan wondered as she went into the kitchen and poured herself another coffee. There would be no harm in that, as it wouldn't cost Camile anything. She knew the basics – how to replace a bulb or fuse or spot where a wire had come loose. Her father had shown her. A loose wire could blow a fuse. It had happened to a lamp in the flat and she'd been the one to repair it. Yes, instead of contacting Camile she'd have a look at the sensor light first to see if she could work out what was wrong.

Setting down her mug in the kitchen, Jan exchanged her slippers for shoes and opened the back door. Tinder stayed on his rug. She stepped outside and felt the fresh air. Even in daylight she was reminded how countrified and isolated the cottage was. Bushes and trees on two sides and a dense wood at the bottom. It was quiet, with only the occasional chirp of an unseen bird or stirring of dry leaves. Camile had said the cottage had been built around 1830. Originally a tenanted farmhouse, it retained many of its original features, although the thatched roof had been replaced by slate tiles.

Jan stood on the stone patio and looked up at the sensor light. It was on the wall just above the living-room window. She'd seen it before but hadn't taken much notice. Now as she looked, she could see it was quite new. Why install a new sensor light and not use it? she thought. That was odd. Camile must have felt she needed it, and Chris had offered to look at it to see what was wrong, but she'd refused. It didn't make sense.

She couldn't see an electric cable running from the light, so logically that meant it went straight through the wall behind the light as it did on the sensor light at her parents' house.

Returning indoors, Jan took off her outdoor shoes and went upstairs. The cottage had two bedrooms. The main one at the front was Camile's and she'd cleared it out so Jan could use it. The second, a smaller bedroom, was at the rear of the cottage and Camile used it for storage. Jan had looked in when she'd first arrived but not since. There'd been no need to.

She went in. As well as a single bed, a small wardrobe and a chest of drawers, it was full of Camile's belongings, some from the main bedroom to make space for Jan. Clothes she didn't need were in sealed polythene bags on the bed, and the storage boxes on the floor seemed to contain books, photograph albums, old CDs, DVDs, china ornaments and other knick-knacks.

Jan carefully picked her way around the boxes to the window. The sensor light was just below it on the other side. However, the bed was pushed right up against the wall, so she couldn't see where the cable came in. She pulled the bed away from the wall and the junction box came into view. She squeezed into the space between the bed and the wall. She would need a screwdriver to take off the front of the box to get to the fuse. But then, as she took a closer look, she saw the on–off switch was set to off. Surely it couldn't be that simple? She flicked it on. Could it have accidentally got switched off when the bed had been pushed against the wall to make room for the boxes? But wouldn't Camile have checked that?

Jan went downstairs. The more likely explanation was that the light had broken and Camile had switched it off at source. Without bothering to change out of her slippers, Jan stepped outside and looked up at the light. She stared in amazement as the small infrared light flashed, suggesting it was working. The real test would come after dark. She'd check it as soon as the daylight faded, but now she had to go to the village shop for the milk she needed.

FIVE

Detective Constable Beth Mayes sat at her desk in the open-plan office at Coleshaw Police Station. It was Saturday and she was doing overtime alongside a few colleagues. With no major incident currently under investigation, most of the others were at home with their families. Beth was catching up with some administration work, form-filling and report-writing, which was mainly done online now and stored digitally.

The door to the office opened and closed behind her and then Detective Sergeant Bert Scrivener appeared at her side.

'A Mrs Angela Slater has just telephoned in,' he said, placing a report form in front of her. 'Can you follow it up, please? It's probably a misunderstanding, but it needs checking ASAP as it's about a baby. Mrs Slater says her neighbours Mr and Mrs Jennings had a baby, but it's disappeared, and the mother hasn't been seen for a while either.'

'Perhaps they're staying with relatives,' Beth suggested, feeling she was stating the obvious.

'Exactly. The PNC checks have come back negative so neither of them has been in trouble before. There are no children registered at that address and no child-protection issues. I'll leave it with you.'

As the DS left, Beth saved the file she'd been working on and picked up her desk phone. Drawing the report form towards her, she keyed in the telephone number for Mrs Slater. The phone was answered after a couple of rings. 'Mrs Angela Slater?'

'Speaking.'

'I'm Detective Constable Beth Mayes. You contacted Coleshaw Police Station earlier today.'

'Yes, I did indeed. I live at fifty-five Booth Lane. There's something very suspicious going on next door. Emma and Ian Jennings are the couple who live there, and they seemed very nice to begin with. Didn't make any noise and were polite when I spoke to them. She was expecting a baby and I think she's had it, but it's disappeared.' Beth could tell from the mounting excitement in her voice that Mrs Slater enjoyed a drama.

'Do you know for certain your neighbour has had the baby?' Beth asked as Mrs Slater paused for breath.

'As certain as I can be. She told me she was going to have a home birth because they'd had a bad experience in the hospital with their previous baby. It died. She used to talk to me, but then three months ago she stopped. Her husband used to speak to my husband, but he began avoiding us too. I can't think of anything I said that could have upset them. I've caught glimpses of her hanging out her washing, but that's all.'

'When was the baby due? Do you know?' Beth asked, making a note.

'Not for a few months, I thought. It must have come early. On Tuesday morning I was looking out of my bedroom window and I saw a woman leave with a Moses basket. It was about eight o'clock.'

'Did you see a baby?' Beth asked.

'No, the blanket was pulled right up over its face, which

struck me as odd. I mean, I wondered if it could breathe. From the way she was carrying the Moses basket – careful, like – I'm sure there was a baby in it. Then she spent some time strapping the basket into the back of her car. If it was empty you wouldn't bother, would you? Then, about two hours later, I saw her return without the baby or the basket. She was in their house for an hour. I think she's a nurse or midwife.'

'What makes you say that?' Beth asked.

'When she left the second time she was carrying a black bag like midwives use and an oxygen cylinder.'

'Perhaps Ian or Emma has a lung condition,' Beth suggested.

'Not when I used to talk to them. They were both very healthy. I remember Emma telling me she couldn't understand why she'd had such a damaged baby the first time as she was fit and well, and had done everything right, like taking iron tablets and not drinking alcohol. I told her sometimes these things happen and it wasn't her fault.'

'No, quite. When was the last time you saw them?'

'I haven't seen her this week, but he has been in and out a couple of times, carrying shopping.'

'Can you give me a description of the woman you saw leaving their house with the Moses basket?' Beth asked.

'She was around fifty, I guess. About five foot six inches tall, dark, chin-length hair, a bit on the dumpy side, like she could do with losing a few pounds.'

'And the car?' Beth asked as she wrote. 'Can you give me a description of that?'

'It was a grey Vauxhall Corsa. The only reason I know the make and model is because my sister has one the same. I didn't get the registration, but if I see it again, I'll make a note and call you.'

'Thank you, that would be helpful.'

'You're welcome,' Mrs Slater said. 'I mean, you hear of such strange things happening. I wondered if they'd sold their baby or maybe she was a surrogate mother. But that didn't seem to add up as she wanted the baby. They'd even chosen a name for it, David.'

'I suppose it could be ill and in hospital,' Beth suggested.

'I wondered that, but wouldn't the parents be with their baby if it was sick? I'm sure Emma's at home, and he's certainly in and out. Parents who have a sick baby usually stay with them in hospital. I know I did with mine. I never left her side.' Which Beth supposed was true.

'I'll look into it, thank you. You've been most helpful.'

'Will you be visiting them?' Mrs Slater asked.

'Yes.'

'What time? I'll arrange to be at home in case you need me.'

'That shouldn't be necessary, but thank you anyway. I have your phone number. I'll contact you if I need anything further.'

Beth wound up the conversation and Mrs Slater said a reluctant goodbye.

While Beth would certainly investigate the disappearance of the baby, she didn't share Mrs Slater's enthusiasm for it being a mystery with sinister undertones. The most likely explanation was that mother and baby were in hospital after a home delivery had developed complications. She would visit Mr and Mrs Jennings, but first she needed to check the register of births online.

Beth stayed at her computer and a few minutes later she had the information she was looking for. The birth of David Jennings hadn't been registered. But parents had forty-two days to register the birth of their baby, so there was still plenty of time.

Twenty minutes later Beth parked the unmarked police car in the road outside 57 Booth Lane. There was a car on the Jennings's driveway and a small window was open on the second floor, suggesting someone could be in. All the houses in the road were built in a similar 1980s terrace style with a driveway at the front just long enough to take a car. As Beth got out she glanced over at Number 55 where Mrs Slater lived. There was no sign of her, but Beth noted that if she stood at her front-bedroom window, she would have a good view of the Jennings's drive and the road outside. It was different on the other side, Number 59; their view was obstructed by a tree.

Beth went up the path of Number 57, pressed the doorbell and waited. No one answered, so she pressed it again, waited some more, and then the door opened.

'Mr Ian Jennings?' she said, showing her ID. He nodded. 'I'm Detective Constable Beth Mayes from Coleshaw CID.'

'Yes?' he asked sombrely.

'Can I come in?'

'Why? Is something the matter?'

'It would be better if we discussed it inside.'

He moved aside to let her in and closed the door. Of average height and build, Ian Jennings was dressed in blue jeans and a navy sweatshirt. His only distinguishing feature was his blond hair. Beth followed him into the living room, which was at the front of the house and minimally furnished, with a long sofa, television and bookcase. Beth saw there was no sign of any baby equipment.

'Is your wife Emma here?' Beth asked.

'She's resting upstairs. She's not well.'

'Oh dear, I am sorry. What's the matter with her?'

Ian hesitated. 'I don't mean to be rude, but why are you here?'

'We've received a phone call from a worried member of the public. I understand your wife was expecting a baby?'

He looked shocked. 'Yes, she was, but I don't understand what that has got to do with anyone else.' He was clearly

31

struggling to contain his emotions – a mixture of anger and upset, Beth thought.

'Has she had the baby?' Beth asked.

'Yes, but that's our business, surely?'

'Where is the baby now?'

'It was born dead,' he said bluntly, and his eyes filled.

'I am so sorry,' Beth said. 'Please accept my sincere condolences.'

Ian nodded stiffly.

'Will there be a post-mortem?' Beth asked. If the baby was full-term it was likely.

'I don't know. Why? The midwife took him away. We were too distraught to deal with it. We still are.' He wiped his hand over his eyes.

'I am sorry,' Beth said again. 'But you understand we have to follow up concerns like this from the public.'

'Like what?' Ian asked. He hadn't suggested they sit down and continued to face Beth across the room.

'If a baby is missing.'

'He's not missing. He's dead,' Ian said tearfully.

'I understand that now. If I could just go upstairs and see your wife, I'll be on my way.'

'Why do you want to see Emma?'

'So I can say I've seen her in my report, and to give her my condolences.'

'Report?' Ian questioned.

'It's procedure. I'll conclude my report by saying I've seen you both and close the file.'

'All right, this way,' he said. 'Sorry if I was rude. We've had a dreadful week, as you can imagine.'

'Yes.'

Beth followed Ian out of the living room and upstairs to the bedroom at the front of the house. The curtains were half open and Emma Jennings was dressed and lying on top of the bed.

'It's the police,' Ian said, going in first.

Emma immediately looked worried and heaved herself up the pillow as Ian went protectively to her side. The poor woman looked dreadful, Beth thought, with deathly pale skin and dark circles under her eyes. Beth was struck by how much she looked like her husband. She'd read that couples grew to resemble each other over time and here was a perfect example.

'I'm so sorry for your loss,' Beth said. Going over, she showed Emma her ID.

'I lost my baby,' she said in a small, pitiful voice. 'Why are you here?'

'We received a call from a member of the public who thought a baby had disappeared from this house.'

'It has,' Emma said, even more upset. 'He's gone and I'll never see him again.' Tears spilled onto her cheeks.

'I am sorry,' Beth said again. 'You understand why I had to check?'

'Yes.'

'I'll leave you then. Do you have everything you need?'

Emma nodded.

'Look after yourselves. I'll let myself out.'

Leaving Ian to comfort his distraught wife, Beth returned downstairs and left the house.

She felt very sorry for the couple – their grief was raw. But the mystery of the disappearing baby had been solved. There'd been no foul play, their baby had tragically been born dead. Of course the midwife would have covered its body with the blanket in the Moses basket while she'd carried it out, and then secured it on the rear seat of the car as she drove to the morgue. It was awfully sad, but it appeared no crime had been committed and in this respect Beth was pleased.

SIX

It shouldn't be this frigging difficult to start a lawn mower! Jan cursed.

Taking hold of the starter cord again, she summoned all her strength and gave it a sharp pull. The engine turned once, the cord sprang back into place, and then nothing.

'Bloody hell!'

Her right arm was aching from repeatedly pulling the starter cord, and now there was a strong smell of petrol! She'd probably flooded the engine, she thought, with all the attempts she'd been making to get it going. An electric lawn mower, like her parents had, would have been much easier. You just plugged it in and off you went. Chris had said Camile's mower could be temperamental in damp weather, but the weather wasn't damp. The day had stayed fine, which was why Jan had decided to cut the grass after she'd returned from the village store.

She pulled the cord again and the smell of petrol grew stronger. If she had flooded the engine, the only solution was to leave it to dry out. Then, if it still wouldn't start, she'd have to phone Chris, which might not be such a bad idea anyway.

She may as well put the time to good use while she waited,

she decided. Taking the rake from the shed, she began raking up fallen leaves. Tinder was indoors as he was scared of the lawn mower. Once she had a decent-sized pile of leaves, she scooped them up and dumped them on the compost heap, which was at the bottom of the garden to the left of the shed. The garden had a large central lawn flanked by borders of shrubs, so there wasn't much to do at this time of year. Camile had written in her notes that if Jan could cut the grass and clear up the leaves that would be great. She didn't think Camile would be impressed by her efforts so far to cut the grass, but then Jan had never had to do it before.

She continued raking leaves from the lawn, working her way down one side and then across the bottom. How different it was out here in daylight. Peaceful, idyllic – she felt at one with nature. As she cleared away the leaves from the hedge where the shadow had disappeared the evening before, she saw the gap it had gone through and track marks in the mud. There were a lot of prints merging together that could have belonged to anything but suggested there might be more than one animal, and that they had been coming into the garden for some time – not just the last four nights when Tinder had become spooked. The prints seemed rather large for foxes, but she could be wrong. It crossed Jan's mind that perhaps Camile had been encouraging them in by feeding them, although she was sure she would have included this in her detailed notes: *I feed the family of foxes so would you . . .*

Raking away the last of the leaves, Jan dumped them on the compost heap, put away the rake and returned to the lawn mower. Any excess petrol should have evaporated by now. One last try and then she'd give up and call Chris, although it was a bit late for him to come today. The sun would be setting soon, so it would be dark by the time he arrived, assuming he was free, of course.

Taking hold of the starter handle, Jan focused, took a deep breath and gave the cord a hefty pull – her very best and final effort. The cord snapped back into place as the engine fired and then amazingly spluttered into life. Success! The engine was running, but raggedly, as though it could cut out at any moment. Moving the lever on the handle, Jan increased the revs until it was running more smoothly, then, releasing the hand brake, she let the mower pull away. The roller was powered so no pushing was required. She began going up and down the lawn and soon found it quite satisfying. She could see why Camile preferred this type of mower. Once it had started it mowed the grass by itself. There was no pushing and no long electricity cable to avoid severing. All Jan had to do was steer it up and down and keep the lines straight.

The result was starting to look rather professional, she thought. She was pleased she'd persisted in getting the mower started without having to call Chris for help. It was another small accomplishment, giving her confidence a much-needed boost. Silly really, taking pride in cutting the grass, but losing her job and long-term partner in one go had damaged her confidence like nothing else had before. Now she was rebuilding it gradually, bit by bit, slowly adding to her achievements.

However, the mower was noisy, she had to admit; it blocked out any other sound. Little wonder Tinder preferred to stay indoors.

It was only when she stopped to empty the grass box that she heard it.

A noise, a rustle coming from the hedge behind her. She turned, but there was nothing to be seen at the bottom of the garden where the sound had come from. She remained where she was, listening and watching. Perhaps it was one of the foxes coming to investigate. In daylight? Chris had said they were hungry at this time of year and approached homes looking for food when they wouldn't normally. Or perhaps the noise of the lawn mower had disturbed them. But wouldn't they have been scared off like Tinder?

Slightly unsettled, Jan removed the grass box from the back of the lawn mower and emptied it onto the compost heap. As she shook it clear she heard the noise again. The shed was blocking her view. Moving quietly, she came out from beside it. The garden was empty. She went over and looked at the gap in the hedge where the track marks had been. Were those fresh prints? She couldn't be sure. The air remained quiet and still.

The sun would be setting soon. She needed to finish cutting the grass. Silencing her unease, Jan returned to the mower and started it again. The engine fired up easily now it was warm. She continued cutting the grass. Up and down, creating neat stripes. But as she worked, she had the strangest feeling she was being watched. It was weird, unsettling and completely irrational, she told herself. Yet the feeling grew so that she had to keep taking her eyes from the lawn in front to look behind her.

She chided herself for being silly, but eventually the feeling became so strong she stopped the mower and went to the hedge at the bottom of the garden for a closer look. Leaning in, she pulled aside some branches so she could see into the hedge more clearly. Camile's garden was separated from the woods by shrubs forming a hedge. She looked at the hole Tinder and the shadow had gone through.

'Hello? Anyone there?' she called, then felt foolish.

Did she expect an animal to reply? Unless it wasn't an animal. Perhaps there were scouts camping in the woods or a homeless person living there, she wondered, as she had before. Now she'd cleared the leaves and parted the shrubbery she could see the gap was big enough for a child to get through, or even an adult if they crouched down and crawled

37

through. Was that what was making those marks? Someone crawling through?

Jan pulled aside more branches and saw another cluster of prints, which again could have belonged to anything. Whatever had been here had gone now, as had the feeling of being watched. It could have been her imagination all along. She needed to finish cutting the grass before sunset. The light was failing fast. If she didn't finish cutting it now, she'd have to go through all the palaver of starting the mower from cold again tomorrow.

Returning to the mower, Jan started it without a problem and finished cutting the lawn. She emptied the grass box again and then wheeled the mower into the shed where it was stored. As she returned across the now freshly cut grass to the back door of the cottage, she heard a noise again. She spun round. There was nothing to be seen. Whatever was out there was well hidden on the other side of the hedge.

With a shiver, she quickly continued indoors. If the sensor light was working, once it was dark it should show her what was coming into the garden and hopefully put her fears to rest.

Tinder appeared from the living room ready for his dinner. Jan fed him and then checked her phone. There was a missed call from her mother – she'd speak to her once she'd made herself a hot drink. The temperature outside had dropped while she'd been cutting the grass and her fingers were cold. She cupped her hands around the mug of steaming tea and stood at the living-room window looking out onto the garden. The sun continued on its descent and at 6.30 Jan thought it was dark enough to test the sensor light.

She opened the back door and stepped out. To her disappointment, the light didn't immediately flash on. But when she took another couple of steps across the patio and moved into its range, light flooded the area. It was working and it would cover the patio just outside the living-room windows.

Pleased with herself, Jan returned indoors as Tinder went out for a run. Closing the back door, she picked up her phone and texted Chris.

Hi! Success! I got the lawn mower and sensor light working! It was switched off. Just waiting to see who my nocturnal visitors are. Jan x

Making light of it helped ease her disquiet.

Five minutes later Chris replied, not congratulating her as she thought he would, but raising some concern.

Camile might have switched it off for a reason so maybe leave it off.

She texted back, feeling she should justify her actions: *I thought it might have accidently been turned off.*

His response was: *I think you need to ask Camile before you change anything in her cottage.*

She felt the censure of his words and was sorry. He was right: of course she should have checked with Camile first.

SEVEN

'Do you think that police woman suspects?' Emma anxiously asked Ian.

'No,' he replied a little wearily, glancing up from his laptop. 'She has no reason to.'

'But supposing she contacts Anne?'

'She doesn't know who our midwife is, and anyway Anne will know what to say.'

'You'd better warn Anne the police have been here,' Emma persisted. 'I wouldn't want her getting into trouble. She's helped us so much, seeing to everything, even though she shouldn't have.'

'I've already spoken to her,' Ian replied.

'What did she say?'

'That what we told the officer was right. But if she comes back, it's probably best to pretend we're out so we don't have to answer any more questions.'

'Comes back!' Emma exclaimed in alarm. 'I thought you said she went away satisfied. Why would the police come back?'

Ian sighed. 'I don't think she will, I'm just telling you what Anne said, as you asked.'

Emma fiddled nervously with the sleeve of her jumper as

Ian returned his attention to his laptop. It was evening and they were in the living room, but she couldn't concentrate on the book she was supposed to be reading. She felt even more wretched now, with the worry of the police visit on top of the trauma of losing the baby. She'd been in bed all day, but Ian had persuaded her to come down for dinner, which he'd made. Now she was regretting it. Sleep gave her some respite from the horror of it all, but when she was awake it was full on. All she did was sit and remember – right from the start, when she'd first found out she was pregnant again and the baby was damaged the same as the first one. Day after day, week by week, until the unimaginable horror of giving birth. Thank goodness it hadn't been full term and thank goodness for Anne, she thought. She wouldn't have managed without her. It had shot out, she remembered grimly, as pleased to be rid of her as she was of it. Her stomach clenched at the recollection.

David, they'd decided to call him, which meant loved one. He would have been so loved had nature not played another cruel trick on them. A baby that wasn't viable was the clinical term, but it had only been confirmed when it was too late for a termination. Ian seemed to be doing better than she was, Emma acknowledged, and was able to concentrate on work. But then he hadn't been pregnant, carried it all those months, hoping for the best but fearing the worst. It was easier for him.

'I think I'll go back to bed,' Emma said, and closed her book.

'No, don't, please,' Ian said imploringly and, standing, went to her. 'Don't shut yourself away any longer. We need to talk about what's happened and discuss what we're going to do in the future.'

'I'm not trying for a baby again if that's what you mean,' Emma said sharply, tears springing to her eyes. 'You said lightning never strikes twice in the same place, but it did for us. And this time it was worse than the last.' Her face crumpled and she dissolved into tears.

Ian put his arm around her and held her as she wept. 'I would never put you through that again,' he said gently, stroking her hair. 'Never. It's too much. I'm hurting too. I love you. But before we give up completely on our dream of starting a family, there's something I want to talk to you about.'

'What?' she asked, looking at him through her tears.

Ian took a tissue from the box and gently wiped her eyes. 'I wouldn't want us to try again for a child unless we could be certain it wouldn't happen a third time.'

'But we can't be certain!' Emma cried. 'That's the problem. We don't know until it's too late. Anne told us we shouldn't try again because the same thing was likely to happen.'

'I know, but please hear what I have to say. I've been doing some research on the Internet.'

'Go on then, tell me.'

'You remember when we were told about how David would be, after the scan?'

'Yes, vividly,' she said. 'It was awful and I was hysterical.'

'I know. You kept saying over and over again that there must be something wrong with you. I reassured you there wasn't.'

'I remember. Are you saying now you've found out there is something wrong with me after all, so it's my fault?'

'No, listen, please. It's not your fault any more than it is mine. But supposing there was something in our genes that's causing the problem? Lots of conditions can be passed down through genes without anyone knowing, and then it suddenly appears.'

'But what happened to us has never happened in my family before,' Emma said.

'Neither in mine, but supposing there is something a long way back we don't know about?'

'Like what?' Emma asked. 'You're scaring me.'

'I don't mean to scare you, love. But if we could find a reason for what's happening then it would reassure us, and there might be a chance it could be corrected. Medical scientists are doing wonderful things, manipulating DNA so babies can be born healthy, without inherited conditions.'

'It was more than a condition,' Emma said, grimacing. 'But how could we find out?'

'I've been researching and a good place to start would be to look at our family trees. It's pretty easy now online. Then we can apply for death certificates, which will tell us what our relatives died of. I've already started on my family. Let me show you.'

Emma watched as Ian fetched his laptop and returned to sit next to her on the sofa. She hadn't seen him so enthusiastic about anything in a long while.

'What made you think of this?' she asked him.

'I watched a programme on television a few nights ago about the way information is passed down through our genes. It was fascinating. It said marrying a cousin is often a bad idea because inbreeding can lead to genetic conditions and mutations. It got me thinking about us. I know we're not cousins but there could be something in our families that has lain dormant for generations and would have continued to do so had we not met and tried to have children. Many inherited conditions are only passed on if both parents are carriers – cystic fibrosis, for example. Do you see what I'm getting at?'

'Sort of. But if you do find something, do you think the doctors will be able to treat it and stop it from happening again?'

'I think we're in with a chance. It will depend on how far the research has progressed. And even if there's nothing that can be done, at least we'll know for certain and can look at alternatives like adoption or fostering.'

'I suppose you're right,' Emma agreed.

But as Ian began to show her the research he'd started on his family tree, she felt a surge of fear. There *was* something in her family, a secret that she'd never shared with Ian. Whether it could have any bearing on what he was trying to uncover, she wasn't sure. But she couldn't say anything to him until she'd spoken to her mother first.

EIGHT

Jan wondered if she should switch off the motion-sensor light because Chris had said in his text message Camile might have switched it off for a reason. Perhaps the wiring was unsafe, in which case it could catch fire. But if it was dangerous, surely Camile would have included a warning in her notes: *Don't use the light on the patio. It's not working properly.* Or something similar. There was no smell of burning coming from the switch box in the small bedroom. Jan had checked, and the light outside seemed to be OK too.

It had crossed Jan's mind to text Chris back and apologize, but she'd decided against it – least said, soonest mended. Instead, she did what she should have done in the first place and messaged Camile: *I've switched on the sensor light on the patio. Hope that's OK?*

It took Camile nearly half an hour to reply: *It gobbles electricity so best keep it off.*

So that was the reason it was off. It made sense. She would switch it off again once it had served its purpose and illuminated whatever it was that was coming into the garden.

Jan had topped up the meter and was now waiting for eight o'clock – the time when whatever it was had visited the last four nights. Animals were creatures of habit, she'd read online. Once she knew what it was and that it wouldn't harm her or Tinder, she could relax. Tinder was feisty but small and wouldn't be able to protect himself if attacked.

It was pitch dark outside now. Jan had finished dinner, washed up and was now sitting on the sofa, the television remote and her phone within reach. Although she was miles away from her family and friends, they were keeping in contact by phone and text. Some of her friends said they were envious of what she was doing – taking time out. An 'enforced sabbatical', one had called it. Put like that, it sounded as though she'd made an informed decision, had had a choice, rather than being made redundant and then dumped by her boyfriend.

When Jan had spoken to her mother on the phone earlier she'd delicately asked if she'd had any thoughts about her future. Jan had mumbled something about a possible career change, maybe retraining as a teacher or social worker, but she was looking into it. It was enough to satisfy her mother, although Jan was pretty sure she didn't have what it took to be a teacher or social worker. She wasn't sure where her skills lay or what she wanted to do in the future.

Tinder jumped onto her lap and then spent some moments turning in a circle until he was comfortable. Jan absently stroked his head while looking at the gap in the curtains. As soon as the motion-sensor light flashed on she'd pull open the curtains and hopefully get a good look at what was there. It was 7.30 now. Half an hour to go. Her pulse stepped up a beat.

She picked up the remote control and switched on the television, more as a distraction than to watch anything. With the volume on low, she flicked through the channels. Tinder closed his eyes and began to doze.

An old film was running and Jan glanced between the

television and the time on her phone. Eight o'clock gradually approached. A few minutes before eight Jan turned off the television and listened. Tinder was still asleep. She watched him carefully. He'd probably hear it first. He slept on.

Eight o'clock came and went. Jan's sense of expectation and foreboding increased. Where were they? She gently lifted Tinder from her lap and resettled him at the other end of the sofa. He looked at her inquisitively as she knelt on the sofa and then peered through the gap in the curtains into the dark beyond. There was nothing to be seen but the ghostly outline of the trees in the woods.

Jan stayed where she was, her breath shallow. She held the edge of the curtain and glanced at Tinder for any sign he'd heard something. Five minutes passed and he began dozing again. Perhaps they weren't coming tonight. Perhaps they wouldn't ever come again. Animals changed their dens and burrows. She'd give it another fifteen minutes and then switch off the sensor light.

It crossed Jan's mind as she waited, looking through the gap in the curtains, that perhaps she'd become a little obsessed with whatever was visiting the garden. Chris clearly hadn't been worried. But she knew she wouldn't sleep easy until she'd seen whatever was out there. She couldn't shift the feeling she'd had in the garden of being watched. It had been intense and she didn't think it was just her imagination.

A few more minutes passed, then Tinder slowly raised his head. His ears pricked up and his eyes rounded as he began a low, guttural growl. He'd heard something, but the motion-sensor light hadn't come on. Perhaps whatever it was had just entered the garden and was now making its way over the lawn towards the cottage. Jan clutched the edge of the curtain, ready to pull it open. Tinder was still growling.

Suddenly a noise at the back door made her jump. Tinder leapt off the sofa and ran to the door, barking. But the light outside still hadn't come on, so whatever it was must have avoided the sensor and gone straight to the back door.

Jan went after Tinder. He was pawing the door, desperate to get out. She gingerly opened the back door, aware that any noise would probably cause whatever was outside to run away. The cold night air rushed in, but there was nothing to be seen. As she stared into the darkness, door held ready to close, Tinder ran to the bottom of the garden barking furiously, then disappeared through the hedge. Drat! The barking stopped, then Jan heard a yelp of pain come from the woods. A cry that suggested an animal – possibly a dog – had been injured.

'Tinder?' she called, praying he would reappear.

Nothing.

'Tinder!'

A lone owl hooted in the distance.

Shit! She needed to find him and fast. Not giving herself time to think, she ran out over the lawn towards the place where he had disappeared.

'Tinder!' she shouted. The air was still. 'Tinder!' He could be hurt.

Suddenly her blood ran cold as she heard a noise come from behind. She spun round, just in time to see a shadowy figure run down the side of the cottage.

'Stop!' she shouted, giving chase.

Too late. She arrived in time to see it disappear over the gate. Shivering, Jan returned to the back door. 'Tinder!' she shouted one last time as she went in.

Nothing. Not a sound.

NINE

Jan sat on the sofa, wrapped in the duvet from her bed and sipped a hot toddy. The heating was on, but she couldn't get warm. Even the hot toddy – whisky, water, lemon and honey – wasn't really helping.

Tinder was missing again and she was really struggling to make sense of what she'd seen. Was there more than one of them? Tinder had chased something through the hedge and then that something had appeared behind her, close to the cottage. Had it intended to go in? She shivered. It was possible. It must have been hiding in the bushes beside the cottage, watching her as she went down the garden after Tinder. Had it hidden there before?

Jan took another sip of her drink and tried to steady her nerves. Were the two of them working together, and what or who were they? The way they'd avoided the sensor light could have been luck or intelligence. Squirrels were renowned for their intelligence when searching for food and could break into quite elaborate squirrel-proof bird feeders. She knew because her parents had problems with squirrels in their garden. But what she'd seen wasn't a squirrel. Not by a long way. It was much larger and a different shape entirely.

When she'd caught sight of it before she'd thought it could have been a fox on its hind legs, but now she discounted that idea completely.

The shadowy form she'd seen had appeared more human, child-like, and the word primate came to mind. Could something have escaped from a zoo and was now living in the woods? There was a zoo about forty miles away; she'd seen it on Google Maps. Were monkeys capable of making that kind of journey and then surviving in the wild in the UK climate? She didn't know. Some non-native species like parakeets and the American mink had colonized rural areas, she'd read online. But if something similar had happened here then surely Chris would have told her when she'd mentioned it before. He'd been unfazed and vague and said he couldn't really remember if Camile had said anything about animals visiting the cottage. Perhaps Camile hadn't told him, or perhaps it hadn't happened while she'd been living here. Although judging from the track marks, they could have been coming into the garden for some time.

Or perhaps she was getting this all out of perspective, Jan thought with a sigh. Children or primates living in the wood! Whatever next! Yet she'd definitely seen something go over the gate. She snuggled further under her duvet and turned on the television. She couldn't go to bed until Tinder had returned safely from the woods and she needed to try to think about something else.

Fifteen minutes later she'd finished the hot toddy and made herself another one. The whisky had taken effect and she was feeling warmer and braver. As she waited for the kettle to boil, she unlocked the back door. Holding it open just wide enough to allow her voice to carry outside, she called, 'Tinder! Tinder! Come on, good boy!'

She listened, called him again, and then closed and bolted the door. She'd try again later.

Taking the hot toddy to the sofa, Jan gazed absently at the television, the sound down, while listening for any noise outside. Every so often she checked the time on her phone. Nine-thirty, ten, ten-thirty, eleven o'clock. Tinder had been missing for over three hours, longer than he'd ever been gone before. Had that yelp of pain come from him? She couldn't be sure. Was he lying injured, unable to return?

Jan went to the back door and called him again and again, but there was still no sight or sound of him. She didn't have the courage to go out into the woods to search at night. If he didn't return, she'd go as soon as it was light in the morning. One last call and she returned to sit on the sofa and continued staring unseeing at the television. More time passed. Eleven-thirty, then it was midnight. Outside it began to rain. Tinder hated rain. Surely he would come back now if he could?

'Tinder!' she cried at the back door.

But all she could hear was the steady patter of rain.

'Tinder!'

She closed the door. Something must have happened for him to be missing this long in the rain. That yelp of pain must have been him. Tinder must be lying injured in the woods at this very moment, dying or even dead. A lump rose to her throat. She'd never forgive herself if something had happened to him. Camile had entrusted her to look after her beloved pet and Jan had cared for him as if he'd been her own. Yet now she was too much of a coward to go into the woods and look for him.

Suddenly she started as a knock sounded on the front door. She froze. The hairs on the back of her neck stood up. The time on her phone showed 00.15. Who the hell was here? Not a visitor, not at this time. Her heart raced as all manner of possibilities charged through her thoughts. Perhaps she should call the police? Or could it have been the wind moving the door knocker? Already unsettled, it was possible that's what she'd heard.

She kept very quiet and still, listening for any noise suggesting someone was there. Were they trying to break in? Her stomach churned. Her car was outside, but that wasn't worth much. The only light on was in the living room and that couldn't be seen from the front. Did they think the cottage was empty? Fear gripped her.

The knock came again, more insistent, then the doorbell rang. A burglar wouldn't ring the doorbell, or would they? Perhaps it was a ploy so they could burst in when she answered. She should call the police. She picked up her phone. But what was she going to say? Someone was at her front door? Wouldn't they tell her to see who it was, and anyway by the time they arrived out here, it would probably be too late. Either they would have gone or broken in. An image of being tied up as burglars ransacked the cottage flashed through her mind. The remoteness of the cottage that had attracted her in the first place had turned into a living nightmare.

Suddenly Jan's phone buzzed with a text message. Her hand trembled as she looked at the screen. The message was from Chris: *I'm at the front door. Are you in? I've got Tinder.*

Utter relief. Chris was here with Tinder. She could have cried with joy. Running to the front door, she threw it open and nearly kissed them both.

'Here you go,' Chris said, placing Tinder in her arms.

'Thank you so much. I've been worried sick. Where on earth did you find him? Come in from the rain.' She cuddled and petted Tinder as Chris came in.

'He was sitting outside the village store in Merryless waiting for it to open,' Chris said. 'It was lucky I spotted him on my way home. Goodness knows what he was doing there.'

'Thank you,' she said again, rubbing the top of Tinder's head. 'I'm so grateful.'

Chris smiled. 'You're welcome. I would have kept him overnight and phoned to say he was with me, but you know how he pines if he's away from home. It makes him ill.'

'Yes,' Jan said. 'He's a big softie, aren't you?' She tickled Tinder's chin. The reason Camile had wanted someone to rent the cottage who could look after Tinder was because he didn't do well in kennels or being left with someone else – even someone he knew.

'Would you like a drink?' she offered. They were still in the hall.

'If it's not too late,' Chris replied, and took off his wet coat. 'I walked here.'

'You walked here from the village in the dark and rain?' Jan exclaimed. 'Along Wood Lane!'

'Yes,' he laughed, following her into the living room. 'There's nothing in the woods that can hurt you. It's people who do the harm.'

'There are people in the woods?' Jan asked.

'No. I'm just saying it's people, not the dark, who can do you harm. Are you all right? You seem a bit on edge.'

'I'm OK. I've just been worried about Tinder.'

Now Chris was here her previous fears and conjecture had gone and she was starting to feel safe again.

'What would you like to drink?' she asked, placing Tinder on his rug.

'Whatever you're having,' Chris replied. His gaze went to the bottle of whisky she'd used for the hot toddies.

'Whisky. Anything in it?'

'Just a splash of water, please.'

As Chris sat in his usual armchair, Jan poured two generous whiskies. 'Ice?' she called from the kitchen.

'No, thanks.'

She added water and carried the glasses into the living room, handed one to Chris and then sat on the sofa. Tinder immediately jumped onto her lap and she began stroking him.

'You seem quite at home here,' Chris remarked, sipping his drink.

'I suppose I am.' How different the cottage felt now she had company. 'You were out late?' she said.

'I was returning from seeing a friend.'

'Sorry, I didn't mean to pry.'

'It's fine. We're old school friends. We get together every couple of months and sink a few beers. Quite a few, in fact, which is why I didn't take my car.'

'I'm so pleased you found Tinder,' Jan said. 'I'll know next time where to look for him.'

'He's never gone that far before. I guess he chased something into the woods and got lost.'

'He did, but what made you think that?' Jan asked.

'You said before he'd chased something from the garden.'

She nodded and took another sip of her drink. 'Whatever is coming into the garden was here again tonight. I think there could be more than one.'

'Where are they getting in?'

'Through the hole in the hedge at the bottom of the garden. But tonight . . .' she stopped. It seemed ridiculous to try to describe what she'd seen scramble over the side gate. Chris was a regular down-to-earth type of guy. Someone who could happily walk along Wood Lane at night and not get spooked.

'Yes?' he encouraged, looking at her carefully.

'I'm worried they might get indoors,' Jan said. 'One got very close tonight.'

'And you don't know what they are?'

She shook her head.

'Would you like me to board up the hole in the hedge?' Chris offered. 'I'm free tomorrow morning. There's bound to be some wood in the shed here I can use. If not, I'm sure I've got something that will do in my garage.'

Jan suddenly felt very silly. Of course the obvious solution was to block the hole.

'And Camile won't mind?' she checked.

'No, why should she?' Chris said. 'Not if it's causing you a problem.'

He'd clearly forgotten his text telling her she should ask Camile first before she changed anything in the cottage. Jan wasn't going to remind him now.

'I'm sure I can do it,' she said. 'The shed is full of bits of wood.'

'OK, but if you want some help, give me a ring.'

'I will. Thanks.'

Chris emptied his glass.

'Would you like a refill?' she offered.

'No, I should be going now.'

He stood and she saw him to the door where he unhooked his coat from the hall stand and slipped it on.

'Thanks again for finding Tinder. Do you want to take my car to get home?' Jan offered.

'I'd better not. A large whisky on top of all the beer. It would be my luck to be stopped by the police.'

'There are police in the village?' she asked. 'I thought the old police house was empty.' She'd seen it when she'd walked through the village exploring.

'It is empty, but a patrol car from Coleshaw comes through every so often. You can never be sure when.' Which Jan found quite reassuring. 'Night then,' Chris said, opening the door. 'Thanks for the drink. Give me a ring if you want any help tomorrow.'

'I will. Thanks again for returning Tinder.'

She watched Chris go down the short garden path and then right onto the lane that led to the village. He glanced back and gave a little wave before he disappeared from view. Rather him than me, Jan thought, walking alone at night, and she quickly closed and locked the door.

TEN

Emma was worried about whether she was doing the right thing as she let herself into her parents' home while calling, 'Mum, it's me!' Her father would be out at work. She'd purposely chosen a weekday for that reason.

Her mother, Mary, appeared from the kitchen, smiling warmly. 'Hello, love, how are you? It's great to see you out and about.' She kissed and hugged her daughter. 'Tea, coffee?'

'No, thanks.'

'Come and sit down. Is Ian looking after you?'

'Yes, Mum, very well. Don't worry. He returned to work today. I need to make the effort to go back too before long.'

They settled on the sofa in the living room. It was largely unchanged since Emma had left home five years ago to marry Ian. She loved returning – it was comforting and reassuring.

'You look so much better than the last time I saw you, the day after . . .' Mary began, and stopped as her eyes filled. 'I'm sorry, love. I'm still struggling to believe it's happened again.'

'I know, Mum.'

'Will there be an autopsy to try to find out what went wrong?' Mary asked after a moment.

'No.'

'Isn't it usual when something like this happens?'

'It depends, but Ian and I don't want one, and we're not having a funeral either.'

'Really? I know it's different with a very early miscarriage, but he would have been a fully-formed baby.'

'Not fully formed,' Emma grimaced.

'No, sorry, love, bad choice of words, but you know what I mean.'

Emma did know what her mother meant and it caused her pain. 'Ian and I couldn't cope with a funeral,' she said. 'So no funeral.'

'Sometimes it can help give closure. Even a small service with just family,' Mary persisted.

'Mum, please stop!' Emma cried. 'This is difficult enough as it is. I want to forget and try to move on.'

'I'm sorry, love. I was just trying to help. I won't mention it again, I promise. But you know you can talk to me anytime.'

Emma nodded.

'Now, what was it you wanted to ask me that you couldn't over the phone?'

Emma took a breath and chose her words carefully. She was worried her mother wouldn't understand the importance of what she was about to say and would be upset, even angry. She didn't need any more upset in her life right now.

'Mum, Ian's doing some research online about our ancestors.'

'Oh yes.'

'He's trying to find out if what happened to us has happened before to other family members. He's applying for copies of death certificates. He thinks if it is something that has been passed down – you know, genetic – then it could be treated.'

'Well, good luck to him,' Mary replied. 'But why are you looking so anxious?'

'Because he doesn't know Dad isn't my biological father.'

'And neither must he, ever. No one knows apart from the three of us, and the clinic where we were treated, of course. When I told you we agreed it would remain our secret. Your father is a proud man and was mortified he couldn't father a child. He's been good to you, a proper father. He couldn't have loved you any more.'

'I know that, Mum. That's not the point.'

'What is it then?' Mary asked, worried. 'You haven't told anyone, have you?'

'No, but I think I should tell Ian.'

'Why? Whatever for?' Mary exclaimed, the colour draining from her face.

'Because obviously there's no point in him researching Dad's family as I don't have his genes,' she said, slightly frustrated.

'I realize that, but don't tell Ian, please. It would destroy your father if it got back to him. He's your real father, always has been. All that other man gave was his sperm. Let Ian do his research, but please don't tell him.'

'But supposing there is something in the genes of the donor – my biological father – that's causing our problem. We won't know so it can't be corrected. Ian and I have decided we won't try again for another child unless we know for certain the same thing can't happen. I was thinking I could trace the donor myself and then tell Ian.'

'There's no chance there could be anything wrong with the donor's genes,' Mary said. 'All donors are thoroughly screened. The clinic explained to us how thorough their screening was. The donor has a detailed medical and lots of tests. They examine their DNA too. I remember the doctor saying only the healthiest sperm donors are selected, so it can't be him.'

Emma looked at her mother and felt sorry for her. She was so immersed in protecting her father she couldn't see the logic in what Emma was saying. But this was too important to let go.

'Ian wonders if it's something in our genes that lies dormant and only appears if two people with the same defective gene have a child.'

'It can't be. The clinic tests for that too. They test for everything, love, trust me. If there is something wrong, it certainly isn't with the donor. I suppose it could be me, but I've never heard of anything like this happening in my family. My guess is that Ian will find something in his family. If indeed there is anything to be found. Sometimes nature gets it wrong and it's no one's fault.'

'Ian's checked your family,' Emma said. 'What details were you given of the donor?'

'Everything except his name and address. The donor's identity was kept secret to protect everyone involved.'

'The law has changed since then, so I could trace him now if I wanted to.'

'Oh, Emma, you wouldn't! It would destroy your father. And it's not fair on the donor either. He made that gift to help childless couples like us, not because he wanted a family of his own.'

'I don't want to be his daughter!' Emma cried passionately. 'I don't even want to meet him. Dad is my father and always will be. I was just thinking of contacting the clinic and asking for details about the donor's genetic history.'

'No, love, let it go. Don't go looking for trouble. You and Ian have each other. Not everyone is meant to have children.' Which was ironic, Emma thought, coming from her mother, who'd gone to such lengths to conceive her.

'I'll give it some more thought,' Emma said. It was the only truthful reassurance she could give her.

ELEVEN

DC Beth Mayes was driving the unmarked police car on the return journey to Coleshaw Police Station. Her colleague DC Matt Davis was in the passenger seat. They'd just come from interviewing Charlie Bates, a member of a local family of hardened criminals. He'd only been released from prison the previous day and was already suspected of taking part in an armed robbery.

The car phone rang and Matt answered it. 'Have you finished with Mr Bates?' DS Bert Scrivener asked.

'For now,' Matt replied. 'We're on our way back.'

'Can you take a detour to 55 Booth Lane and visit Mrs Angela Slater? Beth knows what it's in connection with.'

'I phoned her yesterday, sir,' Beth said. 'I told her the outcome of my visit to Mr and Mrs Jennings, and that their baby was stillborn.'

'She's not convinced,' DS Scrivener said. 'She's phoned twice this morning. She says she has new evidence, but it's too delicate to explain over the phone. She wants to speak to someone "involved in the case", to use her words. So that's you, Beth.'

'But there is no case, sir,' Beth said. Matt glanced at her, puzzled. 'The baby was born dead. That's all there is to it. I told Mrs Slater that.'

'Tell her again, please. Then come back here.'

'Very good, sir,' Beth said, and Matt ended the call.

'What was all that about?' he asked as Beth indicated right to make the detour.

'Mrs Slater reported that her neighbours, Ian and Emma Jennings, had a baby but it disappeared. I interviewed the couple and filed my report. They had a home birth but sadly the baby was born dead. I can't imagine what "new evidence" there could be.'

'Perhaps she's claiming they murdered it,' Matt suggested.

'Impossible. There was a midwife present at the birth and she took the baby's body away. There was nothing suspicious. Mr and Mrs Jennings are just an average couple who are struggling to come to terms with their loss. They've probably had enough of Mrs Slater's prying.'

'So neighbour dispute then?' Matt said.

'Could be.'

A few minutes later Beth parked the car outside the home of Mrs Slater. Her neighbour's drive was empty, suggesting that Ian and Emma Jennings were out, possibly at work, hopefully trying to pick up the pieces of their lives, Beth thought.

'Do you want to wait in the car? I shouldn't be long,' Beth asked Matt. It didn't really need two of them to speak to Mrs Slater, unlike the notorious Bates family when they always went in pairs.

'No, I'll come in. I'm intrigued,' Matt said, and opened his car door. 'I wouldn't want you to miss a vital piece of information.'

'Joker,' Beth said with a smile. She'd worked with Matt before and they enjoyed some light-hearted banter.

Beth pressed the bell at Number 55 and the door was immediately opened.

'Mrs Slater, DCs Beth Mayes and Matt Davis,' Beth said as they showed her their ID cards. 'We spoke on the phone.' Mrs Slater was in her early sixties, Beth guessed, and smartly dressed.

'I'm glad they've sent you. I didn't want to go over it all again with someone who didn't know the case.' She ushered them into her neat living room, which was at the front of the house. 'Would you like a drink?'

'No, thank you,' Beth said. 'We're needed back at the station as soon as we've finished here.'

'Sit down then. It will take a few minutes for me to explain what I've found out.'

Beth and Matt sat on the sofa as Angela Slater took the slightly higher armchair and looked at them as if addressing an audience. A glass-fronted display cabinet stood against one wall, containing ornaments, family photographs and an empty glass decanter with six matching glasses. Matt took out his notepad.

'I'm convinced my neighbours, Ian and Emma, are hiding something,' Angela Slater began with a sense of intrigue. 'I don't believe their baby is dead. They haven't arranged a funeral, nor have they registered its death.'

'How do you know that?' Beth asked, surprised. Matt's pen hovered above the notebook.

'I saw Ian going to work yesterday. I asked him when the funeral was so I could attend or at least send some flowers. He said they weren't having a funeral, which I thought was very odd.'

'Perhaps it's family only,' Beth suggested.

'I wondered that and thought maybe they hadn't liked to tell me and hurt my feelings, so I telephoned my friend Nora. She works at Lovells funeral directors in town. She's a good friend and we often have a chat and a laugh about the goings on behind the scenes at the funeral parlour. You wouldn't believe some of the things she tells me!' So much for confidentiality, Beth thought. 'My friend Nora said Lovells hasn't been contacted to arrange the funeral of David Jennings,' Angela Slater concluded with satisfaction.

'Perhaps they're using a different funeral director,' Beth said, suggesting the obvious.

'That's what I thought too,' Angela said in a conspiratorial tone. 'But I've checked all the funeral directors within a twenty-mile radius, and none of them has been contacted to arrange the funeral.'

Beth stared at her while Matt remarked dryly, 'That shows some dedication.'

Beth threw him a warning look. They got on well together, but he wasn't renowned for his subtlety.

'Not only that,' Angela Slater continued, leaning forward slightly. 'There isn't a death certificate. I got Nora to check the register of deaths. The baby isn't listed, which it should have been. You have to register a baby's death just like you do an adult's.'

Beth was momentarily speechless, not so much because of what Mrs Slater was saying, but the lengths she'd gone to.

'If a baby is stillborn then it has to be registered on the stillborn registry, but you have forty-two days to register.'

'I know that,' Mrs Slater said impatiently. 'But if a baby is born alive and then dies, its death has to be registered within five days as with any other death. Even if it only lives for an hour.'

Beth held Mrs Slater's gaze. 'It was stillborn,' Beth said, as Matt wrote.

'No. It wasn't stillborn. It was alive. I heard it cry.'

'You didn't mention that before when we spoke,' Beth said. 'You told me you couldn't see the baby's face because it was covered by a blanket in the Moses basket.'

'I couldn't see it, but I heard it.'

'So why didn't you tell me that the last time?' Beth asked.

'I didn't think I had to. I just thought you'd assume it was alive. It was only after you said that the Jennings had told you the baby was dead that I realized the significance of what I'd heard.'

Beth paused for a moment and looked thoughtful. 'When exactly did you hear it cry?' she asked.

'As the midwife lifted the Moses basket into her car. I was upstairs looking out of my bedroom window. The fanlight window was open and I heard it cry. A funny little mewing sound.'

'Could it have been a cat you heard?' Matt asked, which Beth thought was a reasonable question.

'Don't be ridiculous!' Mrs Slater exclaimed, glaring at Matt. 'I know the difference between a baby's cry and a cat.'

'They can sound similar from a distance,' Beth offered.

'I'm telling you it was a baby I heard,' Mrs Slater said vehemently. 'Their child was alive when it left the house.'

'So what do you think happened to it?' Matt asked.

'I've no idea. That's for you to find out. I've told you all I know.'

'So that's everything?' Beth asked.

'Yes.'

'Thank you,' Beth said. Matt put away his pen and notepad.

'Will you go next door now?' Mrs Slater asked as they all stood. 'Emma Jennings is in.'

'I'll discuss what our next step will be with my colleagues,' Beth said diplomatically.

Mrs Slater saw them out.

'What do think?' Matt asked Beth as they went down the path. The front door had closed behind them.

'I think she's mistaken about hearing it cry, and the baby was stillborn.'

65

'Or perhaps she did hear it cry and it died shortly after,' Matt suggested.

'It's possible, but in that case there should be a death certificate. Mrs Slater was right when she said a baby's death has to be recorded in the same way as an adult's. Even if it only lives a short while. We'd better speak to Mrs Jennings.'

Having reached the end of Angela Slater's driveway, they went right and walked up the drive next door to Number 57. Beth rang the bell and they waited, then she rang it again. A few moments later the door opened on a chain, just enough for Emma Jennings to see out.

'Hello, Mrs Jennings, Detective Constable Beth Mayes,' she said, showing her ID. 'I visited you before when your husband was here. This is my colleague, Detective Constable Matt Davis.'

'Yes? What do you want?'

'Could we come in?' Beth asked.

'Why? Ian isn't here, he's at work.'

'We don't need to speak to him. I'm sure you'll be able to help us. It won't take long.'

Emma hesitated, and then removed the chain to let them in.

'I'm sorry for your loss,' Matt said as they entered.

'Thank you,' Emma said.

Beth thought Emma looked significantly better than the last time she'd seen her when she'd been in bed and was being looked after by her husband. But she still had a way to go and seemed fragile.

'Shall we sit down?' Beth suggested.

Emma led the way into the front room.

'We won't keep you long,' Beth said. 'We've been contacted by a worried neighbour.'

'I can guess who that is,' Emma said dourly. 'We made the mistake of being friendly with Mrs Slater when we first moved in. Now she won't leave us alone.'

Beth nodded. 'I know this may sound insensitive, but I need to ask you a difficult question in connection with your baby.'

'What?' Emma asked anxiously.

There was no easy way to put it. 'Was your baby born alive and then died or was it stillborn?' Beth said.

'Why would you want to know that?' Emma cried, immediately distressed.

'It appears there is no record of the death yet.'

'I don't know about that. It's nothing to do with me. The midwife was seeing to it all.'

'The problem is, you only have five days to register a death,' Beth said. 'And that time has gone.' Emma looked at her, confused. 'If a baby is stillborn you have longer – forty-two days, but it still has to be registered.'

'I suppose it was stillborn then,' Emma said, her eyes filling.

'I'm sorry,' Beth said. 'Don't you know?' she asked gently.

'No. I was in such a bad way. I couldn't bear to see it. He was born very early, premature, and wasn't right. We haven't talked about it since.'

'So you didn't see or hold your baby before the midwife took him away?' Beth asked in the same sensitive tone. She knew parents could spend some time with their dead baby if they wished.

Emma's reaction wasn't what she'd expected.

'No! Of course not. What a dreadful idea. I just wanted him out of here and gone. He wasn't right. Ian didn't see or touch him either. The midwife took him and then came back to see to me.'

'I see, thank you,' Beth said, as Matt wrote. 'Are you planning on having a funeral?'

'No, my mother asked me that. But I don't understand why you want to know. It's private.'

'I'm sorry,' Beth said. 'I'm just trying to establish a timeline.

There is some suggestion that the baby may have been alive when he left here.'

'That's ridiculous! Of course he wasn't. Can you go now, please?'

'Yes, I'm sorry I've upset you. I don't need to bother you further. Your midwife will be able to give me the details. What's her name?'

'I don't know,' Emma replied agitatedly.

'Her name will be on your maternity records,' Beth prompted.

Emma didn't reply.

'I won't trouble you further,' Beth said, standing. 'I can get the information from your health-service provider. They will have her details.'

'It's Anne Long,' Emma suddenly said. 'Now I want you to go. I'm not feeling well. I need to lie down.'

'I'm sorry. Can I call someone to be with you? Your husband?'

'No. Just go.'

Emma remained in the living room as Beth and Matt let themselves out.

'What do you make of that?' Matt asked, once in the car.

'Not sure. I need to speak to the midwife.'

TWELVE

Beth saw their boss, DS Scrivener, glance pointedly at the clock on the wall as she and Matt returned to their office in Coleshaw Police Station.

'Seeing Mrs Slater took longer than expected, sir,' Beth said, pausing by his desk.

'We had to interview her neighbour, Mrs Jennings, the one who lost the baby,' Matt added.

'Why?' DS Scrivener asked.

'Because Mrs Slater's new evidence is that the baby was alive when it was taken from the house,' Beth explained. 'She's claiming she heard it cry. If she's right then its death should have been registered by now, but it hasn't been. We spoke to the mother, Emma Jennings, but she isn't sure what happened. She was too distressed at the time. I'm going to phone the midwife who was involved to clarify the position.'

'OK,' DS Scrivener said. 'Then I want the two of you to return to Mr Bates and arrest him. We have the evidence we need now.'

'Yes, sir,' Matt said.

He and Beth went to their desks. They sat opposite each other, their computer screens back to back.

'I'd better check the registry records first,' Beth said, logging on to her computer. 'Just in case Mrs Slater's friend, Nora, has got it wrong and the death has now been registered.'

'Good idea,' Matt said, then turned his attention to his screen and the case he was working on.

Beth began by checking the register of births, then deaths and finally stillbirths. Fifteen minutes later she had the confirmation she needed. Nora was right: there was still no record of David Jennings ever having been born or dying. Beth then spent a few moments finding the contact details for the midwife, Anne Long. Her name appeared as a member of staff at Coleshaw Health Centre. Beth keyed in the number for the centre.

'Coleshaw Health Centre,' a trim voice announced.

'Good afternoon. I'm Detective Constable Beth Mayes, Coleshaw CID, I'd like to speak to one of your midwives, please – Anne Long.'

'I'll put you through to midwifery.'

'Thank you.'

Beth waited, then a female voice sang, 'Midwifery. How can I help you?'

'Good afternoon. It's Detective Constable Beth Mayes, Coleshaw CID. I'd like to speak to one of your midwives, Anne Long.'

'She's out at present on a call. I could ask her to phone you on her return.'

'Does she have a work mobile?' Beth asked.

'Yes, but she won't be able to answer it if she's with a patient.'

'No, I appreciate that. If she doesn't answer, I'll leave a message.'

'No problem. Just a moment, please.'

A few seconds later she came back on the line and read out the number for Anne Long as Beth made a note. 'Has Anne worked there for many years?' Beth asked.

'Oh yes, she's one of our longest-serving midwives. She's very highly thought of. Many mums request her.'

'I'm sure she is excellent,' Beth said. 'My enquiry has nothing to do with her competence. I'm doing a routine follow-up after a baby's death. David Jennings. It was a home delivery.'

'Oh yes, that was so sad. Anne was very upset, as we all were. But Anne is the best person to support the parents.'

'Does Anne carry out many home deliveries?' Beth asked.

'Yes, that's her speciality. She loves home births.'

'Thank you for your help. I'll give Anne a call now.'

'You know that sometimes, despite the best care in the world, a baby can't survive. It's heart-breaking for all involved, but it's no one's fault.'

'No, I understand that,' Beth said. 'Thanks again for your help.'

Beth took a sip from the bottle of water on her desk and then keyed in Anne Long's mobile number. Matt was concentrating on his screen as he typed.

Anne's phone was answered after a couple of rings. 'Hello, Anne Long speaking.'

'Good afternoon. It's Detective Constable Beth Mayes, Coleshaw CID. Is this a convenient time to talk?'

'I have a few minutes, yes. Why? What's it about?'

'I understand you were the midwife for Emma and Ian Jennings?'

'Yes, that's correct. Emma's just called me. She was very upset by your visit.'

'It wasn't my intention to upset her,' Beth said, meeting Matt's gaze as he glanced up from his computer screen. 'I'm hoping you can answer my questions.'

'I'll try.'

'I understand Emma had a home delivery?'

'Yes.'

'And their baby didn't survive?'

'That's correct.'

'Was the baby full term?' Beth asked.

'Nowhere near.'

'So it was stillborn?'

'No. A late miscarriage.'

'Oh, I see. How many weeks' gestation was it, if that's the right term?'

'It is, but I'm sorry, this is very personal information. I should like to know the reason you're asking before I share it.'

'Of course. I am following up on a call from a member of the public who thought their baby had been born alive and is now missing.'

'They are wrong. It was twenty-three weeks, more a foetus than a baby. At that stage it is known as a late miscarriage, not a stillborn. Stillborn is after twenty-four weeks.'

'Do late miscarriages have to be registered?' Beth asked.

'Not at present, although there is some feeling there should be a register for late miscarriages as it could help give the parents closure.'

'So it wasn't alive when you took it from the house?' Beth asked as she wrote. Matt was still watching her, listening to the one-sided conversation.

'No. Some foetuses can survive at that stage, but not many. Mr and Mrs Jennings's baby couldn't, even if it had been born in hospital. It wasn't properly formed. It's all in my report.'

'I see. So it couldn't have cried?'

'No. It might have made a sound, but not a proper cry like a full-term viable baby does. No one would have attempted to resuscitate it, not even in hospital.'

'I understand. I believe you disposed of the body?'

'Yes, at the parents' request. It was cremated at the hospital. Is that everything now?' Anne asked. 'Only I'm on my way to see a mum who's in active labour.'

'Yes, thank you.'

'And you won't have to visit Mr and Mrs Jennings again? I believe it's the second time you've been, and they're very upset. They have enough to cope with at present.'

'There won't be any need for me to see them again,' Beth confirmed and, winding up the conversation, she said goodbye.

'It was a late miscarriage,' Beth told Matt. 'Which explains why it's not on any of the registers. You don't have to register until twenty-four weeks. It was a foetus and not fully formed.'

'That also explains why the parents didn't want to see or hold it,' Matt said, grimacing. 'I wouldn't have wanted to, would you?'

'Probably not. I'll just complete and file my report and then we can go and arrest Mr Bates.'

THIRTEEN

On Tuesday evening, after Jan had finished her dinner, she settled on the sofa with her laptop and a mug of tea. She was feeling positive and determined to write the first page of her novel. *A Difficult Romance*. At least she had a title now! No excuses. The night-time visits had stopped, and Tinder was peacefully asleep at the other end of the sofa, eyes closed and ears relaxed.

Jan had spent most of Sunday afternoon in the garden boarding up the hole in the hedge, using what she'd found in Camile's shed – pieces of wood, wire netting and a roll of twine. Doubtless it was a makeshift job by Chris's standards, but it had held when she'd tested it. She'd wedged strips of wood across the hole, then covered it with wire netting, securing it with twine to the hedge. It had worked. Whatever had been getting in wasn't any longer. She and Tinder had enjoyed an uninterrupted and peaceful Sunday and Monday evening. Her confidence received another small boost.

That morning she'd switched off the motion-sensor light at the socket in the spare bedroom. It wasn't needed any longer and, as Camile had said in her text, the light gobbled electricity. It wasn't just when the floodlight came on; the sensor used electricity too, so it was a steady drain on the power. She'd texted Chris to say she'd successfully blocked up the hole and all was well. He'd replied with a thumbs-up emoji. She'd also texted Camile – *I've used some of the wood and netting from the shed to block up a hole in the hedge at the bottom of the garden. Hope that's OK.'*

She'd replied straight away. *Yes, fine with me. Sorry you've had a problem with something getting into the garden.*

Which, Jan thought, was slightly odd because she hadn't told Camile something was coming into the garden. She supposed Chris had.

She took another sip of her tea and set the mug down within reach. Her fingers were poised expectantly over the keyboard, ready to begin. She stared at the page before her, blank except for the title and *Chapter One.* It was so hard getting started, and she knew a good opening was crucial. Those considering buying a book based their decision on the blurb on the back and the first page. Online advice for new writers stated: *Don't worry about writing the perfect first page, just get down what is in your head. You will revise and edit it once the book is complete. Just start.*

Easier said than done, Jan thought.

She forced her fingers to start typing with the thought in her head: *It was a cold winter's night and a frost was already beginning to settle on the lawn.* She stopped and read what she'd written. It seemed OK, so she continued: *At 11 p.m. Melissa was the only one in the house still awake.* She stopped again. She thought she'd heard a noise outside. She listened but it wasn't repeated. Tinder was still fast asleep, so it was nothing to worry about. There were plenty of noises in and around the cottage, especially at night, that Tinder was used to and she was not. He was her barometer.

Jan looked at what she'd written and then deleted it. It would be better if it was set in summer, as it was a romance.

She began again: *It was a hot summer's night. At 2 a.m. the temperature had hardly dropped. Melissa lay naked below a single sheet, her bedroom window wide open.* Yes, that sounded much better. She was pleased. Her fingers hovered above the keyboard as she waited for the inspiration to continue.

Then she heard it again. A noise on the other side of the patio window. She looked at the closed curtains and went cold. Tinder was awake now too, on guard, hackles up, staring at the curtains and growling. 'What is it?' she asked quietly, her voice unsteady.

Was it back again after two nights? Had it got into the garden? Or was there something else out there? It could be anything, she told herself – a hedgehog, rats, mice. The sensor light was switched off. If she went upstairs and turned it on, whatever was outside would very likely be gone by the time she returned to the living room.

Setting aside her laptop, Jan slowly knelt on the sofa so she was facing the curtain. Tinder, still growling, was watching her. She carefully took hold of the edge of the curtain and then quickly pulled it open. A pair of eyes looked back. She screamed and dropped the curtain. Tinder threw himself at the window as if to attack, but it had gone. He ran to the back door, barking frantically to be let out. But unlike other evenings, Jan wouldn't be letting him out to give chase. It wasn't safe.

Her hand shook as she grabbed her phone to call Chris.

'Thank goodness you're there,' she gasped as soon as he answered. 'There was someone in the back garden. They came right up to the window and looked in.'

'Are you sure?' Chris asked.

'Yes! Can't you hear Tinder barking? He wants to give chase.'

'I'll come straight over. Lock the doors and don't let Tinder out.'

'Shall I call the police?' Jan asked.

'No, wait until I get there and we'll decide then. I'm on my way.'

Trembling, Jan went to the back door and checked it was locked. Then, taking her phone with her, she went down the hall to wait by the front door. It seemed safer to be at the front of the cottage and away from the back garden and living-room window. Tinder, finding himself alone, stopped barking and ran to her side.

What had she seen? She didn't know. She'd only seen a pair of eyes and a shadow before it had fled. Too small for an adult. A child? Surely not. Yet the eyes had shown human expression. Intrigue. If only the sensor light had been on.

With her heart still racing and trying to make sense of what she'd seen, Jan leant against the front door for support as she waited, willing Chris to hurry. Although Tinder had stopped barking, he remained agitated. Every so often he gave a low growl while looking down the hall towards the back of the cottage. Had he heard it return? Or perhaps it hadn't left the garden at all? Jan shuddered. Was there just the one or were there others? She'd only seen one pair of eyes.

A few minutes later she heard a car come down the lane and pull up. Thank goodness. But she waited until the bell rang. 'Is that you, Chris?'

'Yes.'

She opened the front door and nearly fell into Chris's arms. 'I was so scared,' she said. 'Thank you for coming.'

'It's OK. Come on, let's sit you down.' He took her arm and steered her into the living room where he eased her onto the sofa. 'Shall I get you a drink?'

'No, I'm all right. I had a fright. Whatever it was came right up to the window and looked in. Thanks for coming so quickly.'

'I'll get the torch and check outside,' Chris said.

'Do you think it's safe?'

He threw her a reassuring smile, suggesting there was really nothing to be afraid of and that she might have been overreacting, then fetched the torch from the hall, Tinder at his heels.

'Keep him in, I don't want him disappearing,' Chris said as he returned to the living room with the torch. He picked up Tinder and placed him on Jan's lap, then went into the kitchen and unlocked the back door.

'Be careful,' she called.

'Don't worry.' Again, his tone suggested there was really nothing to be afraid of.

Jan held Tinder close; it was comforting, as Chris went out the back door, closing it again after him. Tinder tried to break free and follow Chris, but Jan kept him securely on her lap, stroking his fur to calm him. She supposed she could have gone with Chris, but even with him beside her there was no way she was going into the garden now, and she wondered if he should have. How could he be certain that whatever – whoever – was out there had gone and wouldn't harm him?

A few minutes later the back door opened and Chris returned.

'It's all clear,' he said.

She let go of Tinder and he ran into the kitchen.

'Good boy,' Chris said, patting him. 'It's OK, there's nothing out there now.'

Taking off his muddy shoes, he came into the living room. 'Whatever you saw has long gone, but they've made short work of your repair. The wood is strewn all over the lawn. I'll come over at the weekend and fix it.'

'They?' Jan asked.

'I'm guessing there was more than one. Foxes can live in groups, although they usually hunt alone.'

'You think it was a fox?'

'Most likely. They've been trying to get into my chicken coop again.'

'It didn't look like a fox to me,' she said. 'And the wood was in place this afternoon. It must have happened after dark while I was in here.' She shuddered at the thought. 'I think there was someone in the garden and we should call the police.' She picked up her phone.

'So you can give a good description of them?' Chris asked, sitting in his armchair.

Jan paused and thought about what she'd seen. 'I can't. It was too dark. I switched the sensor light off to save electricity. I only saw their eyes at the window. But the outline looked similar to the last time I saw them.'

Chris looked at her. 'You've seen someone in the garden before? You didn't say.'

'It was the night you returned Tinder, and I'm not saying it was definitely a person. I didn't tell you at the time because I couldn't make sense of what I'd seen. I still can't – even less so after this evening. But . . .'

'But what?' Chris asked seriously, holding her gaze.

It seemed ridiculous now. 'Whatever I saw the last time was very agile and went over the side gate. I thought it could have been a child, but now I'm not sure. I'm sorry, this sounds crazy. I don't know what I saw,' she finished lamely.

Thankfully Chris wasn't laughing and appeared to be taking her concerns seriously. 'You've obviously had a shock, seen something, and been very scared by it. But it was dark on both occasions, and our eyes can play tricks on us in the dark.' He glanced at her open laptop. 'I know you want peace and quiet to write your book, but do you think you've been overdoing it? It's very isolated here and you've been spending a lot of time by yourself – just you and your imagination.'

He had phrased it so delicately Jan found she couldn't

take offence. It wasn't her imagination, but she didn't feel like arguing the point now. His face lightened and lost its seriousness as he said, 'Perhaps I could help ease your isolation by taking you out to dinner one evening?'

'Oh, I see. I don't know,' Jan said, surprised. 'It's very kind of you to ask.'

'Well?' He was waiting for her to reply.

'Won't I be treading on someone's toes?' she asked. 'I sort of assumed that you and Camile . . .' But Chris was already shaking his head.

'It's true, we had a relationship some years ago, but for various reasons it didn't work out. We've remained good friends. That's all we are now – friends. So no, you won't be stepping on Camile's toes if you come out to dinner with me.'

Jan smiled. 'Then yes, please, I'd like to.'

'Good. Tomorrow?' She nodded. 'I'll collect you at seven o'clock – that'll give me a chance to shower and change after work.'

'Perfect.'

'And as for whatever is getting into the garden, I'll fix the hole in the hedge at the weekend. I'll also go into the woods and see what's happening on the other side. Then I can reassure you.'

'Thank you.'

FOURTEEN

Jan let Tinder sleep on her bed that night. She felt safer with him beside her. Even so, it was a long time before she fell asleep. Every noise seemed to suggest that whatever was out there could have come back. Tinder was restless too and kept rising from his sleep to pace the bed, ears up and alert, as though he might have heard something. It didn't help Jan's nerves at all. Eventually she must have fallen asleep in the early hours. The last time she looked at the clock on her phone it had been 2.15 a.m. and now it was 8.05, and daylight. She breathed a sigh of relief.

Getting out of bed, she threw on her dressing gown, pushed her feet into her slippers and opened the bedroom curtains. Tinder, tail wagging, was at her side, ready for breakfast and his morning run.

'Come on then, good boy,' Jan said, and went downstairs.

Life here seemed so much better in the daytime and she was seeing Chris this evening for dinner. She was looking forward to it, more than she cared to admit. She'd liked him from their first meeting and would like him more now she knew he wasn't in a relationship with Camile. Good friends, he'd said. Did that mean friends with benefits? Then she caught herself. Chris had asked her out for dinner – to help alleviate her isolation, he'd said – and that was all. His 'friendship' with Camile was nothing to do with her. And anyway, she wasn't ready for another proper relationship yet – with Chris or anyone.

Downstairs, Jan opened the curtains in the living room. How different the garden seemed by daylight: clearly visible, peaceful and non-threatening. She went into the kitchen, fed Tinder and then filled the coffee machine and dropped two slices of bread into the toaster. As usual Tinder ate half his breakfast and then trotted to the back door to be let out for a run. As Jan opened the door she saw the pieces of wood she'd used to block up the hole in the hedge strewn across the lawn as Chris had said. It was nice of him to offer to repair the damage at the weekend, but she couldn't wait until then. Not three or four nights with a gaping hole – an open invitation to whatever it was to return. She would have another attempt at repairing it, make it stronger. It had lasted two nights before, so if she made it more robust, hopefully it would stay in place.

Tinder finished in the garden by sniffing around the wood and then returned indoors to eat the rest of his breakfast. Jan buttered her toast, poured some coffee and took her breakfast upstairs to have as she showered and dressed. *Bring warm clothes suitable for the country*, Camile had included in her emailed instructions. She had, and was now dressed in jeans and a thick woollen jumper.

Returning downstairs, Jan took her padded zip-up jacket from its hook in the hallway and went into the kitchen. Tinder looked at her, hopeful for a walk.

'I'll take you into the village later, but for now we're going in the garden,' she told him. She knew she could trust him not to disappear through the hedge in daylight. It was after dark when he gave chase and vanished into the woods.

Tucking her phone into her jacket pocket, Jan went into the garden and began gathering up the pieces of wood and stacking them to one side. They hadn't been broken or damaged, just removed from where she'd fixed them over the hole. She found the wire netting with the twine she'd used to tie it in place still attached. As she looked more closely she could see that it hadn't been gnawed through; the knots had been unpicked. Could foxes do that? No. What animal could? None that she knew of.

She crossed the lawn to the hole in the hedge and, squatting down, examined the track marks. There were fresh ones, but it was still impossible to identify them. On the branches either side of the hole was more twine.

Puzzled and unnerved but wanting to cover the hole again as quickly as possible, Jan began bringing over the wood she'd used previously and started boarding up the hole again. Tinder sniffed around the patio. She fetched more wood and wire netting from the shed and secured it in place with twine. It was much better fortified now, stronger and more robust, but as she worked she had a strange, unsettling feeling that her efforts could all be in vain. Anything that had the intelligence to untie knots and disassemble wood and wire netting wouldn't be kept out by this. The more she thought about it, the more she was convinced an animal hadn't done this. It must have been a person or people and she trembled at the thought. Chris had been wrong to dissuade her from reporting it to the police simply because she couldn't give a good description.

Half an hour later, satisfied she'd done her best and the repair would hopefully keep them out for a while at least, Jan returned the tools to the shed and went indoors. She sat on a kitchen stool and phoned Coleshaw Police Station.

'I want to report an intruder,' she said to the call handler.

'Is the intruder on the premises now?'

'No.'

'I'll put you through to an officer as soon as one is available.'

Jan then had to wait a few minutes before an officer came on the line.

He introduced himself as 'Detective Constable Matt Davis', and asked for her full name and contact details. Jan then explained that she was renting Ivy Cottage, Wood Lane, and that someone, or possibly more than one person, had been coming into the garden after dark. She said she thought they were getting in through a hole in the hedge at the rear of the property, which backed onto Coleshaw Woods. He asked for the dates and times of the incidents, and then said, 'Did you get a good look at the intruder?'

'No, it was too dark. Just a shadow, really. But there are prints in the earth where they're coming through.'

'OK. I'll take a look. Will you be in at around three o'clock this afternoon?'

'Yes, I can be.'

'I've got to visit someone in Merryless first, so I'll stop by after. Although hopefully now you've secured the gap it won't happen again.'

'Thank you,' Jan said, pleased he was taking her concerns seriously. 'Have you had any other reports of this happening? I've only been in the cottage a few weeks, but judging from the footprints it could have been going on for some time.'

'Not as far as I'm aware,' Matt Davis replied. 'In the summer we sometimes have problems with teenagers messing around in the woods and making camp fires, but that's usually at the other end, up near the quarry. I believe Ivy Cottage backs onto the thickest part of the forest.'

'Yes, although I haven't been in that part of the woods.'

'Oh, you should,' he said enthusiastically. 'They're at their best in autumn. The colours are amazing. Keep to the foot-paths and you can't get lost.'

'I might give it a try,' Jan replied. The local police seemed far friendlier than those in the towns and cities.

Matt confirmed he would be with her soon after three and, winding up the conversation, said goodbye.

Jan was pleased she'd phoned. Justified and exonerated, her spirits lifted. She'd done the right thing in reporting it, and although she hadn't been able to provide a description, it was being investigated. Now she needed to go to the village store to make sure she was back in plenty of time for his visit.

'Tinder! Come on, walkies!' she called.

She checked the back door was locked, then went into the hall and unhooked the dog lead from its peg. Although Tinder could run freely along the lane, she would need to use it when they neared the village and had to cross the main road.

'Tinder! Walkies!' she called again. He didn't usually need telling twice. 'Tinder!'

He appeared at the top of the stairs, tail wagging and with a mischievous look on his face. As he came down, Jan saw he had something white in his mouth.

'What have you got?' she asked, and took it away.

It was a small white bootee belonging to a baby or large doll, now covered in saliva. 'Where did you get that?'

Tinder looked back guiltily. Jan went upstairs and found the door to the second bedroom wide open. She couldn't have closed it properly after she'd switched off the sensor light. The contents of a number of Camile's carefully packed boxes were scattered across the floor.

'Tinder! You naughty boy!' she called. She'd have to clear it up later. She needed to go to the village store now, before DC Matt Davis arrived. 'Naughty boy,' she said again as she came downstairs.

Tinder looked at her with large, sorrowful eyes. 'It's OK,' she said, rubbing his head. 'It's not your fault. I shouldn't have allowed you upstairs. Your mistress doesn't.'

She ruffled his fur again and then, lead in hand, opened the front door and set off for Merryless. As well as milk, she needed to top up on loose change to feed the meter. Also, she'd have a look at the food in their freezer. They kept a reasonable selection for a village store to try to persuade villagers to shop there rather than going to the supermarkets in Coleshaw.

Jan walked briskly along Wood Lane with Tinder not far behind. The day had started off bright but now the clouds were gathering. She could feel the temperature dropping. It was early November and the weather forecast was predicting ground frost by the end of the week. Her mother was already asking about Christmas and hoping that Jan would spend it with them. But she couldn't leave Tinder alone. Her good friend Ruby had texted asking if she had any plans for Christmas and suggesting they could spend it holed up in the cottage with wine and movies, which she liked the idea of.

'Come on, Tinder! Keep up!' Jan called. He kept stopping to sniff and forage in the undergrowth at the edge of the woods.

'Come on. Good boy!' Jan called again, and turned.

Tinder was nowhere to be seen.

'Tinder!' she shouted. 'Here, now!'

There was no sign of him. She stayed where she was and listened for any sound suggesting he could be close. But the woods were eerily quiet. 'Tinder! Come on. Here, boy!'

Still nothing. Worried and annoyed that she was having to retrace her steps, Jan went back along the lane. He'd been following her the last time she'd looked, not half a minute ago, but now he'd completely disappeared. She kept going, calling his name and looking into the woods on both sides. He must have chased something. But in which direction? There were trees to her left and right on both sides.

'Tinder!' she shouted at the top of her voice. Then she heard a rustle.

She spun round and looked into the woods where the noise had come from – just in time to see Tinder reappear, running flat out towards her. But what was that behind him? A flash of someone also running, the briefest glimpse before they disappeared into the woods. An image, an outline, the size and shape of a child, similar to the one she thought she'd seen scramble over the side gate of the cottage. Was it possible there could be a child or children living feral in the woods? Surely not. And yet . . .

FIFTEEN

Shaken, Jan ran along Wood Lane, her thoughts spinning. She kept her eyes straight ahead and didn't look into the woods either side and certainly not behind her for fear of what she might see. Tinder was running flat out beside her, his little legs working hard to keep up.

It could have been a child and yet something in its shape and the way it had moved between the trees suggested otherwise. Could it have been an adult trying to keep low to avoid being seen? She thought it was possible, which made her more afraid. Were they following her? If so, why? What did they want with her? Thank goodness she'd reported it to the police and an officer was coming this afternoon. It gave her some reassurance.

Perspiring and out of breath, Jan finally stopped running when the lane met the main road. She put Tinder on his lead and then continued at a brisk walk towards Merryless. Tinder was also out of breath and panting heavily, his tongue drooling. He seemed as unnerved by what had happened in the woods as she was.

Further up, she crossed the road and continued along the pavement to the village shop. Her pulse rate and breathing began to settle. Her biggest worry now was that she had to return along Wood Lane. The clouds were still gathering – thick grey clouds causing the sky to darken and the light to go early. If only she'd brought her car.

Entering the store, Jan took a wire basket from the stack, quickly gathered together the items she needed and approached the counter. There were two customers ahead of her and she waited impatiently. Once they'd been served, Lillian, the store owner, greeted her with a big smile. 'Hello, love.' Her first question as always was: 'Is Chris looking after you all right?' Her husband, Jim, was Chris's brother.

'He is,' Jan replied.

'Excellent.'

As Lillian scanned the items into the till she made small talk. Jan replied, although her thoughts were still far away – in the lane and surrounding woods. She paid using a card and then asked for change for the meter.

Lillian disappeared through a door behind her, into the office where the safe was. She returned with a bag of one-pound coins, which Jan swapped for a twenty-pound note. It was an arrangement Camile had begun some time before and worked well.

'Are you managing to keep warm in the cottage?' Lillian asked as Jan tucked the bag of coins into her jacket pocket.

'Yes, although it's not cheap and winter has only just begun.'

'No, indeed,' Lillian agreed. 'Camile keeps meaning to have that old meter replaced but never gets around to it.'

'I'm fine,' Jan said. 'As long as I remember to feed the meter.'

'And Tinder is behaving himself?' Lillian asked, looking at him over the counter. 'Not disappearing into the woods again?'

'He does, given the opportunity,' Jan said. She hesitated, then asked, 'Do you know if there is anyone living in the woods?'

'Apart from you, you mean?'

'Yes. I mean actually living in the woods.'

'No, not as far as I know. What makes you ask?' she frowned, puzzled.

'Coming here today I thought I saw someone.'

'A hiker?' Lillian suggested.

'Possibly.' Jan shrugged. 'Never mind. I just wondered. Thanks for the meter money.'

'You're welcome. Have a good evening. Chris is taking you somewhere nice.' She winked.

'News travels fast,' Jan said, returning her smile.

'He was in here earlier and mentioned it.'

Another customer approached the till so, thanking Lillian for the meter money again, Jan said goodbye and left.

Outside, Jan kept Tinder on a short lead as they crossed the main road and then eased it off a bit as they walked to the end of Wood Lane. What she'd seen wasn't someone hiking in the woods. Yet Lillian hadn't heard of anyone living in them and she was usually aware of what went on around here.

Jan paused at the end of Wood Lane and looked along it as far as she could before it disappeared around a bend. With woods on both sides and the sky grey, the lane appeared like a long, dark tunnel. As usual it was deserted. It seemed a long way to the cottage, but she needed to get going.

Keeping Tinder on the lead, Jan set off at a jog, but it was difficult with a bag full of shopping banging against her leg. Tinder was tired, his little legs were having to work hard to keep up and he kept wanting to stop. Eventually, Jan slowed to a brisk walk, which Tinder could manage. As they turned the last bend in the lane, the cottage came into view. Jan stopped dead. There was someone in the front garden. Someone small. Too far away to identify with the light so poor, a shadow, but now moving towards her front door.

Tinder saw it too and began barking, straining against the lead to be let free.

They turned and ran, disappearing into the woods at the side of the cottage.

'Hey, stop! Come back!' Jan cried, and ran the rest of the way to the cottage. 'Hello? Is there someone there?' she called into the shrubbery, feeling braver now she was home again.

Tinder had stopped barking and was sniffing the air. No noise came from the other side.

'Hello? Anyone there?' she tried again, and listened.

The only sound was the chirp of a distant bird. Tinder had lost interest, suggesting that whoever or whatever it was had gone. But what were they doing at her front door? Trying to get in? She called out one more time and then went indoors where she let Tinder off his lead. He ran around the downstairs barking and then went to his water bowl where he drank thirstily.

Preoccupied and disturbed by this last encounter, Jan quickly unpacked the freezer food and left the rest to do later. Taking off her jacket, she picked up her laptop. There was something she wanted to check. Previously when she'd looked online for information about the creatures that lived in the woods she'd searched for *Animals living in Coleshaw Woods*. Now she typed in *Strange sightings in Coleshaw Woods*.

Up came pages of websites and news articles. The top one carried the headline *Strange Encounter in Coleshaw Woods*. But as she read it soon became clear it was an interview with a man who claimed to have seen an unidentified flying object hovering over the woods. What she'd seen certainly wasn't a UFO, although it could be alien, she thought with a shudder.

Jan scrolled down the pages. There were reports about a body being found in the quarry in Coleshaw Woods two years ago. The police had struggled to identify the woman as she was a stranger to the area, but the crime had been solved. She found another article about a woman, Miss Susan Pritchard, sixty-five, who'd been walking her dog in the woods when it had chased something and disappeared. While she was trying to find it, she'd thought she'd heard a baby cry and had reported it to the police. But after an extensive search nothing had been found and it was decided it was very likely a cat she'd heard. 'It was a strange cry for a cat,' she was quoted as saying.

Interesting, Jan thought, but she hadn't heard a noise like a cat. She continued down the list of articles, pausing to read anything that might be relevant and explain what she'd seen.

Half an hour later she was forced to admit that nothing remotely matching what she'd seen had been sighted in the woods. Unsure if she should feel relieved or disappointed, Jan closed the laptop, finished unpacking the groceries, fed the meter and left the bag of change beside it in the cupboard under the stairs. She made herself a coffee and took it upstairs. She needed to get a move on – DC Matt Davis would be here soon and she was seeing Chris later. But first she needed to clear up the mess Tinder had made in the spare bedroom.

She went in. He had really made the most of his time in the bedroom. Many of Camile's boxes had at least some of their contents removed. Thankfully he hadn't chewed much. The bootee he'd brought to her earlier was a bit mangled, and Jan now saw that some of the polythene bags on the bed containing Camile's clothes had teeth marks. Just as well he hadn't managed to tear them open and chew what was inside!

Setting her mug of coffee to one side, Jan knelt on the floor and began repacking, hopefully returning the items to their correct box. Tinder was exhausted after his long walk and was asleep downstairs so couldn't do any more damage. Jan would tell Camile what had happened, apologize and reassure her it wouldn't happen again, as she was making sure the door to the spare bedroom was kept shut at all times.

In one box she found another white bootee that matched the one Tinder had brought to her. It was still partially wrapped in tissue paper, together with a small white outfit belonging to a baby or doll. Jan had no idea why Camile would have these and it was none of her business. She carefully rewrapped the bootees and outfit in the tissue paper and was about to return the parcel to the box when she saw a photograph album further down. She knew straight away she shouldn't open it; it was personal and wrong of her to pry. But curiosity quickly got the better of her and one little peep wouldn't hurt. Camile need never know.

Jan carefully lifted out the glossy, light-grey, professionally bound album. It was commemorative, the type that could be created online by uploading digital photographs of a wedding, party, holiday or similar event. On the front was a picture of a golden sun setting over a deep-blue sea, and beneath was the title *Our Last Holiday*, with a date three years before. Even more curious, Jan opened the first page and immediately saw whose holiday it had been. Camile and Chris looked back at her from a Caribbean island. How perfectly matched they were. With similar hair colouring, high cheekbones and open smiles, they made the ideal couple. Jan felt a pang of envy and wondered why they'd broken up.

She turned the pages. Photographs of Camile in her bikini on a sun lounger by the pool. Chris coming out of the sea dripping wet from a swim and laughing. He had a strong, muscular body. The two of them eating at a restaurant, climbing a mountain, sight-seeing – either taken by someone they'd asked or with a selfie stick.

As Jan continued to turn the pages it became increasingly obvious that they'd had a wonderful time and had been very much in love. So why had it been their last holiday? What had gone so badly wrong to end their relationship? Chris had admitted he'd had a relationship with Camile but had been vague. Jan had formed the impression it had been a casual relationship, but these photographs said otherwise.

She felt deflated. Camile was an attractive, confident woman who had a successful career. Chris had clearly doted on her. True, he was taking her out tonight, but she couldn't be anything but second best. He had seen her as a lonely singleton who, having spent too much time alone, was imagining things. In short, he'd felt sorry for her, nothing more. He was probably now regretting ever asking her out.

Jan closed the album, returned it to the box, then placed the parcel containing the bootees and outfit on top. She folded in the lid and left the box where she'd found it. The shine had gone out of the evening ahead. She drained the last of her coffee, and then picking up her phone texted Chris. *Will understand if you want to cancel.*

But his reply was instant: *Wouldn't hear of it. Looking forward to it. Pick you up at 7. See you later, Chris x*

SIXTEEN

'Why didn't you tell me before?' Ian asked, upset and angry. 'I don't understand. I didn't think we had any secrets, and then this!' He spread his hands open in dismay.

'We don't have secrets,' Emma said. 'Only this one. I'm sorry. I was going to tell you, but then there was so much going on with the police coming back, it didn't seem like a good time.'

'And now is a good time?' he asked crossly. 'I come home from work early to take you out, only to be told you're not the person I married. Am I supposed to accept it just like that?'

'I am the same person you married,' Emma cried, hurt. 'It's still me.'

'But you don't have your father's genes. I wasted all that time researching your family's tree and he's not even family!'

'He is my family. He's my father and I love him!' Emma's eyes filled.

'But you don't have his DNA!' Ian said, equally frustrated. 'You have the DNA of someone else, a donor, a stranger. You must see that?'

'Yes, I know, but Mum said the donor couldn't possibly

95

be responsible for the defective gene because all donors are thoroughly screened.'

'How can she be certain?'

'They went to a proper clinic and all donors had their DNA checked to make sure they didn't pass on anything.'

'What clinic?' Ian asked. 'Where is it?'

'I don't know,' Emma said helplessly. 'I didn't ask. It doesn't matter to me. It never has.'

'It matters to me and my research,' Ian snapped.

'Too much!' Emma retaliated. 'I know why you're so angry. It's because this has shown I can't have the defective gene. You haven't found anything on my mother's side, you told me that, and now this rules out my father too. So it has to be you! I think you've become obsessed with this, Ian. Look at all these death certificates.' She grabbed a handful and threw them at him. 'It's taken over, Ian. It's ridiculous! Let it go. It's destroying us.'

There was silence as they both glared at each other. Then Ian said more gently, 'What happened to us was unimaginably horrible, and I have to find out what caused it. Whether I am to blame or not.'

'We know we're not the only couple around here to have had a pregnancy go wrong. Everyone says it's the discharge from the power station contaminating the water that causes the birth defects. That's what you should be researching, not us.'

'I will once I've ruled out our DNA,' Ian agreed. 'I'm sorry for shouting. Shall we have a hug and make up?'

'Yes, come on. I love you. We've got each other and that's all that matters.'

Ian put his arms around his wife and held her close. 'Yes, you're right.'

SEVENTEEN

DC Beth Mayes looked up from her computer screen as Matt returned to his desk. 'You've been gone ages,' she said. 'The boss was looking for you earlier.'

'I've seen him. I've been to Ivy Cottage – you know, in Wood Lane in Coleshaw Woods,' Matt replied. Beth nodded. 'I took a call earlier from Ms Jan Hamlin, the young lady who's renting it. She reported intruders in her garden and seeing someone in the woods.'

'Young lady,' Beth said, with a sardonic smile. 'So that's why you were gone so long – rescuing damsels in distress.' Beth knew Matt well enough to be confident that their repartee wouldn't cause offence. 'Find anything?' she asked.

'Not really. There's definitely something getting into her garden, but I don't think it's kids like she does. There were no shoe or trainer prints. She said she'd seen someone outside the cottage and running between the trees in the lane, so I had a look there, and also went into the woods at the back. There was no sign of anyone living there. I wondered if it was Bill Smith wandering again. His dementia is advanced now and he's got lost a few times. But she was adamant the figure she saw was smaller. She's blocked up a hole in the back hedge so hopefully that will put an end to it.'

'Why is she living there alone?' Beth asked. 'That cottage is very remote.'

'She said she needed to get away to do some thinking.'

'OK. I can identify with that.'

'She was asking about Coleshaw Woods. She'd been reading articles online and found some about a body in the quarry, and a baby that had been heard crying. I reassured her that both cases had been closed.'

'Yes, I investigated the baby crying. Susan Pritchard was the woman who reported it. She was very upset, convinced a baby had been left in the woods. We took in sniffer dogs and at one point they picked up a scent, but then it disappeared up a tree, so we guessed it was squirrels. By coincidence I bumped into Miss Pritchard a few weeks ago in Merryless. She still walks her dog in the woods and believes it was a baby she heard, although she was kind enough to appreciate that we did all we could.'

Matt nodded. 'I told Jan Hamlin if she had any more problems to call and I'd be straight over.'

Beth was about to reply when DS Bert Scrivener appeared at her side. 'I need you two to go to Coleshaw Hospital. A body has disappeared from the maternity unit.'

'You mean a baby, sir?' Beth asked.

'No, a body. Apparently, the baby was born dead yesterday, poor little mite, but now its body has gone missing. The parents are understandably upset. The hospital will hold an inquiry, but the parents want the police involved. They are with the chief executive, Antony Bridges, now, and are refusing to leave until they've spoken to the police.'

'Very good, sir, we're on our way,' Matt said, standing.

'Then take yourselves home after,' DS Scrivener said. 'It's nearly knocking-off time, so you don't need to come back here.'

* * *

Twenty minutes later Beth and Matt arrived at Coleshaw Hospital and went to the main reception desk. 'Detective Constables Beth Mayes and Matt Davis,' Beth said as they showed their IDs. 'I understand the CEO, Mr Antony Bridges, is expecting us.'

'I'll call his office and tell him you're here,' the receptionist said, and picked up her phone.

As they waited, Beth glanced along the corridor where a security guard was talking to an elderly couple who appeared to be asking for directions. The hospital was busy even at five o'clock.

'Mr Bridges said please go up to his office,' the receptionist said. 'Take the lift to the third floor and his personal assistant will meet you there.'

'Thank you.'

Matt and Beth went to the lift sited to the left of the main entrance and pressed the button for the third floor. A few moments later the lift doors opened and a young man greeted them. 'Hello, I'm Donald, Mr Bridges' personal assistant. Thank you for coming so quickly. It was getting a bit heated in there. One of our security guards is with them now.'

Beth and Matt followed the PA down the corridor where he knocked on a door bearing the name plate: *Mr Antony Bridges, Chief Executive Officer*. The door was opened from inside by a security guard.

'The police are here,' the PA said, leading the way in.

The CEO was seated behind a large desk, talking to a young couple facing him. 'You can wait outside now, thank you,' Mr Bridges said, dismissing the security guard.

The PA left with the guard. Only once the door was closed did Mr Bridges speak. 'This is Mr and Mrs Ryan – Grant and Chelsea,' he said.

'Detective Constables Beth Mayes and Matt Davis,' Beth said to them.

It was obvious how upset they were; Grant was clearly struggling to contain his anger and itching to have a go at someone. Chelsea's eyes and cheeks were red from crying. Beth drew over a chair so she was sitting at right angles to the couple. Matt remained standing in case quick intervention was required and Grant needed restraining.

'I'm sorry for your loss,' Beth said as she sat down.

Chelsea sniffed while Grant's face grew harder. 'Fucking awful the way we've been treated! Bad enough our kid dies, but then to get rid of her body so we can't even say goodbye! We came back today to be told she's gone for good!'

'That wasn't how I phrased it,' Antony Bridges said in an even, slightly patronizing tone. 'It's regrettable this has happened and we will of course hold an inquiry. Although it will take time to gather together all the information.' Which antagonized Grant even further.

His face bulged with anger. 'I want him arrested!' Grant shouted, jabbing a finger towards the CEO. Matt took a step towards him. 'Then I'll sue the lot of you.'

'I understand how upsetting this must be for you both,' Beth said gently. 'And we're here to investigate. Could we start by going back to what happened yesterday?' She took out her notepad and pen.

'You tell them! I might hit someone,' Grant said to his wife, and cracked his knuckles.

Chelsea sniffed and took a deep breath. 'I had a baby yesterday,' she began, her voice thick with emotion. 'We knew it was going to be stillborn – it was very early and badly deformed.'

'I'm so sorry,' Beth said, looking up from writing. 'My heart goes out to you both.'

Grant seemed slightly less riled now he knew his concerns were being taken seriously.

'Thank you,' Chelsea said. 'I was prepared for it, as much

as you can be. Our midwife was fantastic. She asked us if we wanted to see our baby but advised us against it. She felt it would be too upsetting.'

'But we wanted to see our baby today,' Grant added.

'I understand,' Beth said, and looked at Chelsea to continue.

'When Grant and I went home last night we talked about our loss. I also spoke to my sister. She thought we should see the baby as it might help us come to terms with what happened.'

Beth nodded sympathetically.

'But when we came here today we were told her body had already been disposed of,' Chelsea said. 'Disposed of, like rubbish.' She pressed a tissue to her face.

'It was an unfortunate word to use,' the CEO admitted.

'Yes, but that is what you have done with our daughter,' Grant blurted.

'Is that normal procedure?' Beth asked the CEO.

'Sometimes, although there seems to have been a breakdown in communication here. Even if the parents don't want to see a stillborn baby – which many don't – we usually keep the body in the mortuary for a few days in case they change their minds. Sadly, that doesn't appear to have happened in this case. There will be a full inquiry. I've already spoken to the midwife concerned. She is very upset and has offered to meet with the parents if that will help.'

'It's not Anne's fault,' Chelsea said. 'She was lovely to us.'

'Was Anne your midwife?' Beth asked.

Chelsea nodded.

'Anne Long?'

'Yes, she is one of our most experienced midwives,' Mr Bridges replied. 'She acted on the parents' wishes, convinced that as the baby was not viable they wouldn't want to see it. Incorrectly, as it turned out. She is very sorry. We all are.'

'What happened to the body?' Beth asked.

'It would have been incinerated,' the CEO replied.

Chelsea gave a little cry and wiped her eyes.

'I am sorry for your loss,' Beth said again. She paused and, lowering her voice, said compassionately. 'As it's impossible for you to see your baby, what would you like to happen now? What could the hospital do to help you?'

'Give us compensation,' Grant said, without hesitation.

'Make sure it never happens again to anyone else,' Chelsea said.

'That seems reasonable,' Beth said, looking at the CEO.

'Of course. Once our inquiry is complete, we'll amend our procedure in line with any recommendations that are made to make sure this doesn't happen again. We always learn from our mistakes. In respect of compensation, if we are found to be to blame, our lawyers will be in touch with Mr and Mrs Ryan.'

'Does that help?' Beth asked the couple.

Chelsea nodded, while Grant said, 'You are to blame, and I don't want this inquiry of yours taking forever. I'm too upset to work, so I need compensation soon.'

'Will you write a report too?' Chelsea asked Beth. 'I don't want this all being swept under the carpet and forgotten about.'

'I'll be filing my report first thing tomorrow,' Beth said. 'Do you have any more questions for Mr Bridges?' she asked them both.

'No,' Chelsea said.

'Not right now, but I might in the future,' Grant said.

'In that case I suggest we leave Mr Bridges to get on with his work,' Beth said, and stood.

Antony Bridges threw her an appreciative look.

'I'll be in touch as soon as we have any news,' he reassured Grant and Chelsea. They too got ready to leave.

Outside, Matt and Beth saw the young couple off the

hospital premises and continued to their car. It was only then that Beth asked Matt, 'Did you recognize the name of the midwife?'

'Yes,' Matt said. 'It's the same one who delivered Mr and Mrs Jennings's baby. Two stillbirths in a month – is that normal?'

'Sadly, yes. I looked it up while I was investigating Mrs Slater's complaint. One in every 223 births is stillborn, that's 3,400 a year, so nine a day. And that's just those that have to be registered because of the number of weeks' gestation. The true figure is likely to be much higher. So in that respect Anne isn't to blame.'

EIGHTEEN

Jan was ready by 6.30 p.m. and waiting in the living room for Chris to arrive. She'd fed Tinder, showered, washed her hair and spent some time trying to decide what to wear. It was the first time since she'd come to live in Ivy Cottage that she'd needed to change out of jeans and a jumper. She was now wearing a dress; one of three she'd packed in case she needed to look smart.

DC Matt Davis had been very helpful and thorough when he'd visited that afternoon. Not only had he checked the back garden, but he'd gone into the woods surrounding the cottage and down the lane where she'd seen the shadowy figure running from the front door and between the trees. He hadn't found any signs of anyone living in the woods and suggested it might have been an animal she'd seen. She hadn't told him otherwise. She would wait until she had some firm evidence. He'd suggested again that she went for a walk in Coleshaw Woods at the back of the cottage and she was considering it. Here she was, living in a renowned beauty spot and she'd hardly explored it at all.

At 7 p.m. Jan heard Chris's car pull up outside. Tinder

heard it too and pricked up his ears. 'See you later,' she said, standing, and ruffled his fur.

She shut him in the living room so he couldn't get upstairs and then went into the hall where she put on her coat. Leaving the hall light on so she could see when she returned, Jan opened the front door. Chris was turning his car around as Wood Lane was a dead end. The only light came from his car's headlamps. She waited until he'd completed the turn and then went round to the passenger side.

'Hi,' she said brightly, getting in. Immediately she sensed an atmosphere.

'Hello,' Chris said, his voice flat. He tried to smile but it didn't quite reach his eyes. Perhaps he'd changed his mind about taking her out after all.

'Are you OK?' she asked, pausing before fastening her seatbelt.

'Yes, thanks, are you?' He slipped the car into first gear and pulled away.

'I've had a busy day,' she said, making conversation. 'I boarded up the hole in the hedge again, took Tinder to the village and then had a visit from the police.' She had expected Chris to be surprised by the mention of the police, but he wasn't.

'I know,' he said, concentrating on the road ahead. 'DC Matt Davis was the officer you saw. Not sure why it merited CID. He stopped off at the village store after he'd been to see you. He knows Lillian and my brother.'

'Oh, of course, I should have guessed,' Jan said with a smile. Everyone knew everyone else here.

But there was an awkward silence.

'Have you had a good day?' she asked.

'It was OK. I was working locally. But, Jan, I don't understand why you involved the police. I thought we'd agreed it wasn't necessary.'

She looked at him again, but his face was expressionless. 'I just felt it was wise to report it,' she said. 'Why does it matter? What's the problem?'

'No problem, but news travels fast round here.'

'So? Matt didn't find anything.'

'He wouldn't, not during the day.'

'So he might have found something if he'd come at night?' she asked, with a stab of unease.

'I meant you only have the problem at night, don't you?'

'Mostly. Although I'm sure I saw someone today when I walked into the village.'

Chris didn't reply but stared straight ahead, apparently concentrating on the uneven road surface.

Jan wished she hadn't come. The evening was already a disaster and it had hardly begun. She was about to make an excuse to return home when Chris turned to her. 'I'm sorry,' he said. 'I can be a moody bugger sometimes. Let's start the evening again, shall we? I've booked us a table at a really nice restaurant.'

'Yes, I know,' she said, relieved.

'You do? How?'

'Lillian told me. News travels fast round here.'

'Touché,' he said, and this time his smile did reach his eyes.

NINETEEN

At the same time as Jan and Chris were being shown to a candlelit table in Bon Appetit, a fine-dining restaurant in Coleshaw, Emma and Ian were sitting at their kitchen table, having just eaten egg on toast. It was all they'd wanted as neither of them was hungry. Ian had cooked it. He was calmer and more reasonable now he could see why Emma hadn't ever told him she'd been conceived using donor sperm. Quite simply it hadn't mattered to her. The man who had brought her up was her father and that was that.

Emma, for her part, now accepted that in order for Ian to continue his research into their genetic history – which was important to him – he needed to know who the donor was. She had agreed in principle to finding out but was reluctant to take the first step – to ask her mother for the details of the clinic they'd used. Emma knew she'd be upset.

'Phone her rather than go there again,' Ian said. 'It will be easier than facing her in person.'

'I might,' Emma said, nervously fiddling with her fork.

'Or I could phone her?' Ian offered.

'No, I should. But I know it's going to upset her again.'

'It might not. I mean, you've already told her why I need

the information – to trace our genetic history. It's not such a big step for her to realize we need the details of the donor.'

'I think she's hoping we'll forget about it and you won't continue with your research and just let the matter go.'

'Emma,' Ian said, reaching for her hand. 'I thought we'd agreed we needed to know, whatever the outcome.'

She gave a small nod and slid her hand away.

'Let's phone her now,' Ian said enthusiastically. 'It'll be easier for you if I'm here. If you get upset, I can take over and speak to her.'

'No, Dad will be there. Mum won't discuss it in front of him. She won't have told him I've been asking about the donor. It's never mentioned in my family.'

'OK. So phone and ask her to call you back. All we want is the name of the clinic and I can do the rest. Please, Emma. It's better to do it now and get it out of the way or you won't sleep tonight.'

'All right!' Emma said.

Ian left the table and fetched Emma's phone. Handing it to her, he sat opposite and watched as she pressed the number for her parents' landline. They preferred using the landline to their mobiles if they were at home. A few rings and her father answered. Emma's heart sank.

'Hello, Dad. How are you?' she asked, immediately feeling deceitful.

'I'm good, thanks, pet. How are you?'

'Not too bad.'

'It's lovely to hear from you. Your mother said you'd stopped by. Now you're feeling a bit better, why don't you and Ian come over for some dinner at the weekend? I'll do your favourite curry with my speciality rice.'

'Thanks, Dad, that would be great.' She felt another stab of guilt.

'Good. Everything OK with you?'

'Yes.'

'Did you want to speak to your mother?' he asked guile-lessly. Emma felt even more guilty.

'Yes, please, Dad.'

'I'll put her on. Love you, pet.'

'Love you too, Dad.'

She met Ian's gaze and he nodded encouragingly.

A moment later her mother came on the phone, 'Hi, love, everything all right?'

'Yes, thanks. Is Dad still in the room?'

'No, he's gone to check on our dinner. Why?'

'Ian is here with me. He needs to know the name of the clinic – you know, the one we talked about.'

There was silence before Mary said in a whisper, 'I can't discuss it now, your father may hear me.'

'All I need is the name of the clinic and Ian will do the rest.' She waited. More silence. 'It's not going to go away, Mum, not until Ian's found out. Dad need never know, I promise you.'

'No good will come of this,' Mary said.

'Please, Mum, just tell me.'

'I will, but don't say I didn't warn you. It was called the Moller Clinic.'

'Thank you.'

But already the line was dead.

'There! I knew she'd be upset!' Emma said angrily.

'Did she tell you the name of the clinic?' Ian asked.

'Yes. The Moller Clinic.'

'Did she say where it was?'

'No! And I'm not asking her any more about it.'

'Never mind. There shouldn't be too many clinics with that name.'

Opening his laptop, Ian began tapping the keys.

Emma watched him for a moment and then stood. 'I'm going to bed. I've got a headache.'

But Ian was too engrossed in what he was doing to reply or even look up.

Emma left the table, regretting she'd agreed to make the call. Her mother was right. No good would come of it – just the opposite, in fact.

TWENTY

Although the evening hadn't started well, it had dramatically improved after Chris had apologized for being moody. Jan was pleased she hadn't asked to return home. The restaurant was really nice – the sort of place she'd only have booked for a special occasion. Chris had clearly made an effort to impress her, which Jan appreciated. Gone were his trainers, jeans and zip-up windbreaker jacket; he was now dressed smart-casual in beige chinos, cotton shirt, navy blazer and brown leather shoes. As they'd entered the restaurant he'd complimented her on her appearance – 'You look lovely.' And Jan had felt a warm frisson of anticipation for the evening ahead.

He was being very attentive – refilling her glass and checking her food had been cooked to her liking. Their conversation flowed and became easier with every glass of wine. Chris had ordered a bottle of Merlot, having first checked with her that she liked red wine. She did and they discovered they had similar tastes in wine, as they did in coffee. He was sipping his wine slowly because he was driving, so Jan was drinking far more than him. It was many months since she'd had more than one glass of wine in an evening and she knew she was talking a lot. But Chris didn't seem to mind. He was encouraging her, nodding in agreement and laughing at her jokes. She was making the most of it, as on many days recently she hadn't had anyone to talk to apart from Tinder.

They'd finished the main course and the waiter had cleared away their plates and left the dessert menu. Neither of them had looked at it yet as they were too busy talking. Jan was now entertaining Chris with tales of Tinder's antics.

'He can be so naughty at times,' she said, taking another sip of wine.

'Why, what's he done now?' Chris asked, smiling encouragingly.

'His latest mischief was in the spare bedroom – you know, where Camile has stored the boxes of her belongings? I couldn't have closed the door properly because this morning he came downstairs, guilt written all over his face, carrying a little white bootee in his mouth. I knew it wasn't mine,' she laughed. 'So I went upstairs and found Camile's belongings all over the floor. Perhaps he was missing her and could smell her on them. I don't know. I've repacked them, but I couldn't really tell him off because he gave me one of those adoring looks, the picture of innocence.'

Glass in hand, Jan paused, expecting Chris to be laughing as he'd been doing at her other anecdotal stories. But he wasn't.

'What sort of bootee?' he asked.

'Like a baby's or a large doll's,' Jan said. 'I put it back with the other one and a little matching outfit.'

Chris paused. 'Was there anything else in the box?' he asked, his expression serious.

'Just a photograph album. I've repacked everything. I'll make sure Tinder doesn't get in there again.'

But Chris was still looking at her sombrely, pensive and

deep in thought. Their conversation seemed to have dried up, although Jan didn't know why. He was frowning now. Why? What was he thinking about? She finished her glass of wine.

'Dogs can be mischievous,' she added.

'Yes, I suppose they can. Make sure the door to that bedroom is kept closed in future. Camile would be upset if she knew Tinder had got in there and destroyed her personal items.'

'He didn't destroy them,' Jan said, slightly affronted. 'He didn't do any real damage. I'm sorry it happened, and I will tell Camile. I'm not sure what else I can do.'

Chris nodded, placed his napkin on the table and said, 'As we've finished I'll get the bill.' Without waiting for Jan's reply, he raised his hand and signalled to the waiter.

'The bill, please?' he said, not meeting her gaze.

'Yes, sir. Would you like a coffee?'

'No, thank you.' He was already taking out his wallet.

'I'll pay my half,' Jan offered.

'No. I asked you out. I'll pay.'

She watched him settle the bill with no idea what she'd done wrong or how to put it right. Why should he be so worried about Tinder getting into Camile's spare bedroom? The dog hadn't done any real harm. Perhaps there were things in there he didn't want her to see. The photograph album of their last holiday? But she hadn't admitted to looking at that, thank goodness.

They stood and walked towards the exit in silence. She could have kicked herself for telling him Tinder had gone into the spare bedroom. The wine had loosened her tongue, but she hadn't seen any reason not to mention it. She still didn't.

She walked beside him to his car and they got in.

'Chris, have I done something wrong?' she asked as he started the engine.

113

'No.'

'So why have you gone all quiet on me?'

'I hadn't realized I had,' he said dourly, and starting the car he pulled out of the car park.

'I can get a cab if you like,' Jan offered.

'No, I'll take you home.' And that was all he said for a long time.

TWENTY-ONE

It had been easy for Ian to find the Moller Clinic on the Internet. There was only one listed with that name in the UK. It was situated in a small village on the other side of Coleshaw, about a thirty-minute drive away. *A well-established fertility clinic*, the tagline read, set up by Carstan and Edie Moller thirty years ago, and offering a *sensitive and personalized service*. There was a photograph of the couple standing outside their clinic as if welcoming in their clients. A homely couple in their sixties with greying hair. The clinic itself appeared to be an extension built on the side of what Ian assumed to be their house, but with its own front door. The pictures of the inside of the clinic were like many other private clinics, showing a comfortable waiting area, and a consultation and treatment room.

By 9 p.m. Ian had read all the information on every page of the Moller Clinic's website, including a whole page of testimonials, some with pictures of babies. The clinic, he'd learnt, specialized in intrauterine insemination (IUI). This involved placing donated sperm inside a woman's uterus using a cannula, where it would hopefully fertilize one of her eggs. The clinic treated heterosexual couples, lesbians and single women. All donated sperm was screened for sexually transmitted and genetically inherited diseases – just as Emma's mother had said.

The clinic's mission statement was that treatment should be available to anyone who needed it. Because they were only a small clinic specializing in IUI, they could keep their costs down. Ian was surprised just how little they charged: £300, much less than most other clinics. There was a warning that often more than one treatment was required, but payments could be spread. The couple also offered counselling, with a note stating that clients should be aware that in the UK, children born as a result of donor sperm had the right to know the donor's identity once they reached eighteen.

It was all very reassuring and efficient, Ian thought, and he was hopeful his questions would be answered satisfactorily. After all, Emma had a right to know about her donor. He entered the clinic's number in his phone. He'd call first thing in the morning as soon as they opened. Even the contact page of their website was reassuring, with its pledge that Edie Moller personally answered all enquiries.

Having read all the pages on the Moller Clinic's website, Ian began clicking on other links where the clinic was mentioned. There were reviews praising Carstan and Edie Moller for their wonderful treatment and thanking them for the gift of their child. Ian only found one negative review. *Don't go anywhere near this place! They are in it for their own selfish ends. Ms L.*

Ian dismissed it. There were always one or two negative reviews. The Mollers certainly weren't in it for the money, as they charged so little, so s*elfish ends* didn't really make sense. Perhaps the poor woman hadn't been able to conceive using their treatment. In which case, it wasn't the clinic's fault; they warned the treatment didn't always work.

Ian finally closed his laptop, sat back in the chair and

stretched. It had been a productive evening. He would have liked to share what he'd found out with Emma, but she'd had an early night. He was sorry he'd upset her; he seemed to be doing that a lot recently, and then he struggled to find the words to put it right. They'd both been through a lot and he hoped that once he had the answers to his questions, it would make amends and put their lives back on track.

TWENTY-TWO

The silence in the car was unsettling and Jan was relieved when they turned into Wood Lane. Nearly home, she thought. Moody bugger. One minute Chris had been all over her and the next he was sullen and uncommunicative. And all because Tinder had rearranged some of Camile's belongings!

Sitting upright in her seat, Jan kept her gaze straight ahead as they continued along the potholed road surface of Wood Lane. The car's headlamps were the only light, on full beam and illuminating the road ahead. The brightness of the lights seemed to emphasize the darkness of the woods either side, making them even more unnerving, Jan thought. Although she was inside a car, she didn't feel especially safe surrounded by the dark woods and with Chris beside her not saying a word. She realized she barely knew him.

The last bend in the lane appeared and Jan took out her front-door key, ready. She wouldn't ask Chris in for coffee, but she supposed she should thank him. She'd just say a quick formal thank you as she got out of the car, and that would be it. She doubted she'd see him again.

They turned the bend and the car's headlights picked up the outline of the cottage. But as they did, something shot out of the front garden, across the lane, and disappeared into the woods.

'There!' Jan cried. 'Did you see it?' She thought he had as his gaze had momentarily tracked its movement.

'No, what?' Chris asked, looking ahead again.

'That . . . that shadow, that person. You must have seen it.'

'No.'

He continued to drive steadily towards the cottage.

Jan's heart was racing and her mouth had gone dry. She looked all around, but there was nothing to be seen in the lane or woods now. She was sure Chris had seen it. It was the same figure she'd seen earlier when she'd returned from the village. It had been in the front garden then, just as it had now. Whatever it was seemed to be getting braver. Jan shuddered.

Chris stopped the car outside the cottage but left the engine running. There was nothing in the front garden and as far as Jan could see nothing in the surrounding woods either. She gingerly opened her car door, ready to get out. As she did, Chris turned in his seat and for a moment she thought he was going to apologize, but his voice was flat and his face was set and serious when he spoke.

'Jan, if you're so nervous about living in the cottage, why don't you move out? I can speak to Camile if you like. She won't keep you in the tenancy if you want to go.'

'No, thank you,' Jan said tersely. 'I'm fine.' And got out.

She closed the car door with more force than was necessary and went up to the cottage. The car remained stationary for a moment and then Chris began a three-point turn. As she let herself in, he completed the manoeuvre and began along the lane towards the village.

I'll speak to Camile if you like. She kicked off her shoes. No, thank you, Jan thought, annoyed. I'm not nervous.

Although you'll probably tell Camile anyway. And you did see something run from the cottage and disappear into the woods. I'm sure of it. But for some reason you're denying it. I don't know what's going on here, but I'm not giving up that easily. I'm staying for now, thank you!

'Sshh, Tinder!' she shouted, going down the hall.

He was barking furiously from the living room where she'd shut him in. She opened the door and he shot out past her, straight to the front door. Still barking, he began frantically scratching to be let out. He knew there'd been something out there.

How she would have liked to let him out and then follow with a torch. But she wasn't brave enough for that. Nowhere near. Whoever – whatever – was out there had started coming to the front door. But why? What did they want from her? Food? Or were they coming for her?

TWENTY-THREE

The following morning at 8.30 a.m. Ian parked his car in the firm's car park, took out his mobile and called the Moller Clinic. Their website said they opened at 8.30 and, true to their word, Edie Moller answered in a kind, motherly tone. 'Good morning. The Moller Clinic, Edie speaking. How can we help you?'

'I'd like to discuss donor identification, please, for my wife Emma Jennings. I'm her husband, Ian Jennings.'

'Yes, of course. Just give me a moment. I haven't been in the office long so bear with me while I power up my computer. Then I'll need to find your file.'

'Of course,' Ian said, and waited.

'When we first started our clinic it was all paper files,' Edie said, making conversation as her computer booted. 'Now we have to store everything digitally. How things have changed!'

'Yes, indeed,' Ian agreed, while thinking that modern technology had probably been quite challenging for Mr and Mrs Moller, a couple in their sixties.

'Jennings, Jennings,' Edie said, as she searched the files. 'Ah yes, here we are. Thank you for your patience. Were you enquiring about yourself or your wife?'

'My wife,' Ian said, then stopped. 'Sorry, I don't understand. My wife's mother had the treatment so surely it would be listed under Emma's maiden name. Jennings is her married name – my name – and we haven't been to your clinic.' Ian paused as his thoughts raced. 'I really can't imagine why you would have my details.'

There was silence before Edie said, 'I'm sorry, my mistake. What was your wife's maiden name?'

'But you found something for Jennings, didn't you?'

'It's a common name. I made a mistake. As it's your wife who is interested in tracing a donor, she will need to contact the clinic. Confidentiality, I'm sure you understand.'

Ian paused. 'But just now you were willing to talk to me.'

'That was before – when I thought the enquiry was about you.'

'So you have got something on me?' he persisted.

'As I said, it's a common name and I made a mistake. Please advise your wife to contact the clinic if she wishes to make an enquiry about her donor. Thank you for calling.' Saying a quick goodbye, Edie Moller ended the call.

Ian stared through the windscreen, trying to make sense of what had just happened. Edie Moller's manner had abruptly changed and become very formal and guarded, quite brusque. Very different to when she'd answered the phone. Had she made a genuine mistake? Jennings was a fairly common surname, Ian supposed. As the clinic had been running for thirty years there could easily be another Mr and Mrs Jennings on file. Except. He'd given their forenames too – 'Emma Jennings. I'm her husband, Ian Jennings,' he'd said. It would be too much of a coincidence for another couple with exactly the same forenames to be registered at the clinic.

Ian remained sitting in his car, deep in thought, frantically searching for an explanation. Then he pressed redial on his phone. His call went straight to the Mollers' answerphone, inviting him to leave a message. He didn't. He pressed redial again, with the same result. Edie Moller was there but not answering his calls.

Annoyed, Ian tucked his phone into his jacket pocket, took his briefcase from the passenger seat and, with a feeling of disquiet, got out of the car. He had to go into work now. Preoccupied, he crossed the car park and went in the back entrance of Wetherby Security Ltd, then up the two flights of stairs to his office. Saying a perfunctory good morning to his colleagues, he sat at his desk, took out his mobile phone and called the clinic again. As he thought might happen it went through to answerphone. Edie Moller would see his number on the caller display. He picked up his desk phone and called the clinic from that.

'Good morning. The Moller Clinic, Edie speaking. How can I help you?'

'It's Ian Jennings,' he said. 'You're not answering my calls.'

A pause, then, 'I'm sorry, Mr Jennings, I really can't help you further. It's for your wife to contact us.' He heard the tension in her voice and knew she was very worried about something.

'I appreciate that, but I want to talk about me, not her. Do you have an Ian Jennings listed on your books with the address 57 Booth Lane?'

The silence seemed to confirm they did, and Mrs Moller was scared.

'If you wish to make an enquiry about yourself then you'll need to make an appointment,' she said. 'But I'm afraid we're fully booked until next year.'

'I'm not waiting until next year for answers,' Ian said. 'I want to come in today.'

'I'm afraid that's not possible.'

'We'll see about that,' he said, and ended the call.

123

Next year! He needed answers now. Edie Moller was hiding something and he intended to find out what.

Picking up his briefcase, Ian left the office, telling his boss on the way out he was working from home. 'Family matter,' he added, aware they wouldn't press him as the company knew his wife had suffered a late miscarriage.

Ian took the stairs two at a time and then crossed the car park to his car. Edie Moller hadn't answered the phone when she'd seen it was his number, and when she had answered and found out it was him she'd been wary and guarded. If his details weren't on their file then surely she would have just said that the Ian Jennings she had registered lived at a different address.

But she hadn't.

So why did the Moller Clinic have his details when he'd never been near the clinic? He intended to find out.

Ian entered the postcode of the Moller Clinic in the car's satnav and, leaving the car park, joined the rush-hour traffic through Coleshaw. His thoughts were working overtime in the stop-start line of vehicles and he agitatedly drummed his fingers on the steering wheel.

What was going on? Had Emma been to the clinic without him? Surely not. They'd had no need for donated sperm. She got pregnant easily enough. It was what happened after that caused the problem. Ian shuddered at the thought. Two pregnancies that had ended the same way. He couldn't bear the thought of another, neither could Emma, unless they found out what was going wrong and were able to put it right. But what had the Moller Clinic got to do with that? Nothing, as far as he knew.

Once out of the congested town, Ian drove as fast as the country lanes would allow, and fifteen minutes later he was parking outside the Moller Clinic. The house was set apart from the rest of the village by being situated at the top of the hill on the other side. It looked exactly like the photograph on their website, except for the CCTV cameras. They had either been added after the photograph had been taken or, not wanting to discourage clients, purposely left off the photo.

Ian got out of the car and went up the front garden path that ran alongside the drive. A shiny new BMW sat on the forecourt, suggesting the Mollers were doing quite well. The brass plaque on the door to the clinic announced *The Moller Clinic* in bold black lettering. He pressed the doorbell and heard it chime inside. A few moments later the door opened and Ian recognized Edie Moller from her photograph on their website, although clearly she had no idea who he was.

'Good morning,' she said, with a bright, welcoming smile. 'Do you have an appointment?'

'No. I'm Ian Jennings.' He watched her face change.

'You'd better come in,' she said, obviously unnerved by his arrival. 'I'll get my husband to speak to you.'

'Thank you.'

Ian followed Edie Moller down the hall and into the waiting room, which was exactly like the picture on their website. Cream curtains, white leather sofa and a glass-topped table with magazines and a vase of fresh flowers.

'I'll tell him you're here,' Edie said, and hurried out, closing the door behind her.

Ian sat on the leather sofa and glanced around. Had Edie Moller already told her husband of her error or was she telling him now? He was half expecting her to return and say her husband couldn't see him and he'd have to make an appointment. In which case he'd stay put and insist he saw him now. There was no one else waiting, Carstan Moller was here and this was too important to leave. He needed answers to his questions now.

Ian checked his phone – there were no new messages – and

set it to silent. A few moments later footsteps sounded in the hall. The door opened and Edie Moller appeared.

'Mr Moller will see you now,' she announced formally.

'Thank you,' Ian said, and stood.

She led the way along the hall towards the rear of the house where she stopped outside a door marked *Office*. Giving a brief knock, she opened it. 'Mr Ian Jennings to see you.'

Ian went in.

'Good morning, Mr Jennings,' Carstan Moller said, coming out from behind a large oak desk to shake hands.

Shorter and older than he'd appeared in his picture on their website, he was wearing a white lab coat over a grey open-neck shirt and dark-grey trousers. 'Take a seat,' he said, gesticulating to the leather armchair positioned in front of his desk.

As Ian sat down, Edie Moller went out and closed the door behind her. Mr Moller returned to his chair. A row of filing cabinets filled one wall and shelves crammed with books another. There was also a second, smaller desk with a computer and a printer where Ian assumed Edie Moller worked.

'How can I help you?' Carstan Moller asked evenly. Although Ian was pretty certain he already knew.

'I telephoned earlier this morning to enquire about tracing my wife's sperm donor, but I discovered you also have me listed on your books.'

Carstan Moller nodded. 'That's correct. I can discuss your request, but you'll need to bring your wife with you to discuss her search.'

'I know that now, Mrs Moller said. But the reason I'm here is to find out why you have my details. I've never been to your clinic before today.'

Moller held Ian's gaze. 'We usually offer counselling before a client begins a search for their donor,' he replied.

126

'That's not my question. Why have you got my details?'

Moller drew his hands together and took a breath. 'I would have thought that was obvious, Mr Jennings. You are on our books because you were conceived by donor sperm.'

'No, I wasn't!'

'Your reaction is exactly why we recommend counselling first,' Moller replied.

'I don't need counselling!' Ian snapped. 'Just the truth.'

'I'm telling you the truth, Mr Jennings. You asked me why we have your details and I've given you an honest answer.'

Ian stared at him and felt his stomach loosen. 'Edie Moller said it was a case of mistaken identity, but you're now telling me that isn't so?'

'That's right.'

Ian felt hot and clammy. 'Are you saying my mother came here for treatment?' he asked incredulously.

'That's correct. Although your mother and father came together, as do most couples.'

'My mother received donor sperm?' Ian asked, horrified.

'That's correct.'

'And my parents came together, so my father knew?'

'Yes.'

'It's definitely not a mistake then?' Ian said, struggling to believe what he was being told.

'No. The mistake was when my wife accidentally told you over the phone that you were on our books, for which we are both sorry. It was early and she'd just come into the office. She knows she must be more careful in future. It's obviously come as a huge shock to you.'

Ian stared at Moller. 'It has. My parents never said anything to me. Ever. My father is dead, but my mother knows I've been researching my genetic history. Why hasn't she told me?'

'I can't answer that, but many parents don't tell their children. You'd be surprised just how many people from

127

Coleshaw and the surrounding villages have been conceived from donated sperm and are not aware of it. It's more often that children aren't told than they are.'

'My wife grew up knowing,' Ian said ruefully.

'She is one of a small minority.'

Ian glanced distractedly around the room, then brought his gaze back to Moller. 'Why did you have my wife's married name and our current address?'

'Emma's mother, Mary Holmes, telephoned the clinic and asked if her daughter had been in touch. She said you were researching their genetic history and had put pressure on Emma to contact us. She asked for some advice. We updated our records at the time in case Emma contacted us. She hasn't.'

'She is finding it difficult,' Ian admitted.

'That's understandable,' Moller said in a conciliatory manner. 'It's quite a journey to search out a donor and not one to be taken lightly.'

'So I'm not who I thought I was,' Ian said, struggling. 'And all my research has been a waste of time.'

'Of course you are the same person you've always been. And as for your research, I can assure you that if there is any genetic fault it hasn't come from this clinic. All sperm donors are thoroughly screened, so if there is a problem it's not with your biological father.'

Ian let out a heartfelt sigh. 'I understand,' he said numbly.

'I'm sorry you had to find out this way. I suggest you have a chat with your mother and Emma and then contact me again if you or your wife wish to trace your donors. My advice would be not to.'

'Why?' Ian asked.

'Nothing will be achieved and it could make you both feel unsettled. Emma has the right idea – be guided by her. When we first started our clinic, no one traced their donors and everyone was happy. Then the law changed. Get on with your life and be grateful you are both healthy, intelligent and able to do well. You have me to thank for that for screening your donor. Now, if there's nothing else, I really must be getting on. Thank you for coming to see me. I'll let my wife know you are ready to leave.'

Without waiting for a reply, Moller pressed a buzzer beneath his desk and almost immediately Edie Moller came into the room. 'I'll see you out, Mr Jennings,' she said with a tight smile.

Ian stood and left the room.

TWENTY-FOUR

Ian got into his car but didn't start the engine. He was in no fit state to drive. While he accepted what Moller had told him, there was something about him and his wife Ian really didn't like. They were smug, dogmatic, superior. Yes, that was it. The pair of them exuded a sense of elitism, as though they knew better than others . . . *be grateful you are both healthy, intelligent and able to do well. You have me to thank for that*, Moller had said arrogantly. Ian supposed that playing God for so long and giving infertile clients children had gone to his head. But Ian knew he had to speak to his mother, and it wouldn't be easy.

He took a swig of water from the bottle he kept in his car and, picking up his phone, pressed the number for his mother, Helen. She lived a two-hour drive away and he saw her a few times a year. She'd be at work now, caring for an elderly lady with dementia, but hopefully when she saw his number she'd take his call or call him back straight away if she was busy.

She answered on the third ring. 'Is everything all right?' she asked with a mother's anxiety for her child, regardless of their age.

'No, Mum, it's not,' Ian said bluntly. 'I'm parked outside the Moller Clinic. Does that name mean anything to you?'

He heard his mother's silence and could visualize her face. He hated doing this to her. He loved her but now felt cheated and betrayed. How could she have lived with this secret all these years and not told him?'

'Why are you there?' she finally asked, her voice slight.

'Because I have just discovered that the man I used to call Dad isn't my real father. And I'm the result of donor sperm – a complete stranger you never even met. I can't believe you did this to me, Mum, and didn't tell me.'

'Ian, it wasn't like that,' Helen said sombrely. 'We wanted children and tried for years. But then we had tests and discovered your father had such a low sperm count it would be impossible for me to conceive naturally. We thought long and hard about what we should do before we sought the help of the Moller Clinic. Of course your dad was your father – he loved you. But we felt it was better you didn't know.'

'But why not tell me now, Mum?' Ian asked, screwing shut his eyes. 'You knew I was researching my genetic history so Emma and I could hopefully have a normal baby. Surely that was the time to tell me?'

'I thought about it, but I knew it would come as a huge shock to you after all these years. I wanted you to remember your father as he was – your dad, the man who brought you up. He loved you and was so proud of you, son. You know that, don't you?'

'Yes,' Ian admitted. 'He was a good man. I can't fault him. But this has come as a huge shock, Mum, and straight after finding out Emma was conceived by donor sperm too.'

'Was she? Really?' Helen asked, surprised. 'I had no idea.'

'Neither did I until yesterday, although she's known most of her life.'

'Why didn't she tell you?'

'Same reasons you and Dad didn't.'

'I can understand that. Which clinic did her parents use, do you know?' Helen asked.

'The Moller Clinic, the same as you and Dad.' As Ian said this a new fear suddenly gripped him. 'Oh my God, Mum, you don't think Emma and I could share the same donor? If we did, it would mean we were related, half brother and sister.' Bile rose in his throat and he flung open his car door just in time to throw up in the gutter.

'Ian? Are you OK?' his mother asked on the other end of the phone.

'No,' he said, wiping his mouth. He took another swig of water. 'Mum, if Emma and I do have the same biological father it might explain why we look similar and can't have healthy children. Some defects in DNA only appear if there is inbreeding.'

'But Carstan and Edie Moller are professionals,' Helen said. 'They know what they're doing. They wouldn't have let that happen, I'm certain.'

'Think about it, Mum. Sperm donors donate many times and can father hundreds of children. The Mollers couldn't have predicted that Emma and I would ever get together. If I'd had any idea that Emma and I were the product of donated sperm and from the same clinic I would have checked with them before we married to make sure we weren't related. Otherwise it's incest, Mum!' His stomach churned and he swallowed back fresh bile.

'No! It's not possible. I'm sure you're wrong, Ian.'

'How can you be so sure, Mum? You should have told me.'

'I'm so sorry. I kept quiet for your father's sake. I never thought it would come to this.' Her voice broke.

Ian was silent for a moment and then said, 'I'm going back into the clinic now to confront Carstan Moller. I need to know the truth.'

TWENTY-FIVE

Ian drew himself to his full height as he returned up the front path to the Moller Clinic and pressed the bell. No one answered. They were in all right but would be able to see him on the CCTV. He pressed the bell again, long and hard, then opened the letterbox and shouted, 'I know you're in there. I need to speak to you. I'm not leaving until I do.'

Straightening, he pressed the bell again and kept his finger on it until the door opened.

'Yes, what is it, Mr Jennings?' Carstan Moller demanded. 'You're making a hell of a noise.' Ian could see Edie Moller standing a little way behind him down the hall, her mobile in her hand, probably ready to call the police if necessary.

'Could Emma and I have the same sperm donor?' Ian asked.

'No, of course not!'

'How can you be so certain?'

'I keep meticulous records. I always have done. We're professional. That sort of thing can't happen here.'

'Have you checked your records for Emma and me?'

'No. I didn't know you were coming here today. You just turned up.'

'So can you check now, please?'

'It will take me a while.'

'I can wait.'

'I'll phone you,' Moller said. 'But you're worrying unnecessarily. It's not my clinic that's at fault.'

'Please check now and I'll wait in my car for your call. I'm not leaving until I have the answer.'

'That's your decision,' Moller said, and closed the door.

Ian returned to his car. Arrogant bastard!

He was prepared to wait outside the clinic all day if necessary. He had the right to know if he and Emma shared the same donor, horrendous though that possibility was. If the clinic was keeping proper records as Moller had said then it shouldn't be too difficult to find the information.

Ian stared, unseeing, through the windscreen, angry, upset and fearing the worst. Five minutes later his phone rang and it was Carstan Moller. 'I have checked our records and, as I thought, you and your wife don't share the same donor.'

'Are you sure?'

'Perfectly.'

'So why can't we have healthy babies?'

'I really don't know. There could be many reasons. I'm sorry for you, but it has nothing to do with my clinic. And if you don't mind me saying, I think you're becoming obsessed with this. Take Emma's advice and get on with your lives. Now I really need to do some work. Goodbye, Mr Jennings.' He ended the call.

'Arsehole!' Ian cursed, and started the car. He didn't like the man, but at least he had answered his question. He and Emma didn't share the same donor, so that was a great relief.

Ian drove the 200 or so metres into the village and parked outside the shop. He hadn't smoked in years but now felt desperately in need of a cigarette. Discovering he'd come from donor sperm had been a huge blow.

134

He was the only customer in the store and a teenage lad was behind the counter listening to music. He took out his earphones as Ian approached.

'A packet of Marlboro, please.'

The lad opened the cabinet behind him and placed the cigarettes on the counter, the printed warning on the packet face up – *Smoking reduces fertility*.

'That's all I need,' Ian sighed, taking out his wallet.

The lad grinned. 'You been to that clinic on the hill then?' he asked.

'Yes, how did you know?'

'Most strangers who come in have been or are going there. Eleven pounds fifty pence, please.'

'Jesus! Is that what a packet of cigarettes costs now? Just shows how long it's been since I last smoked.' He gave the lad a twenty-pound note and waited for his change.

'What did you think of Mr and Mrs Frankenstein then?' the lad laughed.

Ian shrugged. 'Why do you call them that?'

'Mum says I shouldn't, but you got to admit they're a bit weird.'

'Do you know them well then?'

'No, they don't come in here much and don't really associate with us in the village.'

'So why do you call them Mr and Mrs Frankenstein?' Ian asked, tucking the cigarettes into his pocket.

'They make babies, don't they? And there are rumours around here they create monsters.' The lad laughed again.

'What do you mean?' Ian asked, with a stab of unease.

'Oh, nothing.' He shrugged. 'Mum says I shouldn't repeat this stuff, but rumour has it that sometimes things go wrong and the babies aren't born right.'

Ian took his receipt and left the store. The babies he and Emma had produced weren't right – not by a long way. But they hadn't used sperm from the Moller Clinic so they couldn't blame the clinic for creating their 'monsters', unless . . .

Unless Moller had made a mistake or lied, and he and Emma *did* share the same donor sperm. Then the chance of a genetic fault being passed on became possible again.

TWENTY-SIX

'You're home early,' Emma said as Ian came into the living room.

Without replying, he threw his briefcase and jacket over the armchair and continued to the table where he opened his laptop.

'What's the matter?' Emma asked, concerned. 'You've been smoking. I can smell it on your clothes. Shouldn't you be at work?'

'Yes, but I need to find out how to do a DNA test,' he said, staring at his laptop screen.

'Not that again!' Emma sighed. 'I've told you I'll phone the clinic, but I have to be in the right mood.'

'There's no need to phone now. I spoke to them this morning. In fact, I've been there.'

'You've been to the Moller Clinic?' Emma asked, amazed, looking at him. 'Why?'

'It turns out it's not just you but me too.'

'What are you talking about? You're not making any sense, Ian.' She closed the book she'd been reading and put it to one side.

'I'm the product of donor sperm just like you,' he said, tapping the laptop. 'From the same clinic.'

Emma stared at him. 'What? How can that be?'

Ian didn't reply but concentrated on the screen.

'Ian, I'm talking to you. Can you tell me what's going on? You're frightening me.'

Ian paused to look at her. 'I phoned the Moller Clinic this morning about tracing your donor and spoke to Edie Moller. She let slip that I was on their files too. I saw Moller himself and he said both our parents used their clinic. I called my mother and she confirmed that she and Dad had gone there.'

'Strewth! That's a coincidence. And your mum never told you?'

'No, not a word.'

'Oh, I am sorry, Ian. I can see how upset you are. It must have come as a huge shock to find out like that.' She went over to give him a hug, but his attention was already on the laptop again.

'You can see now why my mother told me early on,' Emma said. 'It wasn't a shock for me. I grew up knowing I came from donor sperm.'

Ian nodded.

'What are you doing now?'

'Trying to find out how to get our DNA tested. Testing is far more sophisticated now than it was when we were conceived, so it may show up something that wasn't picked up before. Also . . .' He hesitated. Did she have to know this? Yes, she did. 'We're nearly the same age, so I'm guessing our parents must have used the clinic quite close together. I need to confirm we don't have the same donor.'

'What! You mean there's a chance we may have?' Emma stared at him, horrified.

'Not according to Carstan Moller, but I want to check. If – heaven forbid – we do have the same donor, it could explain why we can't have healthy babies.'

'But Mr Moller told you we didn't?' Emma said.

138

'Yes.'

'Well, he's not likely to have made a mistake with something so important.'

'He may have and now he's lying to cover his back,' Ian said, concentrating on the screen.

Emma stared at him incredulously. 'You think that's possible?'

But Ian was still engrossed in what he was doing. 'Here's what we need,' he said, tapping the keys. 'Websites offering DNA tests. This one looks good – MyGeneticHistory.com – £60 each. They send us the kit to take samples of our saliva. The results are back in three working days. Perfect. Can you pass me my wallet, love, it's in my jacket pocket. If I order now, we should have the kits at the weekend.'

'And then what happens?' Emma asked. 'Will you be satisfied or will you not believe them either? I am sure you're wrong, Ian. This is all taking over. Here's your wallet. I'm going for a shower.'

TWENTY-SEVEN

Jan *wasn't* nervous about living in the cottage as Chris had said, she told herself. His comments the evening before were still annoying her, together with his behaviour – first at the restaurant and then denying he'd seen a figure running from the cottage. She still had no idea what had got into him, but today she was going to prove him wrong and show she wasn't nervous, by taking Tinder for a walk in Coleshaw Woods. DS Matt Davis had said how lovely the woods were at this time of year and that she was missing out. So now, empowered by hurt pride and daylight, she was going!

Not wholly at ease with her decision but determined to give her confidence another small boost, Jan tucked her phone and keys into her jacket pocket and with Tinder beside her, tail wagging, she left the cottage. She set off along Wood Lane in the direction of Merryless. It was midday and the wintry November sun was as high in the sky as it would get, flickering through the bare branches of the trees she passed.

A good walk should also clear her head, she thought, after all the wine she'd drunk the night before. The evening had held such promise but had turned into a disaster. Oh well, another one bites the dust, she thought stoically.

Pleased to be off the lead, Tinder ran on ahead, then stopped every so often to look behind him and wait for Jan to catch up. Partway down Wood Lane was the turning on the right that led into the deepest part of Coleshaw Woods that ran behind the cottage. Jan had never ventured down it before, although Tinder often glanced longingly towards it as they passed on their way to the village. Jan didn't know if Camile ever walked him there, she hadn't told her. Her instructions had said that Tinder should be let out in the garden three times a day, and to take him with her when she walked to Merryless, but not to take him in the car as he got travel sick. Jan had only used her car twice since arriving and it was parked on a concrete standing to the right of the cottage, now covered in leaves.

'Come on, this way, Tinder!' Jan called. He'd gone past the turning.

He stopped, looked back and, unable to believe his good luck, ran full tilt towards her.

'Come on, you softie. We're going to walk in the woods today.'

She ruffled his fur and they began along the track. Jan knew from reading about Coleshaw Woods that most visitors came in summer and entered through the road on the other side of the woods where there was a car park, picnic area and signposted walks. There was also a flooded quarry where anglers fished. The woods on this side were at their thickest, and although there were tracks like the one she was on, they were rarely used. But if she kept to it, she shouldn't get lost, and even if she did, she had her phone with her so could call for help.

Despite the reassurances she'd given herself, it wasn't long before Jan began to feel slightly anxious by the complete isolation. It was eerie to be so alone. She'd spent all her life in towns and cities where you were never alone, even at night or in parks. Now there was just her, Tinder and the occasional rustle of woodland life in the undergrowth.

Digging her hands deeper into her jacket pockets, Jan continued resolutely along the track. The air was certainly fresh, fresh enough to get rid of her hangover, she thought. Yet there was also a pungent, damp smell that you didn't get in Wood Lane, which Jan supposed was caused by the fallen, rotting leaves. Tinder didn't seem to mind. His short legs were disappearing into the mulch as he sniffed around, and pieces of leaves and twigs stuck to his fur. But although he didn't mind the litterfall sticking to his coat, Jan noticed he was keeping very close to her. He seemed apprehensive and she supposed it was because he was in unfamiliar territory.

While it was somewhat creepy being all alone, Jan reminded herself that nature wouldn't harm her. She wasn't sure how far the track went, nor where the cottage lay in relation to it. She knew it would be on her right, but that was all. A few moments later she made a snap decision to try to find the cottage. Leaving the track, she turned right, further into the forest. Tinder stayed close and their pace slowed as the piles of rotting leaves deepened. In some places there were such small gaps between the trees she had to step around them and part bracken and ivy to forge a path. There was no sign of anyone else having ever been here.

Every so often Jan paused to look behind her to check she was walking in a straight line, so she would know how to get back to the track. It was disorientating being surrounded by so many tall trees. There was no horizon or landmark from which she could take her bearings. But she was as sure as she could be that she was heading in the right direction to where she hoped the cottage lay. The air was still and chilly here.

A few minutes later she was rewarded as the boundary hedge at the bottom of the cottage garden appeared between the trees. She made her way up to it and then found the gap in the hedge with her repair work visible on the other side, the crisscrossing pieces of wood still blocking the hole. It appeared to be standing up well, she thought.

She looked around. This was the spot where whatever it was had been getting in, though there was nothing to be seen now but more leaves and twigs. Nothing to suggest anyone or anything had been here. How brave she was in daylight, she thought, but best not overdo it.

She turned away from the hedge, ready to retrace her steps. She'd accomplished what she'd intended to and her confidence had grown by coming into the deepest part of the forest. She'd also been able to check the boundary fence.

'Come on, Tinder, time to go,' she called. Her voice sounded strange and far off in the otherwise quiet forest.

He was a little way to her left. Having picked up the scent of something, he was sniffing around the base of a tree close to the hedge. 'What is it?'

She went over. A ball of green twine just like the ones Camile kept in the shed and which Jan had used to tie the wood in place lay partly covered by leaves. Moving Tinder aside, Jan picked it up and examined it. She was sure it had come from Camile's shed, but what was it doing here? Had Chris or Camile used it for repairing the fence in the past? No. Chris would have used something stronger and more robust – hammer and nails, not twine – she was sure. And Camile had been gone weeks. This ball of twine hadn't been here that long. It was barely wet and showed no sign of weathering – days not weeks, she thought.

Tinder was looking at her expectantly, hoping to get another sniff of the ball, but Jan threw it in the direction of her back garden. If it made it in there, she would return it to the shed. She set off towards the track, Tinder at her heels. If she walked in a straight line, she should come out more or less where she'd come off the track. Then it was left towards Wood Lane. As she walked the only sound came from her boots crunching over the dry leaves and twigs and Tinder running beside her. In some places she could see the foot marks she and Tinder had made on their way in, so she knew she was on the right course.

Suddenly Tinder stopped and gave a low growl, his ears pricked up. He'd heard something. Pausing, Jan looked in the same direction, but there was nothing to be seen. 'Come on, good boy, this way,' she said, her voice slightly unsteady.

He gave another growl but came with her.

A few steps further on, she heard a noise coming from the same direction, as though someone else was here. Cold fear embraced her. It was still some way back to the track and even further to Wood Lane and the cottage. Her heart began to race. It had been stupid to come this far into the woods alone, just to prove a point. Who knew what lived here? She began to run, stumbling over the piles of rotten leaves and bracken while trying to avoid the branches overhead. Tinder ran beside her, as eager to be out of the woods as she was.

Thankfully the trees cleared and she found herself on the track again, but the movement in the wood continued. Someone or something was in there, moving parallel to them. Petrified, Jan quickened her pace and took out her phone, ready to call for help if necessary.

She stopped and stared in disbelief as a little further up Chris and a woman stepped from the woods onto the track. It must have been them she'd heard. She took a deep breath and tried to calm her racing heart as Tinder ran to Chris. Dressed similarly in boots and waxed jackets, they continued towards her.

'Fancy seeing you here,' Chris said stiffly, and bent to ruffle Tinder's fur. 'I didn't think you liked the woods.'

'I thought it was time to get over that,' Jan said, equally awkward.

'This is my friend Anne,' Chris said, introducing his companion. 'Anne, Camile's lodger, Jan.'

'Hello, pleased to meet you,' Anne said, but her expression said something different.

Jan saw Chris looking at her. Guilt? Embarrassment? She wasn't sure.

There was an awkward silence and then he said, 'Oh well. We'll let you get on with your walk. Are you heading back to the cottage now?'

'Yes, why?' Jan asked.

'I just wondered. Bye, then.'

'Bye,' Jan replied.

She continued along the track towards Wood Lane, in the opposite direction to Chris and Anne. She didn't look back. How embarrassing that was! And what were they doing in the woods near the back of the cottage? Chris had offered no explanation and Jan certainly wouldn't phone or text to ask him. She felt a pang of jealousy but dismissed it. Clearly he preferred older women, for Anne must be fifty. Homely, mumsy described her, Jan thought, slightly overweight with a practical chin-length hairstyle and no make-up. Jan wondered if Anne knew Chris had taken her out the evening before. It would explain the look she'd given her.

TWENTY-EIGHT

Once safely inside the cottage, Jan poured herself a glass of water and then set about making something to eat. It was 2 p.m. and she was hungry after all the exercise. Tinder was exhausted. He flopped out on his rug by the hearth and was soon asleep. Jan took the frying pan from its hook, threw in a knob of butter and whisked some eggs for an omelette. As she worked, her thoughts returned to Chris and Anne. He was a strange one, for sure. When she'd first met him he'd seemed so upfront and uncomplicated – a what-you-saw-was-what-you-got type of bloke. Yet clearly there was another side to Chris completely, one she didn't like. Secretive, moody, evasive. Just as well it had ended when it had.

Jan added salt and pepper to the frothy egg mixture and tipped it into the hot frying pan. The fat splattered. As the omelette set, she grated cheese for the filling. She was about to chop some tomatoes when the doorbell rang. Tinder woke and looked at her from his rug in the living room. Perhaps it was the postman. He came in his van to the cottage if there was any mail. Sometimes he rang the bell as he pushed the letters through the letterbox to let her know they had arrived. But it was a bit late for him. He usually came in the morning.

Jan removed the pan from the heat and went into the hall. There was no mail lying on the mat. She opened the front door. There was no one outside. No car or mail van either. Strange. She looked around. The lane was deserted as far as she could see in both directions. Then she saw it and her heart missed a beat. Positioned on the doorstep was the ball of twine Tinder had found in the wood and she'd thrown towards the back garden. She was sure it was the same one. It looked identical. It hadn't been here when she'd arrived back. She stared at it in disbelief, then looked up and down the lane again. Kicking it off the step, Jan quickly closed the door.

How had it got there and why? Had Chris and Anne found it and brought it back? No. That seemed ridiculous. The chance of them finding it in the woods was tiny and why would they go to all the trouble of returning it? Assuming they knew it had come from Camile's shed.

But the alternative – that someone she didn't know had brought it back – was even more worrying. It would mean that they had been watching her in the woods – following her – had seen her pick up the twine throw it, and, knowing it had come from the shed, had brought it back. Was someone watching her and playing games to frighten her? If so, they were succeeding.

Calm down, she told herself, don't do anything rash. Going into the living room, she picked up her phone and texted Chris.

Did you leave a ball of twine on the doorstep of the cottage?

He'd probably think she was even more neurotic than he already did. But she needed to eliminate him.

A minute later came his reply. *No, I didn't! Are you OK? I'm fine*, she replied testily.

But she wasn't. Far from it.

Someone was out there, watching her. Perhaps it was time to pack and leave the cottage. She'd have to give Camile notice so she could make alternative arrangements for Tinder. Or should she call DC Matt Davis? But what would she say? That she'd found a ball of twine in the woods that had come from the shed and someone had left it on her doorstep? Surely that would be called wasting police time, and goodness knows what Matt would think of her!

What she needed was someone to talk to, Jan thought, someone who knew her well and could be relied upon to give her an honest opinion and sound advice. Ruby. She'd already offered to stay for Christmas, but Jan couldn't wait that long. Christmas was still weeks away. She needed to speak to her now.

A couple of rings and then, 'Hi, Jan. Lovely to hear from you.'

'And you. Can you talk?'

'For a bit. Why? What's the matter? You sound uptight.'

'I am,' Jan immediately confessed. 'Ruby, there's stuff going on here at the cottage I don't understand. Weird stuff I need to tell you about and get your opinion on.'

'Are you in some kind of danger?' Ruby asked, worried.

'I honestly don't know.'

'That doesn't sound like you, Jan. I've only got a few minutes now. How about I come over and visit you tomorrow? I've already booked a couple of days off work.'

'Oh, would you? That would be fantastic.'

'Sure. I'll drive up first thing in the morning and then come back on Saturday.'

'Lovely. Thank you so much.'

'You'll be OK until then?'

'Yes.'

'See you around midday tomorrow.'

'Thank you.'

148

As they ended the call, Jan's phone bleeped with a text message. It was from Camile. *Everything OK at the cottage?*

Too much of a coincidence, Jan thought. Doubtless Chris had said something to her.

Yes, thanks, she replied.

TWENTY-NINE

Despite telling Ruby she'd be OK until the following day, Jan hardly slept a wink that night. Every noise suggested someone was outside trying to break in or were already in the cottage and coming to get her. The wind didn't help. She kept her phone in her hand, ready to call for help if necessary, and left the hall and landing lights on. Eventually she brought Tinder up to sleep on her bed.

Then at 2 a.m., when she was still wide awake, the lights suddenly went out. Panic gripped her until she realized that leaving all the lights on had drained the meter. She didn't dare get out of bed now and go downstairs in the dark to feed the meter, so she pulled the bed covers up over her head and waited for morning.

Thank goodness Ruby was coming today, Jan thought as the sky outside finally lightened and she could get up. Ruby would know what to do for the best. She was Jan's oldest and probably closest friend. She knew how to have a laugh, but could also be relied on to be level-headed and objective when necessary. Ruby wasn't someone given to flights of fantasy. But then neither had Jan been, she reminded herself, before coming to live in Ivy Cottage.

Throwing on her dressing gown, she went downstairs, fed Tinder and set the coffee to brew. Tinder ate some of his breakfast and then began pawing at the back door to be let out for his morning run. Jan slid the bolts and turned the key. As she opened the door she saw it, and her legs went weak. She couldn't believe it. The ball of twine she'd kicked off the front doorstep the afternoon before was now on the patio, directly in front of the back door. Positioned so she couldn't miss it.

Someone had placed it there on purpose. There was no other explanation. Her legs felt like jelly. So the noises she'd heard in the night hadn't all been her imagination. Her stomach churned. While she'd been in bed, whoever it was had taken the twine from the front garden and brought it round to the back and left it right where she would see it, letting her know they were still out there, watching her. She felt sick with fear. But why were they here? What did they want with her?

Keeping one hand on the door ready to close it quickly if necessary, Jan reached out and with trembling fingers was about to pick up the twine, then she stopped. No. She'd leave it where it was to show Ruby. It would be evidence that what she was saying was true.

Tinder, having done his business, returned up the garden, sniffed the twine and then came in. Jan closed and bolted the back door, her thoughts racing. Was she in danger? Ruby had asked yesterday, and Jan had replied she didn't know. Now she did. Without doubt, she was being targeted. Should she call the police again? And say what? A ball of twine had found its way from the woods to her front doorstep and then the patio? It made her sound ridiculous, unbalanced. She'd wait to see what Ruby had to say. In the meantime, she needed to get a grip and think rationally. There were things she had to do.

Jan poured a mug of coffee and took it upstairs to drink while she washed and dressed. She needed to buy food for dinner so she could make Ruby something decent to eat. But she certainly wouldn't be walking along Wood Lane to the village store, not with the chance of whoever was out there stalking her. Tinder would have to forgo his walk today. She would take her car and drive into Coleshaw. It would do her good to be in a town again with lots of people, and the supermarkets there would have a much better choice than the local store. She should leave as soon as she was ready to make sure she was back in plenty of time for when Ruby arrived.

Jan took her empty mug downstairs, shut Tinder in the living room and, collecting her jacket and bag, left the cottage. The air was chilly and she slipped on her coat as she went to the car. She was about to get in when she noticed muddy streaks over the car roof. As she looked more closely, she could see them on the bonnet too. Most of the leaves had been blown off in the wind last night, revealing these muddy track marks as if something had been on her car. But the marks were fresh, recent.

She looked more closely. They were too large for a cat or fox and not the right shape – muddy prints similar to those she'd seen by the gap in the hedge when she'd cut the grass. She traced their path. Whatever it was had run over the bonnet and up the windscreen, slipping as it went, then across the roof of the car and slipped down the back. Jan looked around her. There was nothing to be seen. The trees and foliage were still, but she had the feeling she was being watched just as she'd had in the garden. She quickly took a photo on her phone of the track marks – more evidence to show Ruby – then got into the car, pressed the central locking system and began the drive to Coleshaw.

THIRTY

Don't go anywhere near this place! They are in it for their own selfish ends. Ms L's online review of the Moller Clinic had read. Ian had dismissed it when he'd first read it, but now he'd visited the clinic and met the Mollers, he thought there might be something in it. But what?

It was Friday morning and Ian was sitting at his office desk trying to catch up with his work. It was proving very difficult. There was so much going on in his private life, it was virtually impossible to concentrate, but he needed to try. He'd taken a lot of time off since Emma's miscarriage and while management were still being supportive and sympathetic, he knew it wouldn't last forever. At some point they would expect him to get over it and start pulling his weight again.

Ian's thoughts drifted to the argument he'd had with Emma that morning. It had started because he'd brought up the matter of the DNA tests again. Then he'd made it worse by saying he thought she should return to work, part-time at least. She was still signed off sick. He thought he'd phrased it well, but she'd burst into tears, accused him of being self-centred and caring more about his bloody research than he did about her. He'd left soon after to come to work and had texted an apology, but she hadn't replied.

His thoughts returned to the review.

Don't go anywhere near this place.

How he would have liked to have spoken to Ms L and asked her exactly what she'd meant. He'd found the review online again but couldn't see any way of contacting her. Clearly she'd had issues with the clinic, but why? Was it their manner or something else?

'There are rumours,' the lad in the village shop had said. But that could be no more than malicious gossip.

Ian fiddled with his pen and stared at the report he was supposed to be writing. The DNA test kits he'd ordered should arrive tomorrow – Saturday. There was no postal service on Sunday, so he'd send them off first thing on Monday. He'd opted for the results to be emailed, which was the fastest method, so hopefully he'd have them early next week.

Of course, it could turn out that Carstan Moller had been right all along and he and Emma didn't share the same genes. That's what Emma believed, and that he'd become obsessed – a witch hunt to find someone to blame for them not being able to have a family. Which is more or less what Moller had said: *Get on with your life and be grateful you are both healthy, intelligent and able to do well.*

If the DNA tests showed he and Emma weren't related, then he would accept it and agree to go to bereavement counselling as Emma wanted.

Don't go anywhere near this place! They are in it for their own selfish ends.

But why? Ms L, why?

THIRTY-ONE

Jan paused to read Ruby's text: *Should be with you at 12.*

Great. See you soon, she replied and then continued up and down the aisles in the supermarket, loading her basket.

It was nearly 11 a.m. and only an hour before Ruby arrived. Jan had been longer than she thought. She'd enjoyed the hustle and bustle of the busy supermarket and had taken her time choosing what to buy. She quickly gathered together the last of the items, then joined the queue at the checkout. It was long – Friday shoppers stocking up for the weekend.

It was 11.20 by the time Jan had paid and left the supermarket. As she was crossing the car park she realized she'd forgotten coffee. Drat! She wasn't going back to stand in that queue again; she'd stop off at Lillian's store in Merryless. She'd also get some more change for the meter while she was there.

The roads out of Coleshaw were busy so it was 11.50 before Jan drew up outside the shop in Merryless. Before getting out, she texted Ruby just in case she got to the cottage before she did. *Will be there shortly x*

She was about to open her car door when she saw Chris go into the shop. Damn and blast! She really didn't want to meet him right now. It would be embarrassing after their disastrous evening and then bumping into him with Anne yesterday. She had nothing to say to him. She waited in the car for a few moments longer, but he didn't reappear. She couldn't wait indefinitely. He might be in there for some time talking to his sister-in-law.

Steeling herself, Jan got out and went into the shop. Chris was at the counter talking to Lillian with his back to her. 'Hi, Jan,' Lillian called, while Chris didn't even bother to turn. Not even a nod of acknowledgement. Well, sod him, Jan thought.

Keeping her gaze away from them, Jan went over to the shelves containing the packets of filter coffee and pretended to browse as Lillian wound up their conversation. 'Give my love to Mel and the little ones,' she said. Jan had no idea who Mel was.

She waited until Chris had left the shop before she took the packet of coffee to the counter. 'Can I have some meter money as well, please?'

'Sure, love. How are you?'

'Fine, thanks.'

Lillian went into the back office to fetch the coins from the safe.

'How did your date go?' she asked, setting the bag of one-pound coins on the counter.

'With Chris?' Jan asked, surprised Lillian had mentioned it. Surely Chris would have told her.

'Well, yes, unless you've been dating others,' Lillian said with a smile.

'It wasn't good. I doubt we'll see each other again.'

'Oh dear, I am sorry to hear that.' She seemed genuinely concerned.

'Didn't Chris mention it then?' Jan asked as she paid.

'I haven't seen him since Wednesday,' Lillian replied.

Jan stared at her and thought she must have misheard. 'He was in here just now. You were talking to him.'

'No,' Lillian laughed. 'That was Robert Jarvis. They look similar from a distance. But Robert is happily married with three children.'

'Oh.' Jan felt foolish.

'You're not the only one to make that mistake. There's a few round here that look similar. Camile does. Have you met her?'

'No, Chris gave me the keys to the cottage.'

Jan thought back to the photographs of Chris and Camile and how alike and compatible they'd appeared.

'Why did Camile and Chris split?' Jan asked, tucking the meter money and coffee into her bag.

'I'm really not sure,' Lillian said. 'I'm sorry it didn't work out on Wednesday. A nice girl like you. I'll tell Chris off when I see him.'

Jan smiled. 'That's kind, but probably best not to say anything. I think he already has someone else.'

'Not as far as I know,' Lillian said, surprised. 'What makes you think that?'

'I saw him yesterday while I was walking Tinder in the woods. He was with someone called Anne.'

'Anne?' Lillian asked, puzzled. 'I've no idea who that could be. The only Anne I know is a local midwife and she's not Chris's type.'

'It doesn't matter, perhaps they're just friends.'

'Possibly.' Lillian shrugged, clearly still slightly baffled. 'Bye then, love. Take care.'

'Bye,' Jan said and left the store. Perhaps they were just friends, Jan thought, but that didn't excuse Chris's weird behaviour on Wednesday evening.

THIRTY-TWO

Friday morning finally drew to a close and at 12.30 Ian stood and took his jacket from the back of his chair.

'Are you coming to Rocco's for lunch?' Mike, a work colleague, asked, also standing. They sometimes went to the café, either eating in or taking out as did others from the office.

'Not straight away,' Ian said. 'I'll catch you up. I've a few things to do first.'

'OK, see you later,' Mike said, and headed out of the office.

Ian needed to phone Emma first to make sure she was all right. It wasn't a conversation he could have with someone standing a little way off, waiting. Checking he had his phone and wallet in his jacket pocket, Ian left the office and went down the back stairs. The front of Wetherby Security was close to the main road where traffic noise made talking on a phone near impossible, but at the back there was just the firm's car park.

Ian found a quiet corner away from the main building and called their landline number. If he was honest, he was dreading speaking to Emma. She was always so down and short-tempered with him these days. He could picture her sitting on the sofa in their living room, whiling away the hours with daytime television or a book, or thumbing a magazine, mournful and dejected.

'Are you OK?' he asked as soon as she answered. Then straight away realized his mistake. He should have said, 'How are you?' For clearly she wasn't OK.

But to his surprise Emma replied, 'I'm good, thank you. A lot better.' Her voice sounded brighter too.

'Are you? That's great. Sorry about this morning. I hate it when we argue.'

'So do I,' Emma said. 'I was partly to blame. You were right about me getting back to work. I'm going to phone them this afternoon and suggest I start back on Monday. Anne, our midwife, persuaded me to. She visited earlier.'

'Oh, I see,' Ian said, slightly disappointed that he hadn't been the one responsible for Emma's change of heart. 'Well, that's good.'

'Yes. We had a long chat. She knows exactly the right thing to say. She doesn't mind talking about what happened to David. She said I could talk to her whenever I wanted to. She understood. I even asked her what David looked like.'

Ian grimaced. 'I thought we'd agreed it was better we didn't know.'

'Yes, but I'm glad I did ask. I was expecting her to describe something horrible, but do you know what she said? That although he was born different, he was beautiful in his own sweet way.'

'Good.'

'Anne said wherever David was now, she knew he was happy and at peace. It really helped, Ian. I should have asked her before about David.'

'I'm glad it helped,' Ian said.

'We also talked about when I should go back to work and she said there was no medical reason why I shouldn't return now. Indeed, she thought it was a good idea, but I should take it slowly. She gave me some literature on contraception. It's part of her job as a midwife. She said perhaps we'd like to consider sterilization, as it's so important we don't have another child given the same thing is likely to happen again.'

'I don't see how she can be so certain,' Ian said. 'We need all the facts before we can make that type of decision. Those DNA kits should be here tomorrow.'

Ian immediately realized his mistake and was expecting Emma to snap at him for mentioning DNA, but she didn't.

'I told Anne about your research,' Emma said. 'She looked shocked and worried to begin with, then seemed to change her mind. She said if you found something to tell her and she'd discuss it with us.'

'What did she mean by that?'

'She wants to help us, Ian. She's so nice. She also said she knows another couple who are going through something similar to us and it might be possible for her to put us in touch, if they agreed. She said that sharing something like this can help. I said I'd let her know.'

'All right,' Ian said, while thinking the last thing he needed was to be saddled with someone else's horror story. 'I'm glad you're feeling better. I'm going for lunch now, so I'll see you later.'

'Yes, bye, thanks for phoning.'

'See you later, love.'

THIRTY-THREE

Ruby topped up their glasses of red wine as Jan gathered together the plates and took them into the kitchen.

'That was delicious, thank you,' Ruby said. 'But you shouldn't have gone to all that trouble.'

'No trouble. It was nice to cook for someone else for a change. When it's just me it's pasta or a jacket potato. We'll have our pudding later, shall we?'

'Oh yes, I'm full. Now come and sit down and tell me what's been going on here. I understand from what you've said so far that Chris turned out to be a bit of a weirdo, but what's wrong with the cottage? It seems idyllic if you want time out, although I think I'd prefer it in summer.'

Jan sat in the armchair opposite Ruby. Ruby was on the sofa, her legs curled under her, Tinder at her feet. Their conversation so far had been mainly catching up – about work, relationships, their families and mutual friends, and village life. Jan had wanted to leave the rest until after they'd eaten and she had a few drinks inside her. She'd mentioned Chris and their disastrous first date, and that she'd seen him with another woman the following day, but nothing about being stalked or the strange happenings around the cottage.

Now she needed to try to explain to Ruby what she'd seen without sounding hysterical.

'It's difficult to know where to begin,' Jan said, taking another sip of her wine.

'Start at the beginning – that's what you always tell me when I have a problem,' Ruby smiled.

Jan nodded thoughtfully. 'OK. For the first few weeks here, everything seemed fine. I mean, living in the country took a bit of getting used to, but I enjoyed the peace after everything that had happened. It gave me time to think and I didn't see or experience anything odd. Then something started coming into the garden after dark when the curtains were closed. I assumed it was an animal, out here in the middle of nowhere.' Ruby nodded. 'It came right up to the window. Tinder always knew when it was there. His hackles would rise and he would run to the back door, wanting to be let out to chase it. One night he disappeared completely and didn't come back for hours. I was worried, thinking he'd got lost. When he did return he was so pleased to see me, as if something had frightened him.'

'I would think just getting lost scared him,' Ruby said sensibly.

'Maybe, but then the next night he came back with food stuck in the fur by his mouth. It was cooked meat, possibly sausage. It hadn't come from here and there are no other houses until you get to Merryless. So I began to worry that there could be someone living in the woods. This cottage backs onto the deepest part of Coleshaw Woods and you'd never know if there was someone in there.'

'Couldn't a bird have dropped the food?' Ruby suggested.

'I suppose so.' Jan hesitated. How easy it was to explain away what was happening if you hadn't been here. 'But the next night I caught a glimpse of something as Tinder chased it through the hedge at the bottom of the garden. It was dark so I couldn't get a good view, but it was really strange, not like any animal I've ever seen. I researched online what animals live in the woods and it just came up with the usual, like badgers, foxes and so on. So I sort of convinced myself it could have been a fox. I told Chris – we were on good terms then – and he thought it could be a fox or a dog that had come from the village.'

'He should know, living around here all his life,' Ruby put in.

'That's what I thought, but then I discovered something that convinced me it couldn't be a fox.'

'What?'

She had Ruby's full attention now. 'I promised Camile, the owner of the cottage, that I would cut the grass, and when I was in the back garden I found track marks coming through the gap in the hedge. It was like a walkway through from the woods into the garden. Lots of prints, so I knew it had been going on for some time, and there could be more than one of them. I continued cutting the grass, but I had this really strong feeling that I was being watched the whole time and kept turning to check behind me.'

'You're giving me the creeps now,' Ruby said, instinctively glancing behind her towards the garden.

'There's a motion-sensor light on the patio,' Jan continued. 'Chris told me it was broken, but when I checked, it had been switched off. Camile said to save electricity – the cottage is on a meter. I switched it on and once it was dark I sat where you are, hoping to see whatever it was that was coming to the window.'

'And it didn't come?' Ruby said.

'It did, but it must have known the light was on – a small red light flashes when it's working. It avoided the sensor and came to the back door instead. I knew then it was too intelligent for a woodland animal. It seemed to know what I was doing. I let Tinder out and he chased it. I followed him but it had gone through the hole in the hedge. Then I heard a noise behind me and I spun round just in time to see a shadowy figure run down the sideway and disappear over the gate. I don't know what I saw, but Chris found Tinder in the village and brought him back at midnight.'

'Did you tell him what had happened?'

'No. It seemed ridiculous.'

'So was that the end of it then?'

'No. I blocked up the hole in the hedge, which kept them out for a couple of nights. But then the next night one came right up to the window. It was dark – I'd switched off the sensor light to save electricity – but it made eye-contact like a person would. I was terrified and phoned Chris. He came straight over and went down the garden. It was pitch dark but the wood I'd used for blocking up the hedge was scattered all over the lawn. Whatever it was had removed it all. I was grateful to Chris for coming and he stayed for a drink. It was then he asked me out.'

'And the rest is history, as they say,' Ruby said, finishing her glass of wine.

'Far from it. The following day, when it was light, I went into the garden and found the twine I'd used to tie the wood in place over the hole had been unpicked, not chewed through, which confirmed it wasn't an animal. I thought it must be a person to be able to do that and I was really worried. I called the police and they sent an officer. He was helpful but couldn't find any evidence of an intruder.'

'Well, I suppose that's reassuring,' Ruby said.

'No, it's not. They're getting braver. When I walked to the village along the lane I saw someone or something running between the trees. They've also been to the front door. Chris saw one of them when he brought me back on Wednesday evening, but he denied it. He suggested it was my imagination and said if I was so nervous about living in the cottage then I should leave.'

'He might be right,' Ruby said, and topped up their glasses again. 'It's very isolated here and maybe being all alone isn't right for you. You lost your bloke and job in the same week, which was very traumatic. I can understand why you wanted to get away, but perhaps you've been by yourself long enough.'

'I thought you might say that, but I have proof,' Jan said.

'Really?'

'You know I said I bumped into Chris with a woman in the woods yesterday?'

'Yes.'

'Just before that, while I was in the deepest part of the woods near the back of the cottage, Tinder found a ball of twine that had been taken from the shed in the garden here. I threw it towards the back garden. I've no idea where it landed. But later the doorbell rang and when I opened the door I saw it on the front door step. There was no one there, just the ball of twine. I'm sure someone saw me pick it up in the woods and was trying to scare me – to let me know they were watching me.'

'Chris?' Ruby suggested doubtfully. 'But why?'

Jan shook her head. 'I don't think so. I left it out the front, but then this morning I found the same ball of twine outside the back door, placed on the patio where I couldn't miss it. I've left it there for you to see.'

'So it's still there?' Ruby asked.

'Yes. I checked just before you came. Come on, I'll show you.'

Jan took Ruby into the kitchen and opened the back door. Her heart sank. 'It's gone!' she exclaimed. 'They've taken it. They know you're here and they're playing tricks on me.'

Jan saw the look of pity on her friend's face and knew she didn't believe her. She began searching the patio and garden as Ruby watched from the back door. It was late afternoon and on an already overcast day, the light was fading fast and the air was chilling.

'Come in now,' Ruby called. 'It's cold. Let's have that pudding and open another bottle of wine.'

Jan checked the sideway but there was no ball of twine. She knew she was making a fool of herself. Reluctantly, she came in. 'It *was* there,' she said helplessly. 'They've taken it while we were in the living room. But look at this, I have more proof.' She grabbed her phone. 'See this photo. I took it this morning. Footprints all over my car. The same track marks I found by the gap in the hedge at the bottom of the garden.'

Ruby peered at the photo. 'I can see muddy prints on your car,' she said. 'But that could be anything.'

Jan heard her friend's rationality. And standing here with her now she could see the muddy marks weren't proof and could indeed be 'anything'.

She felt Ruby gently touch her arm. 'Jan, I think you've seen something and got spooked by living out here all alone. Why don't you come and stay with me for a while? I have a spare bedroom. I'm at work all day so you'd have the place to yourself.'

'I'll think about it,' Jan said, then realized she'd sounded curt. 'Thank you,' she added. 'And thanks for listening. I'm sure you're right, so let me get that pudding and we'll talk about something else.'

The look of relief on Ruby's face said it all.

THIRTY-FOUR

It was after midnight by the time Jan was in bed, but she couldn't sleep. She lay in the dark, staring at the ceiling, with the afternoon's conversation running through her head as if set on a loop. It was torture. Tinder was on the bed beside her, also restless. It was clear Ruby hadn't believed her, and who could blame her? It had sounded so far-fetched. No one else had seen anything apart from Chris and he'd denied it. Perhaps he'd been telling the truth and he really hadn't seen anything. Perhaps there was nothing to see. There was no real evidence, Jan conceded, and began to question her own sanity.

The ball of twine could have been blown from the patio into the shrubbery by the wind as Ruby had later suggested. And the muddy footprints on her car could indeed 'be anything', including foxes, squirrels or large birds. Jan tossed and turned, and kept checking the time on her phone. She'd offered Ruby her bed, but she'd insisted on taking the sofa in the living room, which converted into a bed.

Yet she had seen something, and more than once, Jan thought.

Or had she?

Was it possible that living alone in the cottage, following the trauma of losing her job and partner, she was imagining things, even hallucinating? Ruby evidently thought so.

Perhaps she should take up her offer to stay with her. But she'd have to give Camile notice first and then allow her time to make arrangements for someone else to stay in the cottage and look after Tinder. She'd feel bad letting Camile down, but if her mental health was suffering then she really shouldn't stay any longer.

Half an hour later Jan had made the decision that tomorrow she'd accept Ruby's offer to stay, and go as soon as Camile had sorted out arrangements for Tinder. Jan would email Camile first thing in the morning. Once at Ruby's, she'd be able to take stock of her life and maybe see a therapist to help her deal with all the bad stuff that had been going on.

With the decision made, Jan finally fell asleep. It was nine o'clock when she woke. The sky outside was light. She could hear Ruby moving around downstairs. Getting out of bed, Jan put on her dressing gown and slippers and went down.

'Sorry, I overslept. I'm not much of a host,' she said, going into the living room.

Ruby was dressed. The curtains had been opened and the sofabed put away. Ruby looked tired and drawn and Jan immediately felt guilty. She should have insisted she took her bed. 'I'll make us some breakfast,' she said.

'No. I'm going and I want you to come with me,' Ruby said as she packed the last of her belongings into her weekend bag.

'Why so soon?' Jan asked, surprised. 'I was going to make us breakfast.'

'I don't want anything to eat, thank you. I've had a glass of water. I'm going now and I want you to come with me,' she said again.

'I can't, not just like that. I'll need to tell Camile first so she can find someone to look after Tinder.'

'Bring the dog if necessary,' Ruby said. 'But I think you should get out of here.' She zipped shut her case.

Jan stared at her. 'Why? What's happened?'

Ruby met her gaze. 'It's not your imagination, Jan. I'm sorry I didn't believe you. There is something or someone out there. I heard them last night, tapping at the window. I opened the curtains, but they'd gone. I haven't slept a wink.'

'Tapping at the window?' Jan asked. 'I haven't heard that before. Could it have been the wind causing something to tap on the glass?'

'No, Jan. I know what I heard. It was more of a knock than a tap, as if someone was trying to get my attention.'

'Why didn't you come and get me?'

'And spook you even more? I thought about phoning the police, but what could I have said? That I heard a tapping noise and when I opened the curtains there was nothing there?' She picked up her case. 'Come on, Jan. Please come with me. I'm worried about you.'

'I can't, not straight away. I'm not even dressed, and I need to tell Camile.'

'I'll wait while you dress then. Bring the dog.'

'I can't. He doesn't travel well. I have to look after him here, and the cottage, until Camile can find someone else.'

'And I can't change your mind?' Ruby asked.

'No. It's just not practical for me to up and leave.'

'Are you sure?'

Jan nodded.

'Your decision, but come as soon as you can. Take care and look after yourself. This place gives me the creeps.' Ruby kissed Jan's cheek and then headed down the hall where she opened the front door. 'Sure I can't persuade you?' she asked one last time.

'No. I'll be OK. You drive safely.'

'Speak soon.'

Jan watched Ruby get into her car, turn it around and then drive off along Wood Lane. As Jan closed the front door she felt strangely calm. Exonerated. She had the evidence she needed. She wasn't losing her mind. Ruby had heard something too. Last night Jan had gone to sleep convinced it was her imagination, but Ruby had just proved otherwise. There was something out there and she intended to find out what before she left.

THIRTY-FIVE

Still in her dressing gown, Jan made herself a coffee. Although she was reassured she wasn't imagining things, she didn't feel any less threatened. Far from it. Whatever it was, was getting braver by the day and appeared to be closing in on her. When she'd first arrived, it – or they – had stayed away, hiding in the woods, possibly watching her and waiting to make their move. After a few weeks they'd begun coming into the garden but had been scared off by Tinder. Their confidence had grown and they'd become bolder: making eye-contact at the window, running through the trees in Wood Lane, leaving the ball of twine where she could see it. Then last night was their boldest move yet – tapping on the glass to attract Ruby's attention. Pity they hadn't done it when Chris was here. They were becoming fearless, but who were they?

Jan wondered what would have happened if Ruby had opened the back door as she'd been doing? Would they have run away or stood their ground? Jan thought she knew the answer: they would have stayed. And done what? It was a shame Ruby hadn't woken her. Together they might have found the courage to go outside to investigate. As it was,

Ruby had left saying the cottage gave her the creeps. Jan had to smile – her usually sensible, pragmatic and rational friend had rushed out of the door, more unnerved than she was, which left her no nearer to finding out who or what was out there.

If she slept on the sofa one night, out of sight, with the curtains open and the light off, would they return? If they did, she might be able to get a good look at them, perhaps even take a photograph. There was no point in switching on the motion-sensor light, as they'd already shown they knew when it was operating and could avoid it. Did she have the nerve to stay downstairs in the dark and wait for them to reappear? She honestly wasn't sure. It felt safer to be upstairs in bed.

The doorbell rang, making her start. Ruby? Had she forgotten something? Or perhaps she was returning to try to persuade her to leave again. Jan set her mug of coffee on the table and, drawing her dressing gown closer, went to answer the door. Tinder ran beside her, wagging his tail as if he knew who was there.

'Oh, it's you!' Jan exclaimed, astonished.

'Sorry, I should have phoned first to check you were up,' Chris said apologetically.

'I had a friend stay last night and we were up late. Why are you here?'

'I offered to repair your fence this weekend. I've got the tools in my car.'

'Oh,' Jan said again, amazed. How long ago that offer now seemed. 'I didn't think you'd come after Wednesday evening. I've done it myself.'

'I'm sorry about that. You know me, I can be a moody bugger sometimes. Would you like me to check the repair is holding up?'

Jan thought she didn't know Chris at all, and her first

reaction was to tell him the fence was fine and he needn't bother to contact her again. But she hesitated.

'I can come back later if it's more convenient?' he offered.

'No, come in.' She stood aside to let him pass. 'I'll leave you to check the fence while I get dressed.'

'I'll see what needs doing, then get my tools from the car,' Chris said, and headed down the hall with Tinder at his heels.

Bemused, Jan went upstairs to dress. What the hell! He was right when he said he was a moody bugger. But he had seemed genuinely apologetic. And now he was here he may as well check the fence, although she wouldn't be confiding in him again.

As Jan dressed, she heard Chris come in the back door and then let himself out the front to go to his car. Standing a little way back from the bedroom window so he couldn't see her, she watched him as he opened the boot of his car. He was good-looking in a rugged sort of way – she'd always thought so. Tall, fair, with high cheekbones. But more at ease while doing something practical than making polite conversation over dinner. She watched him take his overalls and a tool bag from the car boot and then close the lid. Oddly, he didn't immediately return into the cottage, but stood in the middle of the lane, looking up and down as if looking for something or someone. Apparently satisfied, he came in.

Jan finished dressing, brushed her hair and went downstairs. She'd shower later. Slipping on her jacket, she went into the garden. It was a cold day. Chris, now wearing an all-in-one boiler suit, was leaning into the hedge using a portable electric screwdriver to insert long screws into the wood.

'You did a good job,' he said, pausing and turning to look at her as she approached. 'Your repair has stood up reasonably well. I'm putting in three-inch screws to reinforce it.'

'Thank you,' she said, and watched him. He knelt as he worked, which made him appear almost vulnerable, certainly

173

approachable, and not temperamental and withdrawn as he had been on Wednesday. 'What do you think is getting in?' Jan asked after a few moments.

'Could be anything,' he replied. 'But it won't hurt you, I'm sure.'

'How can you be sure?'

He paused again to look at her. 'There aren't any dangerous animals in these woods.'

'So why do they keep coming to the cottage?'

'Looking for food.' Which is what he'd said before.

Jan continued to watch him and then asked, 'Would you like coffee and croissants? I haven't had breakfast yet.'

'Yes, please, if it's no trouble.'

'It's not.'

She went indoors, threw her jacket over a chair, then brewed more coffee and put the croissants she'd originally bought for Ruby to warm in the oven. Chris was doing her a favour so she could at least be civil, although she wouldn't be talking any more about the weird sightings.

Five minutes later he came in. 'All done,' he said, and stepped out of his overalls.

'Thank you.'

Jan carried the tray containing the mugs of coffee and a plate of croissants through to the living room and placed them on the coffee table. Chris took his overalls and tool box to the front door.

'So I don't forget them,' he said, with a self-deprecating smile as he returned.

He sat in his usual armchair. 'Help yourself,' she said, offering him a side plate and the croissants.

'Thanks. These didn't come from Lillian's store?'

'No, I drove into Coleshaw yesterday. But I did stop off there on the way back. I met your double.'

'Oh yes, Robert Jarvis,' Chris said. 'We do look alike.'

'Very much so.'

There was an awkward silence and Jan concentrated on her croissant. Then Chris said, 'Lillian gave me a right bollocking for my behaviour, and told me to apologize. I am sorry, Jan. I know my reaction when you told me Tinder had been in Camile's belongings was completely over the top.'

She nodded. 'It's forgotten,' she said easily, and meant it. Any thoughts she'd had about dating Chris had gone, so with no vested interest it was easy to forgive him.

'You see, Camile and I have history,' Chris said, concentrating on his plate.

'It's fine, really,' Jan said. 'That's your business. You've obviously been able to move on.'

He looked up questioningly.

'Anne,' Jan said.

'Oh goodness me, no. Anne is a friend of Camile's and mine, that's all. When I told her of the problems you'd been having, and that I was going to check the fence at the back of the cottage, she offered to go with me.'

'So that's why you were in the woods – checking the fence?' Jan asked.

'Yes.'

But Jan remembered the expression on Anne's face and wasn't so sure.

'You didn't find a ball of twine while you were there?' she asked. 'Like the one I used to tie the planks of wood in place.'

'No. But I can soon get you some more if you need it. They are cheap enough and I'm certain Lillian stocks them.'

'It's all right. There's some in the shed.'

There was another awkward silence. Chris finished his croissant and then asked, 'So you had a friend stay last night?'

'Yes, Ruby.'

'A woman then?'

Jan nodded.

He drained the last of his coffee and, standing, put the china in the sink. 'I'd better be going,' he said, ruffling Tinder's fur. 'Those screws should keep the fence in place, but if you have any more trouble let me know.'

'Thank you.'

Jan went with him to the front door. He was about to open it but stopped and turned to her. 'I am truly sorry about Wednesday,' he said. 'I'd like to make it up to you and take you out again.'

'Really?' Jan said, surprised.

'Yes, really. Lillian suggested I take you to the cinema where I can't talk and put my big foot in it again.'

Jan found herself smiling. 'Let me think about it.'

'OK, thanks.'

She watched him go. Would she accept his invitation? She wasn't sure. Nice of him to apologize and help her out, though.

THIRTY-SIX

As night fell, Jan's unease at being alone in the cottage returned. Ruby had been right when she'd said it was creepy. The cottage was picturesque during the day, but as the sun set it blended in with the woods as if the trees were advancing, laying claim to it and its inhabitants.

Before it was completely dark, Jan went from room to room, switching on lights and closing curtains, then she checked the front and back doors were locked and bolted. She poured herself a glass of wine and sat on the sofa in the living room. Tinder jumped up and sat beside her. Although Chris had secured the wood over the hole in the hedge with very long screws, Jan was sure it wouldn't make much difference. Her repair work had still been there the night before when Ruby had heard something tapping at the window. They were using a different way in.

As she sat there nursing her glass of wine with the night ahead of her, Jan wished she could have taken up Ruby's offer to stay straight away. But not only would she have been running away, she would be letting down Camile big time. She could imagine her disappointment when the purpose of leasing out the cottage was to have someone take care of Tinder in his

177

own home. *Someone reliable and trustworthy who likes dogs
. . .* Camile's advertisement had read. Jan cringed.

Jan finished her first glass of wine and was about to refill
when her phone rang. Camile's number showed on the display.
That was a weird coincidence, she thought, as she answered.
It was only the second time she'd phoned. All their contact
had been by email or text. Coincidence? Or had Chris been
in touch with her?

'How are you doing?' Camile asked brightly.

'All right, thank you,' Jan replied. 'How are you?'

'Work is challenging, but otherwise I'm OK. How's Tinder?'

'He's fine.'

'Do you both have everything you need?'

'Yes, thank you. You left him plenty of food.'

'Chris called a short while ago and said you were having
problems with forest animals coming into the garden.' So it
wasn't pure chance she was calling.

'Yes.'

'Don't worry. It happened to me, but they won't harm
you. Chris tells me he's fixed the hole in the hedge so that
should keep them out.'

'Do you know what they are?' Jan asked.

'No. It was always dark. Tinder used to chase them off. I
guess they get hungry in winter.'

'That's what Chris said.'

'You're not worried, are you?' Camile asked.

'No.'

'Good. Well, hopefully Chris's repair work has done the
trick. It was nice of him to give up his Saturday to fix it.
He's a good guy. Someone you can trust.'

'Yes,' Jan said, while thinking, if he's that wonderful, why
did you two separate?

'Thanks for all you're doing,' Camile said. 'I don't know
what I would have done without you. Tinder can't be left in

kennels. I've tried, but he pines so badly he stops eating. I'm very grateful to you.'

'You're welcome,' Jan said.

Camile wound up the conversation. Coward, Jan scolded herself. It would be even more difficult now to give notice when the time came. Doubtless Chris had told her she was anxious and imagining all sorts of ridiculous things. Without proof it was just that – ridiculous. Jan needed concrete evidence and then she'd give notice. The ball of twine and muddy footprints on the car hadn't convinced Ruby – rightly so. She'd had to hear them before she'd believed her. What Jan needed was a photograph, or better still a video clip. But how to get that? They were fast, and as soon as they saw her they bolted.

Suddenly a noise came from outside. Tinder shot off the sofa and ran to the back door, barking. Surely they weren't here already? It was barely dark. Could this be the opportunity she needed to get a picture? Grabbing her phone and with her heart racing, Jan rushed to the back door and opened it. But there was nothing there. No movement. No shadow in the dark. Tinder ran to the bottom of the garden but couldn't get out. Chris's repair work must still be in place. 'Come on,' she called him. 'Tinder!' The night was cold and she wanted to close the door.

He came out of the hedge and trotted up the lawn towards her. 'Good boy,' she said as he came in.

She was about to close the door when suddenly she heard a woman's voice cry out in the woods. 'No. Stop!'

Jan froze. Someone was out there in the woods at night. A woman. She sounded as though she was in trouble. 'Who's there?' Jan called into the dark. There was no reply. Not a sound. She waited a moment longer, closed the back door, then pressed 999 on her mobile for the emergency services.

'Police,' she said, as the call handler asked her which service.

'Putting you through now.'

'I live in Ivy Cottage. Wood Lane. It backs onto Coleshaw Woods,' Jan began as soon as she was connected. 'I've just heard a woman shout in the woods. She sounded as though she was in trouble. Please hurry. I'm sure she's in danger and could be hurt.'

THIRTY-SEVEN

Jan paced the living room, phone in her hand, waiting for the police. The officer who'd taken all the details had said they'd send someone straight away. Five minutes passed, then ten. Jan summoned her courage and opened the back door a little, just enough to hear, but the woods remained eerily quiet. There'd been that one cry, then nothing.

She closed the door and another five minutes passed. Where the hell were the police? Tinder was at her feet staring up at her, concerned. She patted him and he looked back with large enquiring eyes.

It was now twenty minutes since she'd called the police. They'd said a car was on its way. Surely it should be here by now, together with an ambulance? Perhaps they'd gone straight into Coleshaw Woods, Jan thought, and, kneeling on the sofa, gingerly parted the curtains. She couldn't see any torch beams in the woods or flashing lights suggesting a police car or ambulance was there. She went upstairs into the second bedroom at the rear of the cottage from where she had a better view. But there were no lights in the woods. That poor woman could be lying badly hurt, even bleeding to death. Jan returned to the living room.

A few minutes later she was startled by a sharp ring on the doorbell, followed by a loud knock on the door. Tinder shot under the table. The police? She hadn't heard a siren. With mounting unease, Jan went down the hall and to the right of the door where there was a small lattice window in an alcove. You couldn't see who was at the front door from it, just the lane in front. She eased back the curtain and saw a police car parked in the lane. She opened the door to two uniformed officers.

'Thank goodness you're here,' she said. 'Have you found her?'

'Yes, she's fine. We've spoken to her,' the lead officer said.

'You have?' Jan asked, amazed.

'She was driving out of Wood Lane as we were coming in. We thought you'd want to know she was safe.'

'Well, yes. So she's not hurt then?' Jan asked, confused.

'No. She was shouting at her dog.'

'Really? What was she doing in the woods after dark?'

'She was walking her dogs early this evening when one chased after something and disappeared. She'd been searching for him ever since and then caught a glimpse of him through the trees. That's why she shouted, "No! stop!" She has him now and is sorry she caused you worry.'

'Oh,' Jan said, relieved. 'I thought she was being attacked.'

'No harm done. Always best to call us if you hear anything suspicious. You're isolated out here.'

'Yes, I am,' Jan agreed, not really appreciating the reminder.

'We'll be off then.'

'Thank you. Sorry to have wasted your time.'

'Not at all. Enjoy the rest of your evening.'

They said a polite goodnight and Jan closed and bolted the front door. She returned to the living room deep in thought. Of course she was relieved the woman was safe, but there was something bothering her. The voice she'd heard had sounded panic-stricken, not someone calling her dog. Also, the more she thought about it, the more familiar the voice had sounded. As though she might have heard it somewhere before. But try as she might, she couldn't place it. Perhaps it would come to her in time.

THIRTY-EIGHT

Tuesday couldn't pass quickly enough for Ian. He'd posted his and Emma's DNA tests first thing Monday morning, paying extra for same-day delivery. This came with the option of tracking the parcel online, so he knew it had been delivered and signed for at 3.20 on Monday afternoon. If MyGeneticHistory.com got to work on analysing their samples of saliva straight away, which their website had said they would, then the results could be available later today, Ian thought. He'd been checking his personal email regularly throughout the day even though he was at work. So far all he'd had from the company was a standard acknowledgement that his test kits had been received.

Ian conceded he had little idea of what exactly was involved in analysing DNA. But lots of companies offered the service so he assumed it couldn't be too complicated. At 4 p.m., nearly twenty-four hours after the parcel had been delivered, Ian checked his email again. Still nothing. Their samples were probably in a queue waiting to be dealt with. Perhaps a phone call would help move them up the list.

'Good afternoon, My Genetic History. How can we help you?' a friendly female voice answered.

'I sent you saliva samples yesterday and I was wondering when we could expect the results. Our names are Ian and Emma Jennings.'

'It can take up to three working days,' she replied.

'I saw that on your website, but I'm assuming that includes postal delivery time. I opted for the results to be emailed. Could you check where they are in the system, please?'

'Just a moment. I'll see if I can find out.'

'Thank you.' Ian then had to listen to a few minutes of *The Blue Danube* holding music before she came back on the line.

'I've spoken to our technician and she says the results are waiting to be checked and should be with you this evening. If not, it will be first thing tomorrow.'

'This evening would be better,' Ian said.

'I understand, but all our results are double-checked before they're sent out. We can't afford to make mistakes. Each DNA sample is analysed at more than half a million genetic markers. It's very thorough.' Which Ian had seen on their website.

'All right, thank you,' Ian said. 'Remember, email, not post.'

'Yes. It's noted on our system.'

Ian continued to check his emails every fifteen minutes or so and then again as he left work at 5.30. Still no results. He'd be the first to admit he wasn't good at waiting, never had been, especially when it relied on someone else's efficiency. He hadn't told Emma the results were expected this evening. He wanted time to read and digest them before he shared what he learnt. She was still convinced that a professional clinic wouldn't make errors in their record-keeping. Quietly Ian agreed. He knew it was a long shot and he suspected that the results would vindicate the Mollers and he'd have to accept that.

*   *   *

185

Emma, having returned to work on Monday, was home just before Ian. As he let himself in, he could hear her in the kitchen preparing their evening meal. The talk she'd had with their midwife and then returning to work had done her a power of good. The last couple of days she'd been in a much better frame of mind, so Ian was looking forward to coming home and seeing her again.

'Hi, love,' he called as he hung his coat on the hall stand.

'Hi!' she returned from the kitchen.

He dropped his briefcase in the living room on his way through to the kitchen where he kissed Emma's neck. She didn't immediately pull away, which gave him hope that before too long they'd be completely back to normal.

'Anything I can do?' he asked.

'No. Dinner will be about a quarter of an hour.'

'I'll change out of my suit then.'

Ian went upstairs to their bedroom where he took the opportunity to check his phone again for an email. Still nothing from MyGeneticHistory.com. He would look again after dinner and then every so often during the evening, furtively, so Emma couldn't see. Their relationship was improving and he didn't want to risk doing anything that might spoil that.

At 7.30, after they'd eaten and washed up, Emma settled in front of the television to watch a soap, and Ian surreptitiously stole another glance at his phone. A new email had arrived in his inbox from MyGenticHistory.com with a large attachment marked *Confidential*. Their results! His heart missed a beat. He took his laptop from his briefcase and sat at the dining table. Emma glanced over. 'Work,' he said.

She nodded and returned her attention to the television.

Barely able to contain himself, Ian opened the email. *Dear Mr Jennings, I have pleasure attaching your results* . . . Then there was a paragraph stating that the results should be read in conjunction with the explanatory notes. Ian saved the attachment before opening it. He began to read. Emma's results first – gradually making sense of the graphs, numbers, estimates and percentages. So Moller had been right on that count, at least. She didn't carry any genetic condition. He then looked at his results. Ten minutes later he'd concluded that neither did he. Moller had been telling the truth. The last two pages were the results of their paternity tests. He scanned down to the conclusion and that needed no explanation. His heart stopped. There was a 99 per cent chance that he and Emma shared the same biological father, which meant they were half brother and sister. Ian felt physically sick.

THIRTY-NINE

Jan had decided she needed proof. Something she could show Chris, Ruby and the police. Firm evidence that there was something living in the woods. Evidence that wouldn't disappear like the ball of twine and couldn't be misinterpreted as the muddy footprints on her car had. She needed a photograph so there was no doubt.

The ball of twine had appeared and then vanished again and Jan found she wasn't really surprised. Whoever, whatever was out there was tormenting her, toying with her like a cat playing with a mouse, maybe even having a laugh at her expense. They were trying to make it appear as though she was imagining things and losing her mind, but she knew she wasn't. She was still sure Chris had seen something on the night he'd taken her out, even though he wouldn't admit it. And Ruby had been convinced she'd heard one of them at the window, although she was now trying to rationalize it.

She'd texted on Monday: *Sorry for my hasty departure. I feel a fool. I expect it was nothing. Just the wind in the trees x*

No, it wasn't the wind in the trees, Jan thought. She'd seen how scared Ruby had been. She hadn't been able to get out of the cottage quickly enough. Ruby would receive a photograph once Jan was able to take one. She had a plan.

Chris and Camile had both said that whatever was coming into the garden was probably hungry and looking for food. So the obvious way forward, Jan decided, was to entice them into the garden with food and then take a photograph. But what did they eat? She had no idea. Were they carnivore, herbivore or omnivore? She'd leave out a selection of what she had. If they didn't take the bait this time, then she'd buy other foods – but not live prey. With a shudder, Jan wondered if they'd been trying to hunt Tinder, but dismissed that idea as they would have got him by now if that was their intention. They'd had plenty of opportunities.

Jan hadn't heard them on Sunday night and neither had Tinder. If they had come into the garden, they must have been very quiet. But then last night, as she'd been watching a film, she'd heard a noise outside the living-room window. Tinder had immediately pricked up his ears and shot off the sofa, a sure sign there was something out there. But by the time she'd opened the back door they'd gone. Tonight would be different, though. She was going to summon all her courage and stay downstairs, all night if necessary, to get the photograph she needed.

At seven o'clock Jan let Tinder out for his evening run. It was still quiet in the garden. He returned straight away after doing his business. Jan then gathered together a selection of food, including some fruit, and put on her jacket. She wouldn't switch on the motion-sensor light as it might scare them off. Taking the torch from its hook in the hall and, making sure Tinder didn't follow her, Jan went outside. She began arranging little piles of food on the patio, right outside the living-room window. As she worked, she listened out, but there was nothing to suggest they were close by.

189

Returning indoors, Jan switched off all the lights, opened the living-room curtains and then lay on the sofa where she couldn't be seen from outside. She had brought down her duvet, and her phone, with the camera engaged, was ready beside her. Thankfully it was a calm night with no wind or rain so there was nothing that could put them off or spoil the photograph.

Pulling the duvet over her, she lay still and listened. The minutes ticked by. Eight-thirty came and went. Nine, nine-thirty. Tinder slept at her feet. Another hour passed, but no sound from outside. Jan felt disappointed. She should have asked Ruby what time she'd heard them. They were usually here before now. Was it possible they knew she'd set a trap and was lying in wait to photograph them? She'd never left food out before, or had the curtains open after dark. Were they really so clever that they could see her intention by a change of routine? An icy chill crept up Jan's spine and she pulled the duvet closer around her.

By midnight Jan was struggling to keep her eyes open. She dared not get up and make a coffee, for if they were out there watching they would see her and bolt. They never stayed once they'd been seen; but always ran away. She would need them still for a few moments to take the photo – hence the piles of food.

She shifted position and willed herself to stay awake. As one o'clock approached, her eyes closed. Then suddenly she was awake, startled by a noise outside. Senses tingling and her breath coming fast and shallow, she felt for her phone.

Keeping low and out of sight, Jan carefully slid the phone from beneath the duvet and slowly began to raise it. Just high enough over the back of the sofa so she could take the photo. At the same time she carefully drew herself to her knees. She'd only get one chance. But at that moment Tinder heard it too and, leaping from the sofa, ran towards the back door, barking loudly. Jan took the picture anyway but knew even before she looked at it she'd been too late. Just a view of the reflection of the flash on the glass. Tomorrow she'd try again, shutting Tinder in her bedroom first, and with the flash turned off.

FORTY

Ian was still awake in the early hours of Wednesday morning, angry, upset, confused and agitatedly trying to decide what to do next. Moller had lied. The DNA results had shown that while he and Emma didn't have any inherited genetic conditions, they did share the same biological father. Little wonder they looked similar, Ian thought bitterly. They were half brother and sister! It was the worst possible outcome and Ian was struggling to cope.

He lay in bed, a small light coming from the street lamp outside, plagued by thoughts of what he'd learnt as Emma slept beside him. She was in a deep sleep and her breathing was soft and shallow. Lucky her, Ian thought bitterly. He hadn't told her yet. When he'd finally come to bed shortly after 1 a.m. she'd stirred, turned over and cuddled up to him, wanting to make love. He'd recoiled and feigned sleep. Now he knew they were related he wasn't sure what he felt towards her. Not his wife, more like a friend, or sister, which he supposed in some ways she was. Clearly there would be no more children. This was the end of the road for their hopes of a normal family life, and Ian had no idea how he was going to tell Emma.

He moved his legs away from her and tried to relax. He really needed to get some sleep. He had work tomorrow, but his anger persisted. Moller had ruined their lives and Ian wanted him to pay one way or another. He'd go to the clinic tomorrow and have it out with him. But then, on reflection, Ian wondered if that was a good idea. He doubted he was going to get any more out of Moller than he had the last time. Moller had lied, so why would he tell the truth now? Also, if Ian lost his temper – which he could easily do – he might do something he later regretted. Perhaps it would be better to report him to the police and let them take care of him. Yes, that seemed to be the best plan.

But then again . . . Ian could picture going into Coleshaw Police Station and having to explain to the duty officer about the clinic and donated sperm. How embarrassing that would be! Especially if others were there. Added to which, the moment he began talking about their dead babies, he knew he would cry and make a complete fool of himself.

Emma stirred beside him and, giving a small groan, mumbled something in her sleep, which gave Ian another idea. The detective constable who'd come to see them already knew about the death of their last baby. He wouldn't have to go through it all again with her. She'd seemed clued up and sensitive, and as a detective could investigate. It would be easier talking to her than going to the police station. But what was her name?

Ian tried to remember. She'd introduced herself as . . . what was it? She'd shown her ID, but he'd only glanced at it, not long enough to remember her name. 'I'm Detective Constable . . . from Coleshaw CID,' she'd said, but what name had she given? Her first name began with B, he thought, and it was only a short name. Not Bella, Babs, but something like that. B . . . B . . . Beth. Yes, he was certain her first name was Beth. Try as he might, he couldn't remember her surname.

But there couldn't be too many detective constables called Beth at Coleshaw CID. He'd telephone the station in the morning, although he wouldn't tell Emma about any of this, not yet. Once he had all the facts, he'd have to sit her down and break the news to her as gently as he could. She'd be distraught, of course, just as he was. The longer he could postpone it, the better: that dreadful moment when he shattered her life.

FORTY-ONE

Ian woke before their alarm. He looked at Emma sleeping peacefully beside him and felt envious. Ignorance is bliss, he thought. How he would have liked to take her in his arms, gently kiss her awake and then make love. But that would never happen again, now he knew they were related. It seemed she and her mother had been right when they'd said no good would come of delving into the past. He wished he'd listened to them, for what he'd learnt could not be unlearnt. It was a burden he would carry forever.

Carefully moving away from Emma, Ian slowly lifted his side of the duvet and slipped from the bed without waking her. He silently gathered together his office clothes and went into the bathroom to shower and dress. As he finished, he heard their alarm go and then a few minutes later Emma on the landing. 'You're up early,' she called.

'Yes, I have an eight o'clock meeting at work,' he lied.

'Do you want coffee and toast?'

'No, thanks, I'll pick up something en route.'

Ian waited until Emma was downstairs in the kitchen so he wouldn't have to see her before he came out of the bathroom. He collected his suit jacket from their bedroom, then went quietly downstairs, picked up his briefcase from the living room and called goodbye as he let himself out.

The crisp, cold air hit him. He got into his car and then sat for a minute with the engine running, waiting for the windscreen to defrost. Their neighbour, Mrs Slater, appeared at her bedroom window. He nodded politely, but she turned away. She still wasn't speaking to them, which Ian thought was probably for the best. Heaven forbid she got wind of what he'd found out. They'd be reviled, the subject of local gossip, and ostracized for being unnatural.

It was eight o'clock as Ian pulled into the car park of Wetherby Security. It was largely empty at this time of the morning as the majority of employees started work at nine. Nevertheless, he parked away from the entrance and exit, took out his phone and then searched online for the phone number of Coleshaw CID.

'I'd like to speak to a detective constable there,' he said as soon as the call handler answered. 'My name is Ian Jennings. The officer visited my wife and me a few weeks ago. I'm sure her first name was Beth, but I can't remember her surname.'

'DC Beth Mayes?'

'Yes. That's her. Can I speak to her, please?'

'I'll see if she's in. What is it in connection with?'

Ian hesitated and swallowed hard. 'Our baby. I'm sure she'll remember if you tell her it's Ian Jennings. I live in Booth Lane and she saw my wife, Emma, twice.'

'Hold the line, please, and I'll check if she's here.'

It was a minute or so before he came back on the line. 'I'll put you through now.'

'Thank you.'

'Good morning, Mr Jennings,' Beth said. 'How are you and your wife?'

'All right. Well, actually we're not. We've just had some awful news and I need your help. You see, I've discovered that my wife and I are the children of donor sperm. Do you know what that is?'

'Yes.'

'To make matters worse, I've just found out that we share the same donor. We're related! Emma and I have the same biological father.'

'I didn't think that was allowed.'

'It's not. And the man who runs the clinic where the sperm came from lied to me. He told me we couldn't possibly have the same donor. But I've had our DNA tested and we most certainly do. There's no doubt about it.'

'I see,' Beth said gently.

'This must be the reason Emma and I can't have healthy children, although we don't appear to have any inherited conditions.'

'I'm sorry,' Beth said. 'This must have come as a huge shock to you and your wife, but I'm not sure I can help. How is it a police matter?'

'Carstan Moller, who owns and runs the clinic, lied to me. I'd like you to find out why.' Ian heard Beth's hesitation before she replied.

'From what you've told me, Ian, I don't think it's a police matter. But if you wait a moment, I'll check.'

'Thank you.'

It was a few minutes before Beth came back on the phone.

'As I thought, it isn't really a police matter. In the first instance you will need to raise your complaint with the practice manager at the clinic.'

'There isn't a practice manager,' Ian said. 'It's just Carstan Moller and his wife.'

'In that case, if it's an NHS clinic then you could contact the ombudsman.'

'It's not. It's private,' Ian replied, struggling to hide his impatience.

'I think you'll need to take it up with the independent adjudication service then. There's information about their organization online.'

'So you definitely can't investigate?' Ian asked, disappointed.

'Not unless a crime has been committed, and from what you've told me it hasn't been. I am sorry, but I don't see how I can help you.'

Frustrated and feeling let down, Ian said goodbye and ended the call.

Now what? he thought.

He stayed in his car, staring out of his side window. If he took DC Beth Mayes's advice and contacted the adjudication service, he'd have to go through everything that had happened all over again, and then wait for the outcome of any investigation. How long would that take? Probably forever, especially if Moller prevaricated or lied again. He needed answers now. Perhaps he should return to his first plan and visit Carstan Moller in person. He had the DNA evidence now and that couldn't be ignored. If he showed him the results, Moller would have to tell him the truth, wouldn't he?

Ian couldn't think of a better plan. He'd go now. But before he started his car he sent an email to his boss: *I have a doctor's appointment today so I'll be working from home.* He then switched on his satnav and drove out of the office's car park. The DNA test results proved Moller had lied and Ian was ready for a fight.

FORTY-TWO

It was 9.15 a.m. as Ian passed the village shop with its advertising easel outside. Wound up and ready to confront Carstan Moller, he drove up the hill and parked in the road at the front of the clinic. There were two cars on the driveway, a BMW he'd seen there before and a Vauxhall Corsa. Ian wondered if that belonged to Edie or a patient. If it was a patient it could work in his favour. Moller wouldn't want him creating a scene if he had someone with him.

Ian took his briefcase containing his laptop from the passenger seat and got out of the car. He walked purposefully up the path to the front door. He turned his back on the CCTV as he pressed the bell, although he had little doubt he could still be identified. He waited and pressed the bell again, for longer this time. He'd stay there pressing their damn doorbell for as long as it took them to answer. He wasn't going to be fobbed off again. He had evidence now.

The door opened and Edie Moller appeared, face set to a professional smile. 'Yes, Mr Jennings, how can I help you?'

'I want to speak to Carstan,' Ian said.

'Yes, of course, come in,' Edie replied, to Ian's surprise. He had been expecting excuses. 'Carstan has someone with him,' Edie continued as she showed him into the waiting room. 'Please take a seat and I'll let him know you're here. There are some magazines on the table. Hopefully he won't be long. Would you like a coffee?'

'No, thank you,' Ian replied stiffly, and sat in one of the chairs.

With another polite smile, Edie left the room. Ian glanced around, absently drumming his fingers on the wooden arm rest. He needed to calm down so he could think rationally when he presented his case to Moller. He doubted Carstan would readily admit to his mistake, so Ian would need to prove it. He took out his laptop and opened the file containing the DNA results so it was ready, then returned his laptop to his briefcase. He picked up a magazine and put it down again.

He heard a door open and slam shut in the hall, followed by footsteps hurrying down the hall. The front door opened and slammed shut. Interesting. Whoever it was had left in a hurry and, from the sound of it, angry. Ian would have liked to know the reason.

The door to the waiting room opened and Edie Moller appeared, looking slightly flustered. 'Mr Moller will see you now,' she said tightly.

Ian stood and followed her into Moller's office where he'd seen him before. He was standing beside his desk, apparently not fully recovered from his previous encounter.

'Yes, Mr Jennings?' he said rather sharply. 'You wished to see me.'

Ian took a deep breath. Going over, he stood beside Moller and set his laptop on the desk, angling the screen so they both could see it. Edie Moller was waiting by the door.

'When I asked you before to check if Emma and I shared the same donor you told me we didn't,' Ian began, immediately hot and flustered. 'I now have absolute proof we do. I've had

200

Emma's and my DNA analysed and there is no doubt. We have the same biological father. Here are the results.'

'I'll call you if I need you,' Moller told his wife. Ian saw a muscle twitch nervously in his neck. Edie Moller left the room.

'Read this,' Ian said, pointing to the paternity test results. 'A 99 per cent chance that Emma and I share the same biological father. You can't get a result higher than that. And the only way we share the same father is from donor sperm supplied by your clinic.' Ian drew himself up to his full height and glared at Moller.

Carstan Moller barely looked at the screen and certainly didn't have time to read and digest the results before he sat behind his desk, outwardly composed. 'Take a seat, please,' he said, waving to the chair on the other side of the desk.

Ian picked up his laptop and sat down.

'If those results are correct —' Moller began.

'They are,' Ian put in.

'Then it would appear we have made a dreadful error here, unprecedented in the history of my clinic. Donors are allowed to donate more than once, but we work within the correct guidelines. Statistically there is a very slim chance of this happening, and to make matters worse, it seems I must have made a mistake in my record-keeping. I will of course look into it thoroughly, and if I find we are at fault you and your wife will be compensated.'

Ian stared at him, confounded. He had come here expecting denial, then an ugly scene where he would have to force Moller to admit his mistake. But it seemed he was open to the idea.

'If you could email me a copy of those results,' Moller continued, 'I'll be able to compare them with my records.'

Ian took a moment to connect his laptop to the Wi-Fi and emailed the file. 'It should be in your inbox now.'

'Thank you,' Moller said. 'I will study it this evening when I can give it my full attention and then contact you.'

'How can you check?' Ian asked suspiciously. 'You won't still have the donor sperm. All you've got are your records and if they're incorrect, as they appear to be, what else can you do?'

'Each donor is given a number and that is how they are identified. When I checked your and your wife's records before it showed different numbers, indicating the sperm was from different donors. However, I will cross-check the numbers are correct by using the actual identity of the donors. It will take me a while, but it will be conclusive. Let me assure you, if I find the donor is the same, there will be no cover up. I will take full responsibility and compensate you as best I can.'

'How can I be sure?' Ian asked.

'You have my word.'

'I would like to see your records for myself,' Ian said.

'I'm afraid that's not possible. They are confidential. But why would I risk the reputation of my clinic and lie to you? I'm not stupid. I know if you're not satisfied you will go public, and that would be to the detriment of my practice after all these years. Please give me the chance to investigate and then we can discuss the matter further. It's in my interest to make sure you're satisfied, isn't it?'

Moller was being so reasonable Ian felt he had to give him time to look into it.

'All right,' Ian said. 'Check your records, but I know my test results are correct.'

'Quite possibly,' Moller said in the same convivial manner. 'I will be in touch as soon as I have investigated the matter. Will that be all?' he asked politely.

Ian nodded and, closing his laptop, returned it to his briefcase.

'Thank you for bringing this to my attention,' Moller said. He stood and came out from behind his desk. 'I am sorry you've had all this worry. I will do my best to put it right, I promise you.' He opened the door. Edie Moller was waiting on the other side to show Ian out.

'Goodbye, Mr Jennings,' Carstan said.

'Bye,' Ian mumbled, and followed Edie to the front door.

Outside, Ian saw that the other car had gone. Deflated and confused by Moller's reaction, Ian returned to his car. He'd arrived half expecting not to be let in and for Moller to then deny that any error could have occurred. Yet he'd admitted straight away that a mistake was possible and even mentioned compensation. Ian didn't trust him, though. There was something shifty about the man, and he hadn't been surprised by the DNA results. Indeed, he'd barely glanced at them, almost as if he'd known what they would show. Perhaps he had been using the same donor more than was allowed? How Ian would have liked to see Moller's records for himself. Then it occurred to him – there was a way . . . but it was illegal. If he got caught, he would be prosecuted, lose his job and never work again.

FORTY-THREE

Shortly after three o'clock that Wednesday afternoon, Jan left Lillian's shop in Merryless and returned to her car. Dropping the bag of groceries on the rear seat, she started the engine and headed back to the cottage. She was using her car now to visit the store as it felt safer than walking along Wood Lane. There'd been more muddy footprints on her car that morning and at the front door. They were getting braver and she wasn't taking any risks. Tinder missed his walks, but he could go in the garden.

She turned into Wood Lane and pressed the central locking system. As the car bumped along the uneven road surface, Jan maintained her vigilance and kept a look-out for any movement in the surrounding trees. It was a bright but cold day with good visibility, so it shouldn't be too difficult to catch a glimpse of them if they were watching her, as she suspected they were. She looked through the windscreen, the side windows and in the rear-view mirror, but there was nothing so far. She was uncertain whether she should be relieved or more worried than ever.

As she drew to a halt outside Ivy Cottage, her phone

buzzed with a text message. It was from Chris: *Have I been forgiven enough to take you to the cinema?*

She'd told him she'd think about it.

I can't this week, I'm busy, she replied.

Next week? came his immediate reply before she'd even left the car.

She didn't text back.

Taking the bag of groceries indoors, Jan put the cold food in the fridge and left the other items she'd bought for tonight on the counter in the kitchen. Food had enticed them to the window before and she hoped it would again. All she had to do now was keep her nerve until dark and be ready with her camera.

FORTY-FOUR

Ian spent most of Wednesday afternoon in a secluded corner of The Coffee Shop, laptop open and using their Wi-Fi to work. It was easier to come here than go home and have to explain to Emma why he was back early from the office. She always arrived home before him, so he would return at his usual time and let her assume he'd been at work all day.

But it was proving impossible to concentrate. His thoughts kept wandering to Moller and their meeting that morning. The more Ian thought about it, the more he saw that Carstan Moller had got rid of him very easily by promising to check his records and offering compensation. Ian felt a sucker. He should have stood his ground and challenged him, asked him how many others had received the same donor sperm, demanded that Moller check his records in front of him and show him proof of his findings.

Annoyed with himself for being so easily taken in, Ian finished his second cup of coffee and, staring at his laptop, tried again to concentrate on work. It was now four o'clock and there was at least an hour and a half before he could return home. But the thought of seeing Emma didn't fill him with the joy it had just a few days ago. Before long he'd have to tell her what the paternity tests had revealed. It was going to be dreadful. It couldn't be anything else.

His phone vibrated with an incoming call, and as he picked it up he was surprised to see Moller's number.

'Good afternoon, Ian, Carstan here, phoning as promised.' He sounded very upbeat.

'Yes?' Ian said warily.

'I appreciated you needed an early response, so I cancelled my afternoon appointments to deal with your matter expeditiously. I am sorry to say that the test results you sent me are correct. I've cross-checked our records and a mistake was made. An incorrect donor number was recorded on your file, and I'm afraid you and your wife do share the same donor.'

'I thought so,' Ian said numbly.

'I can only apologize,' Moller continued. 'I am assuming this is an isolated incident, but I will cross-check all my patients and donors right back to when I first opened the clinic. I will also implement a better system of record-keeping for the future.'

'How many others share the same donor?' Ian asked.

'I work within the current guidelines, which is that one donor can be used by ten separate patients.'

'So the odds are this should never have happened?'

'The chances of the two of you ending up together were incredibly slim. But I am sorry.'

'Is it the reason Emma and I can't have healthy children?'

'It's possible,' Moller said. 'But it's more likely due to a genetic defect passed down by one of your mothers that didn't show on your DNA tests. They are never a hundred per cent accurate. I don't know what else I can do but offer my sincere apologies and compensate you and your wife. I hope we can come to an agreement so the reputation of my clinic isn't irreparably damaged. What do you think is a reasonable sum?'

207

'I've no idea,' Ian said. 'This has all come as such a shock. I wanted answers, not compensation.'

'And I trust I have given you those. Discuss the matter with Emma and then come back to me. If you and your wife would like counselling, Edie is very good and of course there will be no charge.'

Ian sighed.

'I understand you need time,' Moller said. 'Call me when you're ready.' Winding up the conversation, he said goodbye.

Ian returned his phone to the table and dropped his head into his hands. He supposed he should be grateful for Moller's honesty, but he wasn't. He was gutted. Compensation, when his and Emma's lives were in ruins. Nothing could compensate them for that.

The hum of conversation continued around him and in the background, the hiss of the coffee machine as the barista brewed more coffee. It felt surreal – sitting here in the midst of normality while trying to process something that was anything but normal. He and his wife were half brother and sister.

Ian raised his head. How the hell was he going to tell Emma? He still had no idea. He supposed Emma's parents and his mother would have to know too at some point. But he couldn't think about that now. What a fucking awful mess! He stared distractedly around him and his resentment grew.

Moller had admitted his error very easily on the phone and had renewed his offer of compensation. Of course he'd want to keep them quiet. If this came out, it wouldn't do his clinic any good at all. How easy it would be to hold him to ransom and demand a huge sum. But there was no price on what Emma and he had been through and had yet to go through. Nothing that could undo the harm that had been done.

Ian stood, went to the counter and bought another coffee. The longer he could postpone going home, the better.

Could others be affected? he wondered, returning to the table with his coffee. Moller had said he worked within the current guidelines – one donor to no more than ten families – so the chances were minuscule. But when had that rule come in? Ian googled the question and found it was only ten years ago, so hadn't applied when his and Emma's parents had used the clinic. Before then, artificial insemination by donor had been largely unregulated and at the discretion of the clinic. Had Moller been purposely misleading him?

Ian took a sip of his coffee and slowly replaced it in the saucer. If there were others, what were the chances of Moller contacting them? Low, Ian decided. The only reason he'd admitted his error to Ian was because he'd shown him irrefutable evidence. Ian was sure Moller wouldn't have told him otherwise. How he would have liked to see his records. But if he asked again, he'd get the same reply and Moller would hide behind patient confidentiality.

Straightening in his chair, Ian closed the file on his laptop he'd been trying to work on and stared at the screensaver. His thoughts raced, going where they shouldn't. He broke out in a sweat as he considered the enormity of what he was thinking of doing. He'd be taking a huge risk. If he was caught, there would be a trial and prison.

So he'd have to make sure he wasn't caught, he told himself. He was good at his job – one of the Information Technology team at Wetherby Security Ltd. The company was in the business of keeping organizations safe. His department specialized in online security, advising clients on how to keep their companies safe from hacking, and minimizing the damage if a company was attacked. In order to do his job, Ian had had to study how hackers worked. He knew how they got into computers and how to keep them out.

Ian paused for a moment longer, took another sip of his coffee, and then moved the cursor on his laptop to go online. He doubted the Mollers' computer was well protected from hackers, so it shouldn't be too difficult to access. And while using the public Wi-Fi came with its own security concerns, it also meant Ian's laptop couldn't be so easily traced. But just to make sure, he'd use a VPN – virtual private network – as he did sometimes at work.

Ian glanced around. The nearest person was sitting far enough away not to be able to see his screen. Even if they could or someone walked past, he was just another customer with a coffee and a laptop. Before he lost his nerve and changed his mind, Ian logged into the VPN and began.

FORTY-FIVE

Five minutes later, Ian had identified the Wi-Fi router the Mollers were using at the clinic. It was only a short step from there into their computer. As he'd thought, it wasn't well protected, but he'd make sure he didn't stay for long. The less time he spent hacked into their computer, the less chance there was of being caught.

Ian looked at the dozens of folders and remembered Edie Moller's exasperation when she'd told him over the phone how they'd had to go from paper record-keeping to digital. The records were a mess.

There appeared to be little logic in the way the folders were listed. Ian opened and closed a few, looking at the files they contained and trying to work out if there was a system, and if so, what it was. Some of the folders bore recent dates while others hadn't been opened for years. All of them seemed to be work related, with no folders or files containing personal material like photographs and music downloads. It was impossible to know if all the paper files had been stored digitally, but Ian thought many had as the oldest was dated thirty years before. Plugging a USB stick into the side of his laptop, Ian began copying over the folders to examine them offline.

When he thought he had them all, he logged out. Using the paper napkin that had come with his croissant, Ian wiped the sweat from his forehead. It was warm in The Coffee Shop, but that wasn't the only reason he was perspiring. He'd just committed a crime, and now, with a mixture of dread and anticipation of what he might find, he began studying the folders and the files contained within them. Only some of the patients' folders were stored alphabetically by surname, as if Edie Moller had given up halfway through and had then just entered them in any order.

A bit of time arranging the patients' files now would save him time in the long run, Ian thought, and he began putting them into alphabetical order. He saw his and Emma's parents' names on folders but didn't open them at this point. He just tucked them into their alphabetical place. He was used to being methodical at work. There were two random folders that didn't contain patient details and he moved those to the end.

He began going through the folders of clients, starting with A. There were many files in each folder – some containing multiple pages. The first showed the patient's name, contact details, age and date of birth. The next their medical history, then diagnosis of infertility, treatment dates and what appeared to be the outcome. In some cases there was a record of a healthy baby being born. There were plenty of medical terms and abbreviations Ian didn't understand, but all the patient files seemed to follow a similar format. It soon became clear that Moller had been tracking all those who'd used the clinic and their children. He felt uncomfortable, voyeuristic, reading all their personal details, but it had to be done.

He left his and Emma's parents' folders until last, then, with trepidation, opened his parents' first. Ian read of his father's low sperm count, how long they'd been trying for a baby and the dates his mother had been inseminated with donor sperm. It had taken three attempts before she'd conceived him. His date of birth was recorded, the sex – boy – and that he was healthy. He opened Emma's parents' folder and found similar information, although her mother had conceived on the first attempt.

While some of this was what Ian would have expected from a fertility clinic, it seemed strange that despite all this information none of the patient files appeared to show a donor identification number – as Moller had said they did. He opened a few more and then the two non-patient folders, but they didn't contain a list of donor IDs either. Somewhere there must be a folder containing donor details their ID numbers, and a file cross-referencing them to the clients, as Moller had claimed. He must have missed it.

Glancing furtively over his shoulder to make sure no one was watching, Ian quickly logged into the Mollers' computer again. It was easier the second time. He had the login details. He began searching for any folders he might have missed, but he couldn't find any more. He then checked the hard drive for any folders or files that might have been deleted. Although deleted files disappeared from view, they could still be found on the hard drive if you knew where to look, which Ian did. It was part of his job. But the only deletions he found were junk mail. He then checked to see if there was any indication Moller was using other storage devices – an external hard drive or cloud, for example. But again there was nothing. Puzzled, Ian logged out and returned to the folders he'd saved on the USB stick.

He opened and skimmed through the other patient files, but not one bore a donor ID number. Ian now looked again more carefully at the two folders that didn't contain patient details. The first was called *Research* and contained published papers in the field of embryonic research – not surprising. The other folder was called *Second Generation* and contained a spreadsheet with single-line entries of couples' names, their contact details, the dates of birth of their babies and if they had survived. They weren't in alphabetical order but date order, with the oldest entry at the top. Ian scrolled down the page and felt as though he was walking through an infant graveyard with so many babies not surviving. What was all this about?

Some entries had the abbreviation of A.L. beside them. He guessed that was something to do with artificial insemination as it was a fertility clinic. He continued through the spreadsheet to the last page. His heart stopped. The penultimate entry was Ian and Emma Jennings. But what was this doing here? They hadn't used the clinic. His mouth went dry. Beside their names were the dates of the deaths of both their babies. The second also bore the abbreviation A.L. What the hell! Why was Moller collecting personal data on them? Not only did it not make sense, but it was a shocking invasion of their privacy.

Ian looked at the very last entry, the one below theirs. Grant and Chelsea Ryan. Their address wasn't far away and they'd recently had a baby girl who had died. The same abbreviation, A.L., was in the last column.

Ian's phone vibrated with an incoming call, jolting him from his thoughts. He picked it up. It was Emma.

'Ian, where are you?' she asked anxiously. 'It's seven o'clock. I've been worried.'

'I'm sorry, I got caught up at work. I'm leaving now.'

'Are you all right, Ian? You don't sound good.'

'I'll explain when I get home. We need to talk.'

'What is it?'

'I'll tell you when I get home.'

FORTY-SIX

With his thoughts in turmoil, Ian tucked his phone into his jacket pocket, returned his laptop to his briefcase and left The Coffee Shop. What the hell was Moller up to? He'd have to tell Emma everything he'd found out. He couldn't put it off any longer. But how and where to start he had no idea. It was horrendous and confusing. Moller had admitted to him that he'd made a mistake and he and Emma shared the same donor, but Ian hadn't found any evidence of that. Indeed, there was no evidence of any donors at all. Yet there must be hundreds, if not thousands, stretching back to when the clinic first opened. Instead, Ian had found that Moller had recorded the deaths of his and Emma's babies and they hadn't used the clinic. It didn't add up.

Moller treated infertility by inseminating the woman with donor sperm, his records confirmed that, but Ian was still no closer to tracing their donors or identifying how the mistake had occurred than he had been that morning. The only conclusion he could come to, he thought, as he drove, was that Moller must have another computer and had split files between the two. Perhaps a laptop? Ian had only seen one computer – on the second desk in Moller's office. But there must be another one somewhere containing this information, perhaps in his house.

Frustrated, anxious and dreading telling Emma, he parked on the drive and, with a very heavy heart, let himself into his house. Emma immediately appeared in the hall looking worried. 'I thought you'd left me,' she said with a nervous laugh, and went to hug him.

Ian stepped back.

'What is it?' she asked. 'Are you OK? Are we OK?'

'Not really,' Ian said.

'Why not?' Her bottom lip trembled.

'Come and sit down, love,' Ian said gently. 'We have to talk.'

Cupping Emma's elbow, he steered her into the living room and to the sofa.

'I'm sorry for being so distant recently,' Emma said, panic in her voice. 'I was down, but I'm a lot better now. I'll make it up to you, I promise. Dinner's ready.'

'I'm not hungry,' Ian said, his voice flat. He sat on the sofa beside her, his briefcase at his feet.

'What is it?' Emma asked again, fear in her eyes. 'You're frightening me.'

Ian took a breath. Where to start? 'I haven't been to work today.'

'No? Are you ill?'

He shook his head. 'I went to the Moller Clinic again.'

'Why?'

There was no easy way to say this. 'Our DNA test results came back and they show we have the same biological father.' He couldn't bear to look at her.

'No, that's not possible. Moller told you it wasn't.'

'I know, but I've shown him the evidence and he's changed his mind.'

'Oh my God, Ian, No! Could he be wrong?'

216

'No. I'll show you the results. You have a right to know.'

Taking his laptop from his briefcase, Ian sombrely lifted the lid, then opened the page showing the paternity test. 'Paternity ninety-nine per cent,' he said, pointing. 'It's definite.'

The colour drained from Emma's face. 'That can't be,' she moaned, her hand going to her mouth. 'It's impossible. We can't be brother and sister!'

'We are. Biologically, at least, we are half brother and sister.'

'That's disgusting!' Emma cried. 'I feel ill. Is that the reason we can't have healthy babies?'

'It's possible,' Ian said quietly. 'I don't know.'

'That clinic has ruined us!' Emma sobbed. 'All that pain and upset. It's too awful for words. We'll never be the same again. They need punishing. We'll tell our parents to sue them. They mustn't get away with this.' She collapsed against him, crying.

'Carstan Moller has already offered compensation,' Ian said.

'When? When did all this happen?' she asked, raising her head to look at him.

'I went to the clinic this morning and showed Moller these results. He got back to me this afternoon, after he'd checked his records. He admitted there'd been a mix up and we shared the same donor. He offered compensation straight away, but . . .'

'But what?' Emma asked.

'I don't know.' Ian shrugged. 'I've just got a feeling there's more to it.'

'What more could there be?' Emma cried. 'Isn't this enough? It's horrendous! A nightmare!' Her tears fell and Ian comforted her as best he could.

'Who is our donor?' she asked at length, wiping her eyes on the tissue Ian passed. 'Did you find out?'

217

'No. That's the thing. I can't find any record of the donors at all.'

'What, none?' she asked. 'I don't understand. Where did you look?'

'Emma, I'm going to show you something, but you must promise never to tell anyone. Not even your mother. I'll be in a lot of trouble if this got out. I could go to prison.'

'What have you done?' Emma cried, more alarmed than ever.

'I hacked into Moller's computer,' Ian said.

Emma stared at him.

'You see all these folders?' he said, showing her. 'They are Moller's files on his patients. But not one of them contains information about the donor or even a donor ID. I've been through them all.'

'So surely that information must be kept elsewhere?' Emma said.

'That's what I thought to begin with, but I've been thinking about it and there's no indication he has another computer. Nothing copied or erased. And why would he store those details separately unless he had something to hide? It was his work computer, his only computer as far as I could see. You'd expect it to contain all his work files.'

'There's the one for my parents,' Emma said, pointing. 'Can I have a look?'

'If you want.' Ian opened the folder and waited as Emma read the information.

'There's a lot of medical jargon, but it's more or less what Mum told me,' Emma said at length.

Ian waited until she'd finished and then closed the file. He moved the cursor down to the last folder. 'And this one is odd,' he said, opening the folder titled *Second Generation*. 'It's a spreadsheet of couples, but we're on it. There are our names and contact details.'

'But why?' Emma asked, staring at the spreadsheet. 'My God! There are the dates our babies were born. Why would Moller have recorded those? How would he know? We've never been to his clinic.'

'Exactly,' Ian said. 'I've been thinking about this all afternoon and the only conclusion I can come to is that this is a record of the grandchildren of those he'd treated. That's why it's called "Second Generation". Their parents were the first generation. But why he should be collecting that type of data I've no idea, especially as we haven't used the clinic. I don't know if any of the others listed here did. And why did so many babies die?'

'Can we report him?' Emma asked with a shiver.

'It would be difficult,' Ian said. 'We can't disclose how I came by this information.'

'What about reporting him anonymously to the police? You can do it online now.'

'We'd need to show that a crime has been committed, and we can't at present. There's no evidence, but look at this last entry,' Ian said, moving the cursor to the line containing the details of Grant and Chelsea Ryan. 'They're local and had a baby recently. I was thinking of phoning them to find out what their experience was of using the clinic. I'd have to think of a reason for having their details.'

'Perhaps you could pretend you're from the hospital health-care team?' Emma suggested. 'I had someone call me after the miscarriages and offer counselling.'

Ian hesitated. 'I don't know. What would I say? I'm better with computers than people.'

'I know.' Emma managed a small, sad smile. 'Shall I phone them?'

'Do you think you could without giving us away?'

'Yes, I think so. I know the sort of thing they say when they phone.'

'Wouldn't talking about our babies upset you?' Ian asked, concerned.

'Maybe, but I'll have to hide it, won't I?' Emma said bravely. 'We need to find out what's going on, but if I'm going to phone them, I'd better do it now before I have time to think about it and lose my nerve. What do you want me to find out?'

'Anything you can about their experience of using the clinic. Shall we practise, have a run through it? You could pretend to phone me and I'll answer. There's just their landline number so be prepared for either of them to answer. If it goes through to voicemail, don't leave a message. We'll set our phone to "private number" so it can't be traced.'

'OK, let's practise,' Emma said, throwing her tissue in the bin.

Ian made the noise of a phone trilling and then answered. 'Hello?'

FORTY-SEVEN

'Is that Chelsea Ryan?' Emma asked as a female voice answered. The phone was on speaker so Ian could hear.

'Yes. Who is this?'

'I'm calling from the Primary Care Trust. How are you?'

'OK, I guess. But I already told that other woman I don't want counselling.'

'No, I understand. That's fine,' Emma said. 'I'm just phoning to make sure you haven't changed your mind, and to ask you a few questions about your experiences if you have a moment.'

'Yeah, sure. Go ahead.' Emma glanced at Ian and he gave her the thumbs-up sign.

'Did you and your husband ever attend the Moller Clinic?' she asked.

'I don't think so. What is it?'

'A fertility clinic.'

'No. We don't need that.'

'Thank you. Do you know if either of your parents attended the clinic?'

'Not as far as I know. Do you want me to ask Grant?'

'Yes, please.'

Emma took a moment to breathe again as Chelsea shouted to Grant, 'Did your parents go to the Moller Clinic? It's a fertility clinic.'

'No idea!' he shouted back. 'Who are you talking to?'

'Someone from the Health Care Team. So I'll tell her you don't know.'

'Yeah, and also tell them to get a move on with our compensation.'

'Did you hear that?' Chelsea asked, returning to the phone.

'Yes. What compensation is that?' Emma asked, glancing at Ian. He looked as nervous as she felt.

'We're going to get compensation because the hospital lost our baby's body. We had nothing to bury, but I thought you would know that.'

'No, I'm sorry, I wasn't given that information. How upsetting for you both. I am sorry. What happened?' Emma asked, fighting back her own emotion.

'She was cremated instead of being kept in the mortuary,' Chelsea said. 'They're going to hold an inquiry. Grant found us a lawyer on a no-win, no-fee basis so we're suing them for compensation. Grant wants the midwife sacked too, but I liked Anne, and anyone can make a mistake.'

'You're too bloody soft!' Grant shouted in the background.

'Your midwife was called Anne?' Emma asked. 'What was her surname?'

'Long. Anne Long. She was lovely. Really kind and caring. She just made a mistake. I don't want her to lose her job.'

'Well, I do!' Grant shouted. 'Anyway, what's that got to do with whoever you're talking to?'

Ian motioned to Emma to wind up the call.

'I am so sorry for your loss,' Emma said again. 'Thank you for your time. I hope you get what you want.' Saying goodbye, she ended the call, then turned to Ian. 'Show me that spreadsheet again.'

'What is it?' he asked, holding the laptop between them. The *Second Generation* spreadsheet was still open on the screen.

Emma was quiet as she looked again at the entries. 'You see those letters – A.L. –beside some of the names?' she said. 'They could be the initials of Anne Long. They're beside our names and Chelsea and Grant's and some others. About thirty of them. Could it be that Moller is making a note of the midwife some of us used?'

'Why would he do that?' Ian asked. 'And the others don't have any initials at all. If you're right, shouldn't they have the initials of their midwives too? A.L. could stand for any number of things. I assumed it was a medical abbreviation to do with infertility. What made you think of Anne Long?'

'When she updated my antenatal notes she always signed them *A.L* . It just struck me. I'm probably wrong.'

'There is a way we could find out,' Ian said. 'By phoning some of the others who have the same initials beside their names and asking them if their midwife was Anne Long. But before we do that, I think we should check the names on the spreadsheet with the patient folders. If the "Second Generation" are the grandchildren of Moller's patients there should be a folder for their parents. We know our parents are there, and I'm sure I've seen one for the Ryans.'

'Yes,' Emma said. 'But before we do that you should have something to eat first. You must be starving.'

'I am,' Ian admitted. 'And exhausted. It's been a very long day.'

FORTY-EIGHT

At seven-thirty that Wednesday evening Jan scooped up Tinder from where he was lying on the sofa and carried him upstairs and into her bedroom. She set him on her bed and came out, closing the door securely. Hopefully he would sleep and not chew things. She'd let him out as soon as she had taken the video clip. Capturing them on film would be undeniable proof, not open to misinterpretation as a photograph could be.

With a mixture of fear and anticipation, Jan returned downstairs. Not long to go now. She'd been waiting all day for this moment and yet, as it approached, she wondered if she was really doing the right thing. Perhaps it would be wiser and safer simply to leave the cottage and try to put all this behind her. But then not knowing was likely to fuel her imagination and haunt her even more. She'd seen something that couldn't be explained and needed to know what it was before she left.

Going into the living room, Jan opened the curtains so the light from the room shone out over the patio. She went into the kitchen and gathered together the food she'd bought to entice them, then opened the back door. It was another cold but dry night. A crescent moon hung in a cloudless sky and the light from the living room fell dimly over the patio. She'd switch it off once she'd finished.

Jan began depositing little piles of food around the patio. Not randomly as she had before, but leading from the outer edges of the patio to the window. Close enough, she hoped, that she'd be able to film them while they ate. For a moment she was startled as she heard a noise in the shrubbery, but then a bird fluttered out. She quickly finished distributing the food and returned indoors, locking and bolting the back door.

She checked that her phone was on silent – the camera flash wasn't on – and then, going into the living room, switched off the light. It was pitch black now. It took a few moments for her eyes to adjust, and she groped her way to the armchair where she took one of the cushions to sit on. She placed it on the floor behind the sofa to the far right of the patio window. Partially concealed by the full-length curtain, she had a clear view of the patio where the food was most concentrated. From here she should be able to take a video without being seeing.

The most likely time for them to come was between eight and ten o'clock, so within the next two hours. She'd have to keep very still and stay in the same position for all that time. One movement and they might see her and flee. She made herself as comfortable as possible and held the phone ready in her lap. They wouldn't be able to see her unless they came right up to the glass and looked in. As soon as they began taking the food she'd start filming, the infrared on her phone camera allowing her to film in the dark.

Jan kept very still and waited. Tinder was quiet upstairs, hopefully asleep. The minutes passed and her breath came fast and shallow.

Unable to risk checking her phone in case they were

approaching and saw, she could only guess the time. She thought it was nine o'clock, not much later. It felt like nearly an hour had gone by, but it was difficult to tell. More time passed. She hoped it hadn't all been in vain. Perhaps they'd been watching her arrange the food and had guessed her intention. She thought they were intelligent enough.

More time passed and then Jan saw a small movement at the very edge of her vision. She didn't dare turn her head and risk being seen. Were they coming, lured in by the food? Investigating or eating it? Would they follow the trail and come close enough to the window for her to film? Her heart raced as her fingers closed around the phone. She kept very still and concentrated hard.

Another minute passed and then she saw a small hand. She had to stop herself from crying out. So she hadn't been imagining it! Petrified but enthralled, she watched as it took a grape. Then a wrist appeared. Lean like a child's but covered in fine hair. What was she seeing? It was taking food, but then the hand abruptly disappeared from view. Shit! Had she lost her chance to film? Jan kept very still, phone at the ready. Willing it to reappear but at the same time dreading it.

A few moments passed and the hand appeared again and then an arm, covered by the sleeve of a jacket. Her heart beat wildly. He was turned away so she couldn't see his face, but he was the size and shape of a young boy. There must be children living feral in the woods like animals. There was no other explanation. She'd discovered something incredible and alarming that no one else knew. Should she start filming now or wait in the hope of getting a better view? She was sure she'd only get one chance.

Senses on full alert, Jan waited as he stayed where he was, turned away and eating. If she waited too long, she might miss her chance.

She was about to raise her phone and start filming when out of the dark a girl appeared. She watched in horror and amazement as the girl joined the boy. She needed to start filming now or she could miss the opportunity. Adrenalin pumped through her as she slowly raised her phone, praying they wouldn't turn and see her at the last moment. Then she was looking at their images on the screen and recording. Jan kept the phone as steady as her trembling hands would allow. They moved from one pile of food to the next. Closer now, closer still, then right up to the window. The boy looked in. Jan stifled a cry and kept filming. But he'd seen her. They turned and fled.

Trembling, Jan pulled herself to her feet and came out from behind the sofa. She switched on the living-room light and closed the curtains, struggling to calm herself. What had she just seen?

She stood in the living room, gripping her phone. It contained the proof she needed, evidence of what she and Chris had seen. There was no pretending or denying they existed now. Trying to silence her racing heart, Jan played the video. The image was dark but with the camera's infrared they were clear enough to see. Two of them, child-like, taking the food and then coming right up to the window, looking straight at her. If she hadn't seen them with her own eyes, she would never have believed it. Children, but not like any she'd ever seen.

She pressed play again and examined the clip more closely. Then she spotted something else and a new fear gripped her. Partially visible in the shadows at the outer edge of the patio was the outline of an adult. She hadn't seen it when she'd played the clip before and had been concentrating on the foreground. She played the clip again. It was certainly a person. Too indistinct to identify or even be sure if it was a man or woman. Were they still out there? What did they want? She needed to call the police.

227

At that moment the front doorbell rang and Tinder began barking from upstairs. Terror gripped her. She felt sick with fear. Keep calm and call the police, she told herself. Press 999. She was about to when her phone began ringing. The caller display showed Chris. What the hell!

She pressed to accept the call.

'It's me at the front door,' he said. 'Can I come in?'

'What do you want?'

'To make sure you're all right. Are you?'

'No.'

'Well, open the door so I can help you.'

'What made you come here now?'

'You're not answering my texts.'

Could he be trusted? Did she have any choice?

FORTY-NINE

Trembling, Jan opened the front door, just wide enough to be able to see it was Chris. 'Why are you here?' she asked again, her voice unsteady. She kept one hand on the door, ready to close it if necessary.

'You didn't answer my texts,' Chris said, looking concerned. 'I wanted to make sure you were all right. Which clearly you're not.'

She stared at him, uncertain.

'When I arrived at the cottage just now I found it in darkness. And why is Tinder barking from your bedroom? You look very pale. Are you ill?'

'No, I've had a shock,' Jan said. 'Was that you in the back garden just now?'

'No, of course not. Is there someone there?'

'There was. I expect they've gone now.'

'Are you sure?'

'Sure that I saw someone or sure that they've gone?'

'Shall I come in and check?' he asked.

Jan looked at him carefully and didn't immediately open the door wider.

'Jan, it's me, Chris,' he said. 'I am not going to harm you. Whatever is the matter?'

She slowly opened the door and let him in.

'I'll check the garden,' he said. Taking the torch from its hook, he walked swiftly down the hall. 'You stay here,' he called.

'No, I'm coming with you.'

Jan went after him, through the kitchen and into the garden. He held the torch out in front and swept its beam around the lawn and shrubbery. There was nothing to be seen. He went to the very bottom of the garden. She followed.

'My repair is still in place,' he said, focusing the beam of light on the planks of wood that still covered the hole in the hedge.

'They can climb over things,' Jan said, and saw his expression of incredulity.

'What can, Jan?' he asked, and shone the torch around the rest of the garden. 'You said there was someone in the garden.'

'There was.'

The beam fell on the food on the patio. 'I'm not surprised creatures are coming in if you leave food out,' Chris said tersely.

'I wanted them to stay long enough to film them.'

'And did they?' he asked sceptically.

'Yes.'

She saw his expression change to astonishment and unease, then he recovered.

'There's nothing here now,' he said firmly. 'You look cold. Come on, let's go indoors and you can show me the video you took.'

She went with him. As they approached the back door he paused to shine the torch down the side passageway. 'That's how your intruder got in,' he said. 'You've left the gate open.'

'It was closed the last time I looked,' Jan said lamely.

Chris shut the side gate. 'Keep it closed and they won't come in,' he said.

He was taking this all too well, Jan thought, but he would struggle to account for the video clip.

'Shall I make you a hot drink?' Chris asked as they went in.

'No, thank you.'

'So where's this film?'

He was standing next to her as she pressed play on her phone. She watched his face, but it gave nothing away. 'Hmm,' was all he said. 'It's rather dark.'

'But you can see them, can't you?'

He nodded.

'Well? Who or what are they?' she asked, and played the video clip again.

'I've no idea. I could ask Camile if she has any idea.'

'Ask Camile!' Jan exclaimed, astonished. 'Why are you trying to normalize what clearly isn't normal at all.'

'I'm not. I've no idea what you saw.'

'And what about that person in the background?' Jan said, her anger growing. She stopped the video at that point and showed Chris.

He looked more closely at the image. 'Perhaps it was Bill Smith from the village. He sometimes wanders after dark and could easily have come down your sideway. Let me have another look.'

Jan passed him the phone and watched his expression as he studied the image. Tinder was still barking.

'I'm going to take it to the police tomorrow,' Jan said.

Chris nodded. 'That's your choice, but can you let Tinder out now? He's getting very distressed up there.'

Jan went upstairs, annoyed by Chris's reaction. Here she was, showing him evidence of something incredible and he was trying to rationalize it! She opened her bedroom door and Tinder shot out and downstairs. By the time she returned, Chris was in the hall ready to go.

231

'I can't tell if it's Bill or not,' he said, handing back her phone. 'I'll check on him on my way home. If he's not in, I'll let the police know. It's a cold night to be out. Are you all right to stay here tonight?'

'Yes. Shouldn't I be? I've nowhere else to go at this time.'

'You can stay with me if you like, I have a spare bedroom.'

'No, I'll be fine,' Jan replied stiffly.

'Give me a ring if you change your mind, and I'll speak to Camile tomorrow. I'm sure there's an explanation and there's nothing to worry about.'

Once he'd gone, Jan closed and bolted the front door.

What the hell was all that about! She couldn't believe his reaction – calm and rational about something that defied logic. His response hadn't been normal. Either she was losing her mind or he was, and she was sure it wasn't her. She had the proof she needed now and tomorrow she'd take it to the police. The video was clear enough, wasn't it? Jan looked at her phone again to check – and went cold. The video clip had gone. Chris! He must have deleted it while she'd been upstairs. The bastard! There was only one reason for him to have done that – he hadn't wanted anyone to see it. But why? He had to be involved with whatever was going on. There was no other explanation.

FIFTY

It had been too late on Wednesday evening to start telephoning Moller's patients, so Emma took Thursday off work. Ian had already taken a lot of time off and she could gather the information they needed just as well – if not better – than he could. She sat at the dining-room table with Ian's laptop open in front of her, making notes.

She'd been very nervous to begin with, but with each call it had got a bit easier, and being able to concentrate on something was helping. Most of the people she phoned were helpful when she explained she was asking for feedback on their healthcare experience. A few couldn't remember the details she needed, and some said they never took part in surveys, so she apologized and moved to the next. It was time consuming and emotionally draining. Often the parent wanted to talk about the loss of their child or grandchild and poured out their feelings. Able to identify with losing a baby, Emma found it upsetting and exhausting as she struggled to hide her own feelings.

By midday she had collected as much information as she could and was able to confirm that Moller's 'Second Generation' file referred to the children of patients treated

233

by him, although they had never been to the clinic themselves – and A.L. stood for Anne Long. In each case where Anne had been the midwife the parents had suffered at least one late miscarriage and sometimes more than one, as she and Ian had. Yet everyone spoke highly of Anne: kind, caring, dedicated and showing great empathy for their loss. It wasn't her fault, they said.

As a longstanding midwife, Anne would have delivered thousands of other babies in addition to those on Moller's list, Emma thought. This high neonatal mortality rate couldn't possibly be present in all her work or she would have been investigated and stopped from practising years ago. It was worrying and didn't make sense. Why was this happening to Moller's babies when Anne was involved? What was going so badly wrong?

Ian had said he would phone in his lunch break to see how Emma was getting on, and she now took the opportunity to make herself a mug of tea. She returned to the table and sipped it as she waited for Ian's call, puzzled and worried by what she'd found out.

A few minutes later Ian phoned, his voice sombre. 'Hello, how are you getting on?'

'I've just finished. Without doubt those listed on the "Second Generation" spreadsheet weren't patients of Moller but their parents were, and A.L. does stand for Anne Long. I'll show you my notes tonight. But, Ian, something else has come out of this and I'm not sure what to make of it.'

'What?' he asked, anxiety obvious in his voice.

'According to Moller's spreadsheet, it seems that when Anne was the midwife, the babies never survived, and also she always took care of the disposal of their bodies. Just like she did with David.'

Emma heard Ian's silence. Her discovery had clearly filled him with dread as it had her.

'What are you thinking?' he asked at length.

'I don't know. The couples were grateful at the time, but later some of them regretted they'd made the decision so quickly, like Chelsea and Grant. But it was too late by then. I feel very uncomfortable and sad about all of this. I mean, we didn't give it much thought either, did we? We were too upset, so when Anne suggested she took David away, we agreed. We didn't even say goodbye.'

'No, but I think that was for the best,' Ian said, remembering the glimpse he'd had of their baby.

'Do you think there's a connection between Anne Long and the Moller Clinic?' Emma asked.

'It would seem so. Why else would Moller have her details? Maybe she's selling body parts to labs. There was that big scandal some years ago.'

'Oh, Ian, don't say that!' Emma cried. 'That's horrible. I couldn't bear the thought of David being in a laboratory.'

'Hopefully I'm wrong,' Ian said. 'Anne wasn't our midwife in your first pregnancy and that went wrong too. I seem to remember we weren't allotted Anne for David straight away. The midwife was changed partway through your pregnancy.'

'Yes, because we decided on a home birth and she was more experienced in home deliveries. If you remember, the hospital tried to talk us out of a home birth and said they couldn't be held responsible. We had to insist. Then Anne came to our rescue.'

Ian was quiet again and then said, 'I think I need to speak to Anne face to face.'

'Shall I ask her to visit us? The last time I saw her she said to phone if we needed to talk.'

'No, I'll visit her.'

'At the hospital?'

'Or her home.'

'Do you know where she lives?'

'No, but I'll be able to find out.'

'Oh, Ian, that's not a good idea. We don't want any more upset. We've had enough to cope with this year. And Anne hasn't done anything wrong as far as we know.'

'Don't worry. I just want to ask her some questions.'

FIFTY-ONE

'Thank you for returning my call,' Jan said to DC Matt Davis.

'You're welcome, although if it's an emergency you should call 999.'

'It's not, or rather it isn't an emergency now. It happened last night. I had another intruder come into the garden.'

'Yes. It was Bill Smith.'

'Really? Are you sure?'

'Positive. He's safely home now. If you'd told the duty officer what your call was about when you phoned this morning, they could have reassured you then.'

'I wanted to speak to you because you'd been here when it had happened before,' Jan said.

'No problem. Anyway, the mystery of your intruder has been solved.'

'Where was Bill found?' Jan asked.

'In Wood Lane. Chris Giles found him and phoned us in case anyone had reported him missing.'

'I see,' Jan said, wondering why Chris hadn't texted her to let her know. 'Well, I'm glad he's home safely.'

'Yes. Was there anything else concerning you?'

Jan hesitated. She no longer had the video to prove her

claims. 'You remember you saw those track marks in the garden? Whoever made them was here again last night,' she said. 'They came right up to the window looking for food.'

'They seem to be getting around,' Matt replied lightly. 'A family in the village has reported seeing a "strange figure", to use their term, in their home.'

'They did!' Jan gasped.

'Yes, it gave them quite a shock. It seems it had come in through a window in the kitchen they'd left open to clear the smell of cooking. The couple's teenage daughter came down in the night for a drink. They heard her scream, but by the time they arrived it had gone. So don't leave any windows open.'

'No. I won't. Did the girl say what it looked like?'

'Not really. She only caught a glimpse of it as it disappeared out of the window. It was most likely a fox.'

'Was there just one?' Jan asked.

'Yes. Try not to worry. Just remember to keep your windows and doors closed.'

FIFTY-TWO

It had been very easy to find Anne Long's address. Ian hadn't had to hack into a database. Her name and address were on the public Electoral Register for all to see – 45 Dells Lane, Melton, CP29 1DA. It was about three miles from Merryless.

Ian was now driving there after work on Thursday, having first told Emma where he was going. She'd tried to dissuade him, but he was determined. He had to go. He needed to know. If Anne was out, he'd wait a few hours and then return tomorrow, and every evening until he had the answers he was looking for. What was Anne's connection to the Moller Clinic and why was her name linked to so many baby deaths? Ian was trying to keep an open mind, but it was becoming increasingly difficult.

It was nearly six o'clock as Ian pulled into Dells Lane. It was on the outer edge of the village. A row of semi-detached houses lined one side of the road, with open common land on the other. The road was dimly lit by old sodium street lamps, which gave it an unhealthy orange glow. Ian drove slowly along the road, checking the house numbers as he went. Number 45 was last. Most of the houses had a small driveway so additional cars were parked on the road. Ian pulled into a space two doors up from Anne's, from where he could see her house.

The house was in darkness and no car was parked on the drive or directly in front, suggesting she wasn't home yet. He would check anyway. Getting out, Ian walked along the pavement, up the drive and pressed the doorbell. He heard it chime inside and waited, but no one answered. He tried again and then returned to his car to wait.

It occurred to him that if Anne was on a night shift she might not return until the following morning. He'd wait an hour or so and then try again tomorrow. He turned on the radio and watched the minutes tick by on the dashboard clock. Half an hour passed. The car chilled and Ian switched on the heater. He stretched his legs and texted Emma to say he was all right. He looked around, out of the side window to the common land, which was just grass and bare trees. He wasn't used to this level of isolation and stillness. It was very different to where he and Emma lived. In the suburbs there was always movement – cars going along the road or neighbours in and out of their houses. Since he'd been sitting here he hadn't seen a single person.

At 7.30, with no sign of Anne, Ian decided it was time to call it quits for this evening. He straightened in his seat and was about to start the engine when a car appeared in his rear-view mirror, having just turned into Dells Lane. Ian waited. The headlamps dipped and Ian watched the car's progress in his wing mirror as it came towards him along the lane. He was half expecting it to turn off into one of the driveways or draw up outside a house. But it kept coming.

He ducked down low in his seat as it passed, then raised his head just enough to see out. It stopped outside Anne's house but didn't turn into the driveway. The door opened and Anne got out. He could see her reasonably clearly in the glow of the street lamp, but her vision of him was blocked by the car in front. She was wearing a dark winter coat, flat shoes, and had a bag over her shoulder. He couldn't tell if she'd come from work or not. Ian watched her walk briskly to her front door, key at the ready, and let herself in. The door closed and the lights began going on inside the house. He'd give her a few minutes before he went to the door.

Ian looked at her car, parked right under the street lamp. It was a grey Vauxhall Corsa, which he recognized from when she'd visited him and Emma, but he now realized he'd also seen it – or one very similar – parked outside the Moller Clinic on his last visit. It had been there when he'd arrived but had gone when he'd left. If that car had been Anne's, which he was pretty sure it was, then she was the person with Moller when Ian had arrived and who'd left in a hurry. Why was she there? And what had happened to make her slam the door as she'd left?

Time to confront her, Ian thought. He opened his car door, but as he did he heard a whirring sound coming from Anne's house. He looked over and saw her garage door slowly rising. He quietly closed his car door again and waited, keeping low in his seat. The garage door rose to its full height and a small navy van with tinted windows pulled out. It turned left down the lane, going past him. The garage door automatically closed. It had been impossible to see who was in the van through the tinted windows. The lights in the house were still on. Perhaps there was someone else living there, Ian wondered, although there was only Anne listed on the Electoral Register.

Getting out, he went to Anne's front door again and pressed the bell. Silence. He rapped on the door. More silence. It seemed no one was in. So that must have been Anne leaving in the van, which was odd. She'd arrived home in her car and gone straight out again in a van with tinted windows. He ran to his car, quickly turned it around, and then sped down the lane after her.

He thought he'd seen the van's indicator flash right before it had disappeared and so he turned right, heading towards Melton. There was no van in sight. He continued along the main road that ran through the village, looking left and right, down the side roads, but there was no van.

At the end of the village he turned the car around and retraced his route until he came to Dells Lane where he turned in. He continued to Anne's house and tried the door again, but no one answered. Annoyed with himself that he hadn't spoken to Anne when he'd had the chance, he went next door to Number 43 and rang their bell. A man in his fifties dressed in overalls answered.

'Sorry to trouble you,' Ian said. 'I was hoping to see your neighbour, Anne Long, but she's out. Do you know when she might return?'

'At this time in the evening she's either working or walking her dogs,' he replied.

'Oh, I see. Her car is still outside.'

'In that case she's walking the dogs. She takes them in the van. We keep well away. Nasty brutes by all accounts. She can only walk them at night when there's no one else around.'

'Thank you,' Ian said. 'Do you know what time she's likely to return?'

'It varies. Recently it's been very late. I heard her garage door at nearly midnight yesterday.'

'I'll come earlier tomorrow then. Thanks for your help.'

FIFTY-THREE

If Chris thought it was going to be that easy to get rid of the video she'd taken then he was very much mistaken, Jan decided. There was no other reason for him to have deleted it from her phone than to stop her from showing others, and especially the police. She couldn't imagine why he didn't want anyone to know, and also why he'd lied about Bill Smith being in Wood Lane, but it was very worrying.

The more Jan thought about what DC Matt Davis had told her, the more worried she was. She was sure Chris had made up finding Bill in Wood Lane after he'd left her. Otherwise he would have texted or phoned her to say he'd been found. The police had taken Chris at his word, but perhaps Bill had been home all the time, and Chris had simply checked on him as he'd told her he was going to.

The other reason Jan believed Chris had lied to the police was that she was certain it hadn't been Bill in her garden last night. She'd seen Bill Smith wandering around the village and he was a big man, over six feet tall, with broad shoulders and a large stomach. Although the image in the video hadn't been clear, the person certainly wasn't tall and broad. They were much shorter, smaller and thinner. But why had Chris lied? Had he recognized the person in her garden and was covering up for them? There was no other explanation.

Jan fully intended to take another video if possible that evening and then go to the police with the full story. Now someone else had reported a strange sighting she felt sure that, together with the video clip, her fears would be taken seriously. She could imagine the teenage girl's horror when she'd gone into the kitchen. The police were putting it down to an animal getting in, but Jan knew differently. Food seemed to entice them, and Jan would be using it again tonight. But she wouldn't be showing Chris her evidence this time. He couldn't be trusted. After she'd gone to the police, she'd call Camile and say she wanted to leave as soon as possible. Enough was enough. This was supposed to have been a quiet retreat to give her time to heal, and it was anything but.

At 7.30 Jan arranged the food she'd prepared around the outer edges of the patio, not close up to the window as she had done before, then returned indoors. She shut Tinder in her bedroom and then, downstairs again, opened the living-room curtains. Hardly daring to breathe, she put on her jacket, boots, scarf, beanie hat and gloves, and, tucking her phone into her pocket, quietly let herself out of the back door, closing it again behind her. The light from the living room shone out over the patio. From outside looking in, it was obvious that no one was in the living room. They would be wary about being caught a third time, so she was using a different tactic tonight and showing them the room was empty.

Struggling to believe she was actually doing this, Jan crossed the lawn to the shed at the bottom of the garden and let herself in. Thankfully Camile had kept it reasonably clean – there were just a few cobwebs hanging in the crevices.

She shivered from cold and nerves and pulled her woollen hat further down over her ears. Taking out her phone, she stood a little way back from the window and prepared to wait. From here she could see the living room clearly lit up. On a cold winter's evening it looked warm and inviting. Despite being well wrapped up, the cold seeped into her. The shed was old and some of the wood had separated at the bottom, leaving gaps. A mouse scuttled past, but Jan had never been frightened of mice. Eight-thirty came and went. An owl hooted in the distance and a light breeze stirred the barren branches of the trees overhead, making them creak and groan.

Then she was aware of another noise. She stood perfectly still and listened. It sounded as though it had come from the roof of the shed. A scratching sound. Was it a branch chafing against the roof? She didn't think so. There it was again. Something was up there. More scratching as it moved across the roof. Her heart raced. It was too heavy for a bird, she felt sure. Then a small hand appeared at the top of the window. It was them; they were on the roof.

Jan clamped her hand over her mouth to stop herself from crying out. Petrified, she forced herself to keep quiet and wait. The hand disappeared from view, but the noise coming from the roof continued. How many were up there? She'd only seen one hand, but the noises suggested more. She looked up and tried to track their movements. Why were they on the roof and not going to the food? Did they know she was in the shed? Surely not. Unless they'd been watching her earlier. Fear gripped her.

More scratching noises, and then it went quiet. What were they doing? Were they still up there? She was half expecting to see them appear on the lawn, running towards the food. She kept her phone camera at the ready and waited, but it went quiet. She listened, straining against the silence. Where were they? Had they gone?

Suddenly she heard a movement at the door. Dear God!

They were trying to turn the key and lock her in. Throwing herself at the door, she forced it open, just in time to get out. Without looking back, she ran up the lawn to the cottage and let herself in. As she did, she heard a woman's voice call from the woods, 'No, don't do that!' The same voice she'd heard before.

Fighting for breath, Jan locked the back door and fled upstairs to the spare bedroom at the back. Without switching on the light, she crossed to the window, dialling 999 as she went. She could barely keep her phone still for trembling, but there was a torch beam in the woods.

'I'm Jan Hamlin, I live in Ivy Cottage, Wood Lane,' she said as soon as she was connected. 'There were intruders in my garden again just now and I think they are in the woods. I can see a torch. Please come quickly.'

'Ivy Cottage, Coleshaw Woods?' the operator checked.

'Yes.'

'We'll have someone there as soon as possible. Stay in the property and keep your windows and doors locked.'

'Yes. I will. Please hurry.'

Jan kept her phone at the ready, but as she looked the torch light disappeared. She had no doubt that by the time the police arrived there'd be nothing to find, just like the last time.

FIFTY-FOUR

A little after six o'clock the following evening, Ian pulled into Dells Lane. He drove to the end of the road and parked a few spaces back from Anne's house, as he'd done the previous night. It had been raining most of the day and although it had stopped now, a damp mist hung in the air. Tinged with orange from the street lamps, it gave everything a ghostly hue.

Anne's house was in darkness, her car wasn't parked outside and the garage door was closed. Ian assumed she hadn't returned from work yet, so he'd wait in his car just as he had the night before, only this time he'd make sure he spoke to her. According to her neighbour she would return to walk her dogs at some point, for they weren't the type of dogs you could ask someone else to walk. Ian struggled to reconcile the Anne he and Emma knew – a gentle, sensitive midwife – with a woman who kept dangerous dogs. But then Ian would be the first to admit he was struggling with a lot of what he'd learnt in the past few days.

At 6.20 he saw headlamps as a car pulled into Dells Lane. He tracked its progress in his wing mirror, but it parked halfway down the lane. Not Anne. Not this time. He blew

247

into his hands to keep them warm and then turned on the car's heater. His gaze wandered to the common. The mist was thicker there, drawn to the damp soil of the turf; it hovered unnaturally in the frost-laden night air.

Ten minutes passed, then another set of headlamps appeared at the end of Dells Lane. Ian straightened in his seat and monitored the car's progress as it came steadily towards him. He ducked as it passed, then raised his head and watched Anne park her car in the road outside her house. He waited until she got out, then opened his car door. 'Anne!' he called, walking swiftly towards her. 'It's Ian Jennings.'

'Ian! Whatever are you doing here?' she asked, shocked.

'I need to talk to you,' he said, and followed her to her front door.

She put her key into the lock. 'Why? Is Emma unwell?'

'No, but I have to speak to you about the Moller Clinic.'

The colour drained from her face.

'It won't take long,' he added. 'I have some questions.'

'What about?' She kept one hand on the door.

'You know the Moller Clinic and the work they do there?'

'I've heard of it.'

'I've found out recently that both Emma's parents and mine used the clinic, and they were given the same donor sperm. Emma and I share the same biological father. It could be the reason we can't have healthy babies.' Ian would have preferred to say all this inside, but it was clear Anne wasn't going to invite him in.

'How do you know this?' Anne asked, turning slightly to meet his gaze.

'Carstan Moller told me, eventually.'

'Did he?' she asked, surprised. 'Did he tell you who the donor was?'

'No. He said it was confidential.' Ian couldn't tell her he'd accessed the clinic's files.

'I am sorry, Ian. That should never have happened. It must have come as a huge shock for you and Emma, but I don't see how I can help you.'

'I'd like you to tell me what you know about the clinic.'

'Nothing. I was just aware of its existence.'

'Have you ever had any dealings with Carstan or Edie Moller as a midwife?'

'No. There's no reason for me to.'

'So you've never come into contact with them?'

'No. Sorry, Ian, I'm afraid I can't help you. Now, I've just returned from work. I must have something to eat before I take the dogs out. Would you like me to visit you and Emma tomorrow?' She turned the key and opened her front door.

'I'll ask her and let you know,' Ian said.

He returned down the path to his car as Anne let herself in.

She was lying. Her name was all over Moller's files and her car had been at his clinic. The expression on her face when he'd first mentioned Moller had been one of shock and possibly guilt. Anne wasn't a good liar – but what was she hiding? She'd been so warm and friendly when she'd been their midwife, but now she was guarded and hadn't been able to get rid of him quickly enough. Yes, she'd just come home from work and wanted dinner before she took the dogs out, but Ian hadn't seen or heard any dogs eager to be let out. He supposed they could be caged out the back, but wouldn't they have barked when they heard her voice?

Ian turned his car around and drove to the other end of Dells Lane. He parked between cars, switched off the headlights and prepared to wait. At some point Anne would leave to take the dogs for a walk and he would follow her and perhaps try again. He'd come here hoping for answers, but now he had even more questions. Some that he could barely consider and made his stomach churn. All those dead babies listed in Moller's files with Anne's initials beside them. She must be involved. Could it be that under cover of darkness she was using her van to transport baby parts to laboratories for research? She would get paid a fee. Is that why she'd been so on edge and had lied? Or even more macabre, was she burying dead babies to cover up a crime? Ian shuddered at the possibility.

At 7.30 Ian saw headlamps in his wing mirror coming from the far end of the lane where Anne lived. Was she in her car or the van? He kept his head turned away as she passed. She was in the van. It stopped at the end of Dells Lane and indicated to turn right, the same as last night. Ian started his car but waited until she'd pulled out and had made the turn before he followed.

He kept a safe distance between them so she wouldn't be able to identify him in her mirrors. The fog helped. It had thickened in the last half an hour, and sometimes all he could see of her van was the red glow of its taillights.

He followed her along the High Road that ran through Melton and out the other side. They were now heading towards Merryless. Ian knew this road. He kept his distance and concentrated on the taillights. A little further along, Anne took the turning signposted to Coleshaw Woods. Ian dropped back so she wouldn't become suspicious. There was only the two of them now, driving on this side of the road, with the occasional car coming in the opposite direction. Half a mile or so further on she turned left down a single-track lane.

Ian waited until her taillights had disappeared before he followed. The lane didn't go anywhere but into the woods. He'd come here for walks in the summer as a child. It had been pleasant then, but now the mist and darkness gave it a sinister edge, which added to his unease. He admired Anne's tenacity to come here all alone. But was it really necessary to come this far to walk dogs? Were they really that dangerous? Surely there were less isolated places she could have gone? Unless she wasn't walking dogs at all but burying dead babies. In which case it would be ideal. Ian grimaced at the thought.

Ian pulled over and stopped. The lane ran out shortly so Anne would have to park before long, and he didn't want to get too close. Slowly opening his car door, he listened. He could hear an engine idling somewhere further up the track, just around the bend. He assumed it was the van. It stopped. From memory he guessed she had parked close to the thickest part of the woods, but it was impossible to see in the dark and mist.

Ian quietly got out of his car and stood very still, listening, senses on high alert. All that could be heard was a light breeze stirring the treetops. He needed to get closer to see what she was doing, but there was no moon to show him the way. Taking out his phone, he pointed it down and switched on the torch. Keeping close to the trees, with the torch beam concentrated on the ground, he gingerly made his way along the edge of the track, until he came to the bend. The outline of her van appeared and he quickly switched off the torch, stepped back, and tucked himself behind the trees. As he watched he saw Anne get out of her van and go to the rear doors. She was wearing a quilted jacket, Wellington boots and jeans, so looked dressed for walking dogs, although he couldn't see any leads. Ian stayed perfectly still and watched as she glanced around and then opened the rear doors.

He stared in horror and amazement, unable to believe what he was seeing, as two little figures jumped out and disappeared into the woods. Not dogs. Definitely not. They looked like children. Jesus! What the hell was Anne doing? It was worse than he could have imagined. Leaving the rear doors open, she went after them, disappearing into the dense woods.

Breaking out in a cold sweat, Ian followed, moving slowly and stealthily through the trees. He couldn't see them, but he could hear them further up. They were in the thickest part of the forest now. They were a lot faster than Anne. He caught glimpses of her jacket through the trees a little way ahead as she struggled to keep up. They appeared to be trying to outrun her. Were they trying to escape? But who were they and why were they here? What in heaven's name was she doing transporting children in a van after dark?

Then he realized, and his heart missed a beat. She was trafficking children. Selling them for money. That must be it. He couldn't think of another explanation. Pretending she had dangerous dogs, she was actually making money from the sale of children. He had to act fast to save them.

Ian took another couple of steps, hiding himself behind the trees as he went after her. He'd rescue the children and then phone the police and let them deal with Anne. Suddenly a twig snapped under his foot. Shit. He froze, hoping they hadn't heard. All movement stopped. The wood fell silent. Then Anne's voice called out, 'Who's there?'

Ian stayed where he was, hardly daring to breathe. His stomach churned and sweat trickled down his neck. Then there was movement from somewhere in the forest. Something was running towards him. He couldn't see what. He should get back to the car and phone the police from there. He turned and fled, ran as fast as he could through the under-growth. Out of the woods and onto the track. He could hear footsteps behind him, gaining on him, then Anne's voice again: 'Stop! Come here, now!'

He looked behind him, lost his balance, tripped and fell. Down, down. No time to save himself before his head hit the ground. Pain shot through his skull as the trees began to shimmer, swimming in and out of focus. He tried to shout for help, but the cry died in his throat as he began to lose consciousness. The last image he saw before darkness engulfed him was of a small face looking down on him. Then nothing.

FIFTY-FIVE

Jan stood at the open window in the back bedroom, her phone in her hand, watching and listening. It was quiet in the woods now. Not a sound. She'd rushed up here, hoping for a better view, one that would allow her to take another video clip, but it hadn't happened. She'd seen two torch beams in the woods, the same woman's voice, and then nothing.

She wasn't going to call the police again. It would only be a repeat of last night. By the time they arrived there would be nothing for them to investigate, and last night she'd got the feeling the officer they'd sent had thought she was wasting police time.

Reluctantly, Jan closed the window and admitted defeat. She wouldn't be replacing the video Chris had deleted, now or in the future. This had been her last chance. She'd already telephoned Camile and said she was sorry, but she needed to leave the cottage as soon as possible as she wasn't happy here. Camile had taken it very well, considering, and said she would book a flight straight away and would text her once she'd landed. Jan had agreed to stay until she arrived.

She came out of the bedroom and went downstairs. Whatever was happening in the woods would remain a mystery. She checked the front and back doors were secure and the electricity meter was topped up, then she sat on the sofa beside Tinder and rubbed his head. She'd miss him, but she couldn't wait to leave the cottage and live in the town again, where electricity was constant and there were no strange happenings in dark woods. As soon as Camile arrived, she'd be off. She'd already begun packing and felt ready to restart her life: apply for jobs, meet old friends, maybe even have another long-term relationship. If she could meet an uncomplicated, honest guy.

Her thoughts went to Chris, who had seemed so honest and straightforward at the start. Now, she had no idea who he was or how he fitted into whatever was going on around here. She remembered the look on his and Anne's faces when she'd come across them in the woods – guilty, almost as if they'd been caught out.

She stopped stroking Tinder and looked up. Of course! Why hadn't she made the connection before! The woman's voice she'd heard in the woods was Anne's. She was sure of it. No wonder it had sounded familiar. But what the hell was she doing in the woods at night?

Grabbing her jacket and keys, Jan let herself out of the front door into the cold, misty air. Hopefully she wasn't too late and Anne was still there. Jumping into her car, she pressed the central locking system and switched on the side lights only. They gave just enough light so she could see where she was going without being seen. She drove as fast as she could along Wood Lane to where it joined the track leading to Coleshaw Woods. She pulled over onto the bank, out of sight, then cut the engine and lights. Just in time. Headlamps on full beam appeared from the turning, flicking through the mist as the car bumped over the uneven surface. Closer and closer, growing brighter, then a small van appeared and turned into the lane heading towards Merryless. Jan couldn't see who was driving – visibility was too poor, and the windows seemed to be tinted. But the rear number plate was lit. Jan made a note of the registration on her phone, then headed back to the cottage to report it to the police. Hopefully this was the proof that was needed to start a proper investigation.

FIFTY-SIX

Ian's eyes slowly opened. Where the hell was he? A light on the ceiling swam in and out of focus. God, his head hurt. Had he been in a car accident? He seemed to remember driving in fog.

Then a voice close by said, 'You're awake.' Anne Long came into view.

Ian started and tried to sit up but collapsed back, his head throbbing. 'Where am I?' he gasped, his throat dry. 'What are you doing?'

'You're safe, you're on the sofa in my house,' Anne said. 'You fell and knocked yourself out.'

'Shouldn't I be in hospital?' he asked, trying to struggle up again. 'How long have I been here?'

'Not long. You should be all right. It wasn't serious. Have a sip of water.'

She held a glass to his lips and Ian drank. Water had never tasted so good.

'What do you want with me?' he asked, confused and frightened.

'Nothing. I brought you back here to recover. You can go as soon as you feel well enough.'

'Why didn't you call an ambulance?'

'There was no need. You're not badly hurt.' She hesitated and set the glass of water on the table. 'What do you remember from before you fell, Ian?'

He frowned, trying to remember. It began coming back. 'I remember driving, following your van. It was dark. You turned off into Coleshaw Woods and parked. Jesus! You haven't got dogs. You're trafficking children!' He struggled up and stared around. 'Where are they? What's going on? Where are those poor kids now?'

'Calm down, Ian,' Anne said, touching his arm. 'They're upstairs, asleep. I'm not trafficking children, far from it. You have to trust me.'

'Trust you! You lied about knowing Carstan Moller and then you lock children in the back of a van and take them to the woods at night pretending they're dogs. You're evil. Sick. I'm going to call the police.' He jabbed his hand into his trouser pocket for his phone, but it had gone. 'Where's my phone?'

'In your jacket pocket, over there.' Anne nodded to where his jacket hung on a chair back. 'You can have it, Ian, but it's not in your interests to call the police.'

'Whatever do you mean?'

She looked at him carefully. 'Ian, things have gone on that you have no idea about. Things you couldn't begin to guess at in your wildest imagination, and it's better for you if it stays that way. As soon as you feel well enough, you need to return to Emma, forget everything you have seen this evening and continue your lives.'

'That's not possible on any level!' Ian snapped. Lowering his feet to the floor, he sat upright and faced Anne. The room tilted slightly. 'Emma and I can't continue our life together. We're half brother and sister! And I'm not taking your word for it that those children are upstairs asleep. Who are they?

You told Emma you don't have children. I want answers, Anne. I already know a lot more than you think. I know you're involved with Moller and his clinic and that the two of you are responsible for babies dying.'

'No, that's not true!' Anne cried, visibly upset. 'How could you believe that? I'm a nurse, a midwife, I *save* lives.'

'Then tell me the truth.'

Anne was silent for a moment, then, bringing her gaze back to Ian, she said, 'If I tell you, you must promise never to repeat it to anyone, not even Emma. Especially not Emma. Or you will regret it.'

Ian felt a rush of fear. 'I'm not making any promises until I know what it is you and Moller have been doing.'

'Then at least keep an open mind.' Anne took a deep breath, as if summoning the courage to begin. 'Ian, you already know that you and Emma share the same donor, but do you know who it is?'

'No.'

'It's Carstan Moller. He is your biological father.'

'No, he's not!' Ian gasped. 'That's not possible.'

'It's true, Ian. He is your and Emma's biological father, as he is to thousands of others, probably going back to when the clinic started.'

Ian stared at her, stunned, and felt sick to the core. 'But how? How is that possible? Both our parents were given details about their donors.'

Anne shook her head. 'He made them up. All the babies conceived by donor sperm at his clinic came from him. There were never any donors. It was all him.'

Ian stared at her as he struggled to take in what he was being told. 'So that's why I couldn't find details of donors in his records.'

'You've been able to see Moller's records?' Anne asked.

'Yes, although he doesn't know. That's how I came to link

259

you to him and the clinic. Your initials are beside some of the entries I've seen, and in each case it seems the baby was born dead.'

'So that's why you thought I was responsible for babies dying?' she asked, her face sad.

'Yes. Aren't you?'

'No, and they weren't born dead, Ian.'

He continued to stare at her.

'I haven't seen the clinic's records, but if Carstan has been putting my initials beside babies' names it will be for those who were born alive but with a life-limiting condition. I told the parents they were stillborn and took them away to save them the trauma, just as I did for you and Emma. Many don't live long.'

'You what!' Ian cried, his hand instinctively going to his throbbing head. 'I don't believe you. Why are you lying?'

'I'm not. I'm telling you the truth. I did it to save the parents the agony they would otherwise have endured. Think about it, Ian. You caught sight of David just after the birth, and you were grateful I took him. You didn't want any fuss or an autopsy. You just wanted me to deal with it, which I did.'

'But that's when I thought he was stillborn. It's different now.'

'How? I saved you and Emma the pain and heartache of the truth. You wouldn't have coped. Remember the looks on the faces of the nurses who delivered your first baby? Emma told me the senior nurse managed to just about hold it together, but the younger nurse couldn't hide her shock. That would have been the reaction of everyone who came into contact with David if I hadn't falsified the records to show him as stillborn.'

Ian held her gaze as he remembered the horror of that first birth, and that he and Emma had been grateful to Anne

260

for taking David away and seeing to everything. He supposed there was some truth in what she said.

'If you are telling me the truth, then Moller is responsible for all of this. He's pure evil. But I don't understand – we're normal. We don't have any condition.'

'The children born from his donor sperm are usually healthy; the only give-away is that they often look similar, as half siblings do. The defects only began to appear in the second generation. Moller got away with it for years, tricking parents into believing they were buying donor sperm when it was him all along. But then some of *their* children began forming relationships with each other, as you and Emma did. It was inevitable with so many sharing the same biological father that this would start to happen. Unaware they were related, they began having babies and that's when this condition began to appear.'

'My God! And Moller did this for money?'

'Maybe in part, but he and Edie can't have children and he became obsessed with his line carrying on. He's very arrogant and believes his genes are superior.'

'That's ironic,' Ian said bitterly. 'When he's responsible for deformed babies.'

'Except they're not deformed, as such.'

'Whatever do you mean?' Ian asked, touching his head again.

Anne paused. 'Have you ever heard of atavism?'

'No,' Ian admitted.

'It's the term for what is sometimes called a throwback – when a trait from our ancient ancestors reappears in the modern day. The most common example of atavism is the human tail. It formed part of the storyline in the film *Shallow Hal*.'

Ian nodded. 'I saw that film.'

'Although rare, there are examples of atavism all over the

world. Including excessive body hair or fur, skulls shaped like Neanderthals, exceptionally large teeth reminiscent of primates, reptilian hearts, and so on. It happens in animals too. These features are hidden deep in our genes and usually remain dormant but can resurface or mutate. In the case of Moller, it happened because the babies of the second generation shared too much of the same DNA. Had you and Emma had children with a different partner who didn't share the same DNA, it would have been lost in the genetic pool and remained dormant. You would have had normal children.'

Ian shook his head in dismay. 'But why haven't you reported Moller?'

'To begin with it was just a suspicion I had that something odd was going on at the clinic. I began keeping records of babies who'd been born with the condition. It took many years to build up enough evidence to confront Moller. He laughed in my face, said I was delusional, and then reminded me of the part I'd played in an illegal abortion. Some years before, a woman came to me, miscarrying after she'd tried to get rid of it herself. I helped her, and I should have reported her, but she begged me not to. She said her brothers would arrange to have her killed to save their family honour if they found out. I don't know how Moller knew, but if he had reported me it would have put her in danger and been the end of my career. Moller promised he would stop what he was doing and use donated sperm. And think about it, Ian, what would happen to the infants if the news got out? They would be considered freaks. The press wouldn't leave them alone and neither would scientists. They don't live long, and I try to make their short lives as happy and comfortable as possible.'

'I saw your car at the clinic.'

'I've been there a few times recently. I wanted proof he'd kept his word and was now using donor sperm as he'd promised. We argued and I left.'

'You left a review online,' Ian said, remembering. '"Don't go anywhere near this place. They are in it for their own selfish ends."'

'Yes, for what it's worth,' Anne said wearily. 'I'm worn out by all this – the guilt, secrecy, lies and trying to protect the children.'

'But how do you know when one of these babies is going to be born?' Ian asked. 'You weren't our midwife to begin with.'

'If Moller knows in advance, he tells me. He agreed. It was one of the conditions for not reporting him. He notifies me so I can provide the antenatal care, then I take the baby and look after it for as long as necessary. It's difficult, working as well, but specializing in home deliveries gives me flexibility.'

'How many are there?' Ian asked, still struggling to accept what he was being told.

'I have three at present. That's the most I've ever had at one time. Sometimes I don't have any. The numbers fluctuate. Some of them only live for a few months, others years.' Her eyes filled. 'They are my children, Ian. I love and care for them, and when they die I mourn their passing. I pray for them and bury them in Coleshaw Woods.'

'Is that why you were in the woods tonight?'

'No. We go there for a walk. They can't be seen so have to stay indoors during the day, but they need fresh air and exercise, just as all children do. I take them in the van after dark to the deepest part of the forest where they can run and play freely. There is nowhere else for them to go.'

'And they really are upstairs now?'

'Yes. I'm telling you the truth, Ian. They'll be asleep, worn out. They're like children, just different. They can be very mischievous sometimes, but they mean no harm. They love to run and can move very quickly. They can't talk, but they understand in different ways. They like to have fun. I can't

263

always keep up as they're too fast. I live in dread of them being discovered. A couple of times when they've run off into the woods it's taken me hours to persuade them to come back. My neighbours believe I have dangerous dogs, which keeps them away. But there's a tenant in Ivy Cottage, which backs onto the woods, who knows far too much. I think she's heard me calling them, and she's been encouraging them into her garden with food.'

Ian fell silent as he tried to come to terms with what he'd been told. He was still struggling. 'So they're genetic throwbacks from our ancient ancestors,' he said at last.

'Yes, although I prefer to call them outsiders, as they live outside the human race and animal kingdom.'

Ian fell quiet again, then said, 'I suppose I should thank you for taking David and looking after him. When did he die?'

'He hasn't yet. Your son is still alive.'

FIFTY-SEVEN

Ian held his head in his hands as the room spun and a buzzing noise filled his ears. He thought he was going to faint. 'David is still alive?' he asked incredulously, finally looking up, his voice far off and unreal.

'Yes, I left him wrapped up warm in his car seat in the back of the van while we took our walk. He's asleep in his cot now with the other two. They're a little older. I love them all for the short time they're with me. Am I doing wrong?'

Ian shook his head in despair. 'I really don't know. I can't take all this in. I wish you hadn't told me. It was easier not knowing. Who are the others?'

'The boy, James, is the son of a single mother, Lydia Wren, and the daughter was born to Grant and Chelsea Ryan.'

'I saw their names on Moller's list. Emma spoke to Grant and Chelsea.'

'Why?' Anne asked, immediately anxious.

'Because we were trying to establish what connection they had with the Moller Clinic.'

'I see. Mr and Mrs Ryan don't suspect anything, do they?'

'No.'

'If they found out, they would sell their story to the

newspapers. They're already suing the hospital for compensation because their baby's body disappeared.'

'So you took her from the hospital?' Ian asked.

'Yes. I had their permission at the time, but then they changed their minds. I've called her Kerris. It means love. She'll miss him after he's gone.'

'Gone? Gone where?' Ian asked.

'When David passes, I mean,' Anne said quietly.

'He's going to die soon?' Ian asked, shocked.

'A few months.' Anne's eyes filled again. 'The gene mutation that gives them this condition means they mature more quickly and at different rates. It's very evident in Kerris. But it also shortens their life expectancy. I know it's nature taking its course, but each time one dies, it's harder for me. I look forward to a time when there are no more being born.'

'I shouldn't have pressed you to tell me,' Ian said remorsefully. 'I don't know how I'm going to deal with all of this.'

'You don't have to. You can go home and let me deal with it, just as I have been doing.'

'I doubt that's possible. Now I know, I can't just walk away and forget.'

'What other choice do you have, Ian?'

He sighed. 'I've no idea. I can't share it with Emma, that's for sure. She'd never cope. It's better she believes David was born dead.'

Anne nodded solemnly.

'And you've told me everything now?' Ian asked.

'Yes. There is nothing else.'

'I'll go then,' he said, standing. 'I need to think about all this and then decide what to do.'

'Put it behind you, that's what you do. Go and get on with your life.'

Ian took a couple of steps towards the door and stopped. 'Does David look like me?'

266

'Yes, he's definitely your son,' Anne said. She paused and then asked, 'Would you like to see him before you go? There is nothing to be frightened of and it might help give you closure. Show you he's not the monster you imagine, but a child in need of love and affection, one who won't be with us for much longer.'

Ian hesitated and then gave an imperceptible nod. 'Yes,' he replied quietly. 'It might help.'

Anne stood and led the way upstairs. Ian followed, full of trepidation and misgivings. Was this really wise? Shouldn't he do as Anne had first suggested and leave now and get on with his life as best he could? Would seeing David really help or make it worse? He honestly didn't know.

They came to a halt outside a bedroom at the rear of the house. The door was bolted from the outside.

'Is that necessary?' Ian asked, concerned.

'Yes. I daren't give them the run of the house in case someone sees them at one of the windows. The glass in the window of this room is opaque, but the others aren't. It would only take one sighting and that would be it.'

Ian watched, his heart thumping, as Anne slid the bolt and slowly opened the door. A small night light cast a pattern of stars and a moon on the ceiling. It was like the outside come in.

Ian followed Anne into the room. There were two small beds and a cot, a chest of drawers and a changing station, much as you'd find in any nursery, Ian thought. Only, of course, this wasn't any nursery.

'This is David,' Anne said quietly, going to the cot.

Ian went over and stood beside Anne as she leant over the side of the cot and adjusted the cover. He looked at the sleeping form. Curled on his side, with a blanket loosely over his body, only his head was visible, and one little hand that clutched the corner of the blanket. The back of his hand was covered in a fine down. So was the top of his head, but there was none on his face or neck as there had been when he'd been born. His features were more like that of an ordinary child too now, as was the outline of his body. After a few moments, Ian found he wasn't experiencing the repulsion he'd thought he would – as he had at the birth – but compassion. David stirred in his sleep, and then turned onto his back. His lips moved and his eyelids fluttered. Was he dreaming? Ian wondered. If so, about what?

'Are you all right?' Anne quietly asked him.

Ian gave a small nod and continued to gaze at the sleeping child. His child, although not like other children. A throwback from the ancestral past or, as Anne preferred to call them, an outsider. A child who should never have been born and would never experience the joy of living with his parents, playing, having friends or going to school. A child who hadn't long to live.

Ian swallowed hard and slowly extended his hand. Reaching out, he lightly touched his son's forehead. It felt warm and smooth, not cool and rough, as he had expected. He touched David's hand, which was still clutching the corner of the blanket. That too was soft and smooth despite the fine down. The little fingernails were all perfectly formed, although Ian noticed his thumb was shorter than that of a normal child.

David's eyes suddenly flickered open and Ian quickly withdrew his hand. He stared up at them, startled and confused.

'It's all right,' Anne soothed. 'There is nothing to be afraid of, love. This man won't harm you.'

'He understands?' Ian asked incredulously.

'A little, combined with my facial expression and tone. Babies do. Say something, talk to him, but don't make any sudden movement as it frightens them.'

'David,' Ian said softly.

The child looked at him.

'Are you all right?'

He looked back.

'Do you have everything you need? Are you well and happy?'

The brightness that came into his eyes suggested he was.

'I'm so sorry,' Ian said, his voice catching. 'Sorry for you being like this. If I'd had any idea this could happen, I would never have had children.'

David looked back with something that looked like sadness in his eyes.

'I'm your father,' Ian said. But there was no response.

'He doesn't understand,' Anne said. 'He's had no experience of a father. They just have me.'

Leaning into the cot, Anne said, 'This man is good. A parent, like me. He loves you.' She touched Ian's arm to show David she approved of him.

David's expression lightened.

'I think he knows who you are,' Anne said softly.

'So do I,' Ian said, and a tear escaped down his cheek.

He was looking at the child he'd never thought he'd have and he could never share it with Emma – it would be too cruel – and Moller was to blame. That man needed to be punished, and at that moment Ian vowed to do it, for David's sake and all those like him. Whatever it took.

FIFTY-EIGHT

The following morning, DC Beth Mayes sat at her desk in the office above Coleshaw Police Station, puzzled and concerned. She'd just filed her report on the arrest of another two members of the notorious Bates family for their involvement in a vicious armed robbery. With the criminals now safely in police custody and the report filed, Beth looked at the other matter awaiting her attention. It was worrying and strange.

Jan Hamlin, the tenant in Ivy Cottage, had reported intruders in her garden again. But last night, ignoring advice to stay indoors, she'd gone to investigate and had seen a van leaving Coleshaw Woods. She'd noted the registration number and had told the officer she believed the owner was somehow linked to the intruders coming onto her property. Uniform had run the registration number through the police computer and had identified the owner, but that was as far as they'd got last night. The matter had been passed to Beth and she was struggling to understand exactly what it meant.

Anne Long was the registered owner of the van – the same Anne Long, midwife, Beth had interviewed in connection with missing babies. While the previous enquiry was closed – there'd been a satisfactory explanation – whatever had

Anne been doing in Coleshaw Woods late at night in the middle of winter? And on many other occasions, if Jan Hamlin was to be believed. According to Ms Hamlin, she'd heard Anne calling some creatures that were getting into the garden and terrorizing her. She'd refused to accept they could be foxes or badgers and was so distressed by what she'd seen that she'd given notice on her tenancy agreement and was ready to leave. When Matt had previously visited her he'd said she didn't seem hysterical or given to flights of fantasy, and it seemed that something *was* getting into the garden. Perhaps there was a rational explanation for all of this, Beth thought, but what it could be escaped her.

She glanced at the office clock. It was 11.30 a.m. and she'd been working since 5 a.m., up since 4 a.m., for the raid on the Bates house. Time to go home, and on the way she'd stop off and visit Anne Long. Closing down her computer, Beth took her jacket from the back of her chair and crossed the near-empty office. There were only a few officers in on a Saturday.

She left the building by the back exit where the cars were kept and got into the unmarked police car assigned to her. Mulling over possible scenarios for Anne being in the woods, Beth drove up the high street, heading in the direction of Melton. Some of the shop windows were already decorated for Christmas, but Beth's thoughts didn't mirror their festiveness. There was something disquieting about Anne Long being in the woods late at night following the previous investigation into missing babies. She dearly hoped she was wrong, but Anne wouldn't be the first nurse to suffer from psychosis and use her position to do harm rather than good to others.

Beth gave the Christmas tree standing in the market square at Melton a cursory glance as she drove past and then, with a growing sense of unease, turned into Dells Lane. Her satnav showed that Number 45 was at the far end on the right.

There was no van parked on the driveway, nor any sign of the other car registered to Anne – a grey Vauxhall Corsa. Perhaps one of them was in the garage; it wasn't large enough to take two vehicles. Beth got out and glanced at the sky. Dark clouds were gathering on the horizon and storms were forecast for the weekend. She rang the doorbell to Number 45 and waited. No one answered. She tried again, knocked on the door, then looked through the letterbox, but a security hood blocked her view.

She returned up the drive and then went next door to Number 43. A woman in a dressing gown answered the bell.

'Sorry to trouble you. Detective Constable Beth Mayes,' Beth said, showing her ID. 'There's nothing to worry about, but do you know when your neighbour Anne Long will be at home? I would like to talk to her as part of a routine enquiry.'

'If she's not there she's most likely at work. She's a midwife and doesn't keep regular hours. If she's late back, she goes straight out again to walk her dogs. Someone else was asking about her and my husband told him the same thing.'

'Who? Do you know?'

'No, just said he was a friend of hers.'

'And Anne keeps dogs?'

'Yes, dangerous ones that have to be kept on a tight leash. She can only take them out at night when there's no one else around. Goodness knows why she bothers with them. I wouldn't go to all that trouble.'

'No, indeed,' Beth said. 'That's very helpful. Do you know what breed of dog they are?'

'No, never seen them. We stay well away. You could try phoning her mobile,' she added helpfully. 'Do you have her number?'

'Yes, I do. Does Anne have a navy van here?'

'Yes, it'll be in the garage if she's at work. She uses it when she takes the dogs out, which keeps her other car nice for work.'

'Thank you,' Beth said, and returned to her car.

The mystery was solved. Anne had dangerous dogs and sensibly walked them at night when there was no one else around. It made sense, but that wasn't the end of it. The Dangerous Dogs Act made it illegal for any dog – regardless of its breed – to be out of control, which clearly Anne's were. It must have been the dogs that had been going into the garden of Ivy Cottage and terrorizing the tenant. Anne would need to be spoken to and warned that in future her dogs had to be kept on a lead in any public space. However, that wasn't a matter for CID and Beth would pass it back to uniform to deal with. Satisfied, she headed for home as large drops of rain began splattering on the windscreen.

FIFTY-NINE

Ian sat at the dining table staring at his laptop, angry and upset. He was at home and Emma had gone to her mother's for the day, which was just as well for he was struggling to hide his feelings. He wouldn't have believed what Anne had told him had he not seen David with his own eyes.

Atavism. When DNA from our evolutionary past reappeared in the present generation. He'd been reading about it on the Internet. It happened naturally sometimes when a gene mutated, but in David's case it was because of Carstan Moller's obsessive need to continue his line. How dare he mess with people's lives. The arrogance of the man! How much Edie Moller knew Anne hadn't been sure, but felt she probably knew and turned a blind eye to what he was doing.

Ian hadn't told Emma what he'd discovered, and he wouldn't. He'd said he'd seen Anne and she'd confirmed that errors had occurred at the Moller Clinic resulting in too many patients sharing the same donor and babies not surviving. It was all Emma needed to know, now or in the future. They'd agreed that soon they'd have to start making plans to separate, for now they knew they were half brother and sister, a future together was impossible.

Ian's anger flared again. Moller had played with the lives of his patients, manipulating and deceiving them for years for his own ends. He had told Anne he had stopped, but Ian wasn't so sure. There'd been no evidence of other donors in the files he had seen. Ian needed to be certain his evil practice had stopped for good, but in a way that didn't expose David or others like him that might follow. Ian thought he knew how.

He was studying Moller's files on his laptop. Not those relating to his patients, but his accounts, including tax returns, which it seemed Edie Moller had been responsible for. The accounts were in a mess, much like all her other filing, but it was clear that the Mollers hadn't made huge sums from the clinic. But then that was probably part of his strategy, Ian thought: keep the fees low to attract as many clients as possible so he could spread his genes far afield. Ian was aware that the quickest, most efficient way to close down a business was as a result of tax evasion and money laundering. HM Revenue & Customs were fast and relentless in their pursuit of offenders.

He set to work. Posing as Moller, Ian began raising capital online using Moller's business and house as collateral. It was ridiculously easy on the Internet, with no face-to-face interview. He electronically signed documents and raised as much as he was allowed from various banks and loan companies. It had increased the clinic's income tenfold – on paper at least – and Ian then introduced two fictitious employees. It was a scam firms used to reduce their tax bill – illegal, of course, but it added another layer of fraud to Moller's accounts.

Ian then set up five offshore accounts in countries that were notorious for tax evasion and money laundering. He'd seen similar on clients' computers and knew how they worked. Ian spent a productive hour transferring money out of Moller's UK accounts and in and out of the various offshore accounts, backdating some of the transactions so it appeared he'd been up to no good for years. Working in information technology at Wetherby Security had taught Ian a lot, and by the time he finished, Moller's accounts shouted money laundering and tax evasion to even the most inexperienced clerk. But just to make sure they weren't missed, and to get an investigation going quickly, he emailed the police fraud department and Revenue & Customs anonymously, whistle-blowing on Moller.

Last but not least, Ian sent an email from Carstan Moller to all his current patients and those whose parents had been treated at the clinic. It informed them that there'd been a dreadful mistake at the clinic and if they were planning on starting a family, they should have their DNA tested as a matter of urgency, as it was possible they might share the same biological father as their partner.

All Ian could do now was watch and wait.

He didn't have to wait long.

Almost immediately, patients began emailing Moller expressing their shock and concern, and asking for more details about the exact nature of the error that had occurred and if they should be worried.

Yes, Ian replied on Moller's behalf, *you should be very worried indeed. Get checked straight away.*

Some asked where they could be tested and Ian sent them details of the firm he'd used – MyGeneticHistory.com.

The emails continued to arrive and Ian wondered what Moller was making of it, or perhaps he didn't check emails on a Saturday, enjoying the weekend off, for there was no reply from him. Was he in for a shock on Monday morning!

An email arrived from Grant and Chelsea Ryan threatening to sue Moller for every penny he'd got, which wouldn't be a lot by the time the fraud squad and HMRC had finished with him, Ian thought with satisfaction. Now heavily mortgaged and with huge debts, Moller would be bankrupt once the fraud squad got hold of him. Sweet revenge. Ian was destroying Moller's life just as he had destroyed his and Emma's, and all the others he'd deceived. Moller had played God and lost.

SIXTY

Jan stood to the right of the living-room window, partially secreted behind the curtain, and stared into the night. The rain had stopped but the sky was dark as fresh storm clouds gathered. She was still hoping the creatures would return. The motion-sensor light outside was off and she had her phone ready. One final chance to get the film she so desperately needed before Camile arrived. But the opportunity was quickly receding. It was after 8 p.m. now and Camile would be here before long. She'd texted from the airport to say her plane had landed and she should be with her by 8.30, depending on the traffic.

Jan had taken up her position at the window as soon as night had fallen, waiting and hoping they might come early. She was already packed and her cases were in her car. Just her coat and handbag remained in the cottage. She'd gone into the village earlier and bought some basic food items for Camile, and flowers to say thank you and sorry, which she'd put in a vase on the coffee table. She'd said goodbye to Lillian, who hadn't appeared surprised to hear she was leaving. Camile had told Chris, who'd told his brother, who'd passed it on to Lillian. That was how news travelled in the village: a grapevine of conversations, as efficient as email or text.

Jan shifted position and continued to keep watch. Surprisingly, Camile had already found another tenant who would move in as soon as Jan had left, which eased Jan's conscience. Camile was coming back to oversee the changeover, spend a few days with her family and Tinder, and then return to her job abroad. Heaven help the new tenant, Jan thought. They would need to be made of strong stuff to live here. Nothing would have enticed her to stay.

Jan had arranged to lodge with her mother for a few weeks while she applied for jobs and looked for a flat to rent. She would also spend a weekend with Ruby and catch up with other friends she'd neglected while she'd been here. Maybe even make a proper start on that book she was supposed to be writing. She had a few ideas, and if she could get a film or photograph, she would also write a feature article about the creatures in the woods. Newspapers and magazines were always keen to buy pieces about the weird and supernatural.

The front doorbell rang and Tinder shot off the sofa and ran to the front door, barking. Jan came out from where she'd been standing and switched on the living-room light. Tinder would be as pleased to see Camile as she was, she thought, and opened the door.

It wasn't Camile, but Chris.

'I wanted to say goodbye,' he said, and handed her a box of chocolates.

'Oh, OK, thanks,' she said awkwardly. She hadn't expected to see him again.

'Do you want to come in?' she offered, feeling she should. 'Camile will be here soon.'

'Yes, if I'm not disturbing you.'

She stood aside to let him in and he headed to the living room.

'You've got the curtains open,' he remarked. 'I didn't think you liked seeing the dark.'

She shrugged. 'I'm getting better. I've had to, living here. Do you want a drink?' she asked, putting the chocolates on the table.

'Yes, please.'

'Scotch?'

'Thanks.'

Chris sat in his usual armchair and Tinder went to him. Jan poured his drink and handed it to him.

'Aren't you joining me?' he asked.

'No, I'll be driving soon.'

She sat on the sofa, her back to the open curtains, as Chris took a sip of his drink. This would be her last chance to challenge him about the video he'd removed from her phone, for as soon as Camile arrived she would leave.

She took a breath and looked at him. 'Chris, why did you delete the video from my phone?'

A brief flash of discomposure and then he recovered. 'I'm not sure what you mean,' he said.

'The video clip I took of what was coming into the garden. I showed you, then left my phone down here while I went upstairs to let Tinder out of the bedroom. After you'd gone, I found it had been erased. You knew that was the only proof I had.'

He briefly met her gaze, but his look was guarded. 'I remember you showing me the video, but that's all. Perhaps I accidentally deleted it.'

She was about to say that was highly unlikely when the doorbell rang again. Tinder shot down the hall.

'That'll be Camile,' Chris said.

'Yes, I know,' Jan said tartly, and went to answer the door.

'Hi, we meet at last,' Camile said warmly, coming in. She hugged Jan and then petted Tinder as he jumped up at her excitedly.

The likeness between her and Chris that Jan had seen in the photographs was even more obvious in person.

'Welcome home,' Jan said. 'Chris is here.'

'Yes, I saw his car outside. I texted him to say I was on my way back.'

Setting her case down in the hall, Camile went through to the living room with Tinder close beside her. Jan followed.

'Hi, love,' Chris said, and he stood to greet her. They hugged with great affection.

'I could do with one of those,' Camile said, referring to Chris's Scotch. 'I'm knackered after all the travelling.'

'How do you like it?' Jan asked.

'Same as Chris, please.'

Jan went into the kitchen and poured the Scotch, feeling slightly uncomfortable at playing hostess in what was Camile's home again. Returning to the living room, she handed her the glass.

'Thank you so much,' she said appreciatively. 'Those flowers are gorgeous. Don't forget to take them with you.'

'They're for you,' Jan replied. 'I put them in water to stop them from wilting.'

'That is kind.' Camile seemed as pleasant in person as she had been in her emails and Jan couldn't help but like her.

'I've put bread and milk in the fridge,' Jan said. 'And I've topped up the meter. The spare change is in its usual place in the cupboard under the stairs, and here are the front door keys.' She placed them on the coffee table and prepared to leave.

'Thank you,' Camile said. 'Sorry I couldn't get here earlier. You've got a long journey. Why don't you stay tonight and then drive home tomorrow?'

'I'll be fine,' Jan said, and instinctively glanced towards the open curtains.

Camile followed her gaze. 'I am sorry you've had problems with the creatures from the woods coming in. They wouldn't have harmed you, but it must have been annoying just the same.'

'Chris doesn't believe they exist,' Jan said, and waited for their reaction.

Camile sipped her drink while Chris concentrated on his glass. Neither of them spoke.

'Goodbye then, thanks for everything,' Jan said, and she picked up her handbag.

'I'll see you to your car,' Chris said.

'There's no need. I'll just say goodbye to Tinder before I go.'

Jan went to stroke him, but as she did he let out a low, threatening growl. She instinctively stepped back. Still growling, he gave a bark and ran to the patio window. Jan's heart missed a beat. It wasn't her he was growling at. He'd heard something. Were they out there? Had they come after all? It was the time they often came. Chris and Camile were looking at the window too.

'I'll close the curtains,' Camile said, and stood.

But as she crossed the room a face appeared at the glass. Jan let out a small cry and delved into her bag for her phone. Too late. The face had gone. She rushed to the back door with Tinder at her heels and opened it. He ran down the garden barking and Jan caught a glimpse of the shadowy figure before it disappeared through the hedge and was gone.

SIXTY-ONE

With blood pounding in her ears, Jan returned to the living room, her phone still in her hand. She looked at Camile and Chris. Neither of them spoke. Camile continued to the windows and purposely drew the curtains. Chris concentrated on his glass of Scotch. Jan looked from one to the other. Were they planning on ignoring what had just happened? The silence was deafening.

'Well?' Jan asked after a moment.

Camile returned to her chair and looked at her. 'Do you still have any photographs or film of them?' she asked.

'No. Chris saw to that,' Jan said sharply. 'But you're surely not going to deny they exist?'

'No,' Camile said quietly. 'Sit down, Jan. We need to talk. Are you sure you don't want a drink?'

'Perfectly.'

Jan sat on the sofa, upright, with her bag still on her shoulder, ready to make a run for it if necessary. She didn't feel safe with the two of them alone in the cottage. They were clearly colluding, and the air was charged with secrecy and foreboding. Perhaps she should leave now while she had the chance, but then she'd never know what was really going on.

283

'You obviously want an explanation,' Camile said, and took a sip of her drink. 'I will explain, but first you must promise never to tell anyone. Young lives could be lost if you did.'

'I want to hear what's happening first before I make any promises,' Jan said, her voice unsteady. 'I doubt anyone would believe me anyway without proof.'

Camile glanced at Chris, who nodded, confirming it was all right for her to continue.

'It won't have escaped your notice that Chris and I look alike,' Camile began.

Jan nodded.

'We are related. We share the same biological father. We are half brother and sister.'

Jan gasped.

'I know, although we didn't know when we began our relationship. We assumed our likeness was the result of our genes being messed up by the power station's chemical waste getting into the water supply. There are others in the villages around here who look alike and everyone believes the power station is to blame. It was only after we'd been in a relationship for some years and had a child that we discovered the truth.' Camile paused to take another sip of her drink. Jan saw her hand shake as she set the glass on the table. Chris was looking at her.

'Our baby was born very different to how nature intended,' Camile continued. 'He was a genetic throwback and didn't live long. It was only by chance we discovered the truth after we saw someone in the garden here and gave chase. It was late at night and pitch black, but we found Anne in the woods locking what looked like a child in the back of her van. Chris blocked her path and demanded to know what was going on. She broke down and told us. Some children, including our son, were being born with a genetic condition, not because of the power station, but because our parents had received the same donor sperm from a local fertility clinic. Chris and I were obviously appalled, angry and upset, and wanted the man responsible arrested. Anne said he was no longer practising, she had seen to that, but begged us not to go to the police as it would jeopardize the safety of the little ones still being born – "outsiders", she calls them. After much soul-searching, we agreed to keep quiet and do what we could to help Anne. Chris and I couldn't continue our relationship as we were half brother and sister, so we parted but have remained friends.' Camile stopped. Her eyes glistened with tears.

Jan looked from her to Chris and didn't know what to say. Was she telling the truth? She could see pain in his eyes too.

'Our son only lived ten days,' Camile said. 'But others with his condition have lived much longer, some for years. They mature quickly, not like human babies. There is a baby and two toddlers alive at present – the ones you've been seeing. When you met Anne with Chris they were trying to work out how to stop them coming into the garden here. Anne keeps them in her house all day, away from prying eyes, then at night she takes them into the woods for some exercise. The woods are thickest at the back of the cottage so it's reasonably safe. There's nowhere else for them to go around here. Some years back a woman heard a baby cry. She reported it to the police, but they searched the area and thankfully found nothing. But as you have discovered they can be very mischievous – undoing your hedge repair and teasing you by moving a ball of twine. They mean no harm. Usually they're wary of strangers. They would probably have lost interest had you not started leaving food out. Anne feeds them well, but they can't resist tempting treats.'

'I'm sorry,' Jan found herself saying.

'It's not your fault. I now realize it was a stupid idea to rent out the cottage. Chris warned me there might be problems, but I wanted to take the contract abroad and I needed someone to look after Tinder. I really didn't think they would bother you. They know me well, but I thought they would stay clear of a stranger, which, according to Chris, they did at first.' Jan nodded. 'Then it seems they got braver and braver as they got used to you. I switched off the motion-sensor light upstairs just in case they came to explore, but you turned it on again and saw them.'

'Sorry,' Jan said again.

'I'm not blaming you. They obviously felt safe and knew you wouldn't harm them – well, not in a physical sense. But, of course, what they can't appreciate is that they would be harmed dreadfully if news of their existence got out. Anne has tried to tell them, but they don't understand. They're only children.' Camile stopped. 'That's it, really.'

Jan took a moment before she spoke. Did she believe them? Yes. 'I knew something weird was going on, but never in a million years would I have guessed what it was. What happens now?'

'We continue as we have been.'

'Who else knows about them?' Jan asked.

'Until recently just Chris, myself and Anne. But Ian Jennings, a father to one of them, has found out and is taking steps to close the clinic permanently. He can be trusted. He understands no one must ever find out. As I hope you do.'

'Does Lillian know?' Jan asked, looking at Chris.

'No,' he replied. 'She and my brother believe our child was stillborn and that's what broke up Camile and me. No one can know, for the sake of these little ones and those like them who haven't been born yet.'

'There will be others?' Jan asked, horrified.

'There will be until all those who have been affected have stopped having children. Ian is contacting them all now.'

'And what will happen to those children who haven't been born yet?' Jan asked.

'Some will die straight away,' Camile said sadly. 'And Anne will look after those who survive. Chris, Ian and I will do what we can to help.'

Jan nodded solemnly. It was an incredible story, and if she hadn't seen the children herself she would never have believed it. But she accepted the explanation she'd been given. 'Anne won't be able to take them into the woods when your new tenant is here,' Jan said. 'It will be too risky.'

'Anne *is* my new tenant,' Camile replied. 'It makes sense for her to live here, in the middle of nowhere, without fear of being discovered. When I return from my contract abroad I will help look after them. Anne will be able to spend time in her own house again without the constant worry of being found out.'

'How did Anne get involved?' Jan asked.

'As a midwife she was seeing and hearing of children being born with the condition. She became suspicious and started asking about their history. She discovered that all the grandparents of the babies had used the same fertility clinic.' Jan nodded. 'These babies are born a lot earlier than human babies. Some are stillborn, but others can survive. Instead of leaving them to die, Anne began taking them away and looking after them for however long they had. She's a saint in my eyes, but if anyone found out she would be prosecuted. I dread to think what would happen to the little ones then.'

'I won't tell anyone,' Jan said. 'No one would believe me anyway.'

They fell silent for a moment and then, glancing at Chris, Camile said, 'I'm sorry things didn't work out for you two. Chris is a good man. He was only trying to protect me. He was upset when you told him Tinder had got into our baby's clothes. I kept one outfit and the rest I got rid of.'

'Those clothes belonged to your baby?' Jan asked.

'Yes.'

'I'm sorry. I had no idea. I put them back carefully and made sure that Tinder never went in there again.'

'Thank you,' Camile said. 'They're all I have to remember him by.'

There was silence again and then Jan said, 'I think I should be going now.' She stood.

'Are you sure you won't stay the night?' Camile asked.

'No, but be reassured, your secret is safe with me.'

'Thank you, and thanks for the flowers.'

'I'll see you to your car,' Chris said.

Jan petted Tinder one last time, said goodbye to Camile and went with Chris to the front door. Outside, the clouds had parted to reveal a full moon. Jan unlocked her car door and got in.

'Goodbye, Jan,' Chris said, one hand on the open door. 'Look after yourself.'

'I will. And you.' She smiled.

'Perhaps, once you're settled at your mother's, I could text you?'

'Yes, I'd like that.'

He ducked his head in and kissed her cheek. 'Drive carefully. I'll be in touch.'

Chris closed her car door. Jan started the engine and slowly pulled away. As she bumped over the uneven road surface, she glanced in the rear-view mirror. Chris was standing in the middle of the lane watching her, a lone figure silhouetted against the night sky. But as she looked, she saw two small figures emerge from the woods and stand either side of him. He held their hands. Guilt enveloped Jan. She'd let Chris and Camile believe their secret was safe with her, but it wasn't.

Far from it. Last night she'd given the registration number of Anne's van to the police. How long would it be before they traced her and found out what she was doing? She'd never forgive herself if she was the one who led to them being discovered.

Once out of sight of Ivy Cottage, Jan pulled over. Sick with fear that it was probably already too late, she took her phone from her handbag and called Coleshaw Police Station.

SIXTY-TWO

'It's Jan Hamlin. I used to be the tenant in Ivy Cottage,' she said. 'I phoned last night and reported a prowler in Coleshaw Woods behind the cottage.'

'Yes, I remember,' the officer said. 'I took your call. I was on duty last night. How can I help you?'

'I made a mistake. I gave you the registration number of a van I thought I'd seen leaving the woods, but I was wrong.'

'No, I think it checked out.'

'Surely not? It was a mistake.' Her stomach churned.

'I'm certain the matter's been dealt with, but if you'd like to hold the line I'll find out.'

'Yes, please.'

Tears stung her eyes and panic gripped her. Please let him be wrong, she thought. What was she going to do if the matter had been 'dealt with'? Say nothing and continue home or return and alert Chris and Camile? Was there still time for Anne to escape with the children? She doubted it.

Sitting there with the full moon shimmering through the trees, she could picture those strange children being captured like animals as Anne tried to protect them. Then what? A media circus, a secure hospital to be tested, analysed and experimented on. And it was all her fault.

'Hello,' the duty officer said, coming back on the line. 'You were right. The lady who owned the van was traced and she has been spoken to.'

'Spoken to? Why?' Jan gasped. 'I was wrong.'

'No, you weren't. She owns dangerous dogs and hasn't been keeping them under proper control. That's what's been getting onto your property.'

'Oh, I see, she keeps dogs?' Jan repeated, hardly daring to believe.

'Yes. An officer has spoken to her and she'll be given a formal warning in writing that they need to be kept on a leash at all times or she will be prosecuted. It's an offence not to keep dogs under control. So thank you for bringing it to our attention. We're always grateful to members of the public for helping us in our job.'

'Thank *you*,' Jan said, and ended the call.

Relief flooded through her. Thank goodness. The police believed Anne kept dangerous dogs, so all she would receive was a written warning. She'd be free to continue her work and those little ones could live out their short lives in her loving care.

SIXTY-THREE

Six months later, Ian sat in his living room, dinner on a tray, watching the evening news. A *For Sale* board had been erected at the front of the house and Emma had already moved out. She was staying with her family until the house was sold, when they would divide the proceeds and furniture and buy a flat each of their own. Emma had taken all her personal belongings and the house felt bare and lonely without her. Ian missed her, but they would remain friends and eventually, he thought, they would hopefully find new partners with whom they could have healthy children.

The signature tune for the six o'clock news began and Ian raised the volume, anticipation coursing through his veins. Today was the day. The climax of the police investigation, which Ian had been monitoring closely throughout. He'd watched and, where necessary, had given an anonymous helping hand, although the fraud squad hadn't needed much help as Moller's guilt was obvious from all the records they'd found.

The fruition of their investigation had come today at 2 p.m. when they had raided the Moller Clinic and arrested Carstan and Edie Moller. Ian had taken time off work to watch it through Moller's CCTV, which he'd hacked into. The media had been there because Ian had tipped them off. Now he was looking forward to seeing their arrest on the evening news, as were others whose lives Carstan had ruined.

The international news items came first: a plane crash in Siberia where no one had survived, a shooter in the US, a bombing in Thailand, and the ups and downs of the stock market. Then the home news began and this item was first, with a presenter giving her report outside the Moller Clinic.

'Earlier this afternoon,' she began, 'this quiet, rural village was left in a state of shock when a husband and wife in their sixties, purporting to be doctors, were arrested at this clinic you can see behind me. They are being detained on suspicion of deception, fraud and money laundering.' The report cut to film taken that afternoon of the Mollers being led away by detectives as reporters took photographs and shouted questions.

'I never claimed to be a doctor!' Moller retaliated.

'But you don't deny you let patients believe you had medical qualifications when you duped them?'

Any reply was lost in the barrage of questions and jeers from onlookers as the Mollers were put in separate police cars and driven away.

The presenter came on screen again. 'Carstan and Edie Moller ran a fertility clinic from their home here for decades. But instead of using donor sperm as they told their patients, they used Carstan Moller's own sperm, charging clients and growing rich on the proceeds. It is thought that Moller could have fathered thousands of children with unsuspecting victims. A despicable and cruel breach of professional trust, it's not the first case like this. There have been similar cases in the UK and abroad. Local MP Sandra Tilsley is calling for tighter legislation.'

A woman who'd been standing off camera moved into view and the presenter pointed the microphone at her.

'The whole village is dismayed and upset by what has happened here,' the MP said. 'Our sympathy goes to those who have fallen victim to this unscrupulous pair. I shall be calling upon the government to make changes in the law so that in future private clinics like this one are better regulated. Clearly this is a scandal on an unprecedented scale and it must never be allowed to happen again. If anyone thinks they may have been affected they can contact me or telephone the number that will be shown at the end of this report.'

The presenter thanked her and then moved to a teenage lad Ian recognized from the village store. 'What did you feel when you heard the news about the clinic?' she asked him.

'I always thought there was something odd about that pair. A lot of people round here did,' he said.

'But you didn't suspect what they were up to?'

'No. They never had much to do with us, really.'

She thanked him and then wound up the report with more film taken earlier, showing the police coming out of the clinic carrying computers and medical equipment. The piece ended with the helpline phone number.

Satisfied, Ian switched off the television, picked up his knife and fork and continued to eat his dinner. He knew there was sufficient evidence to convict Moller without implicating Anne or giving away the existence of the outsiders she protected and cared for. Ian had seen to that. He'd removed all traces of the *Second Generation* file from Moller's computer and had tweaked others. The great advantage of his job was that in keeping hackers out, he knew exactly how they got in and the damage they could do.

Tomorrow he would visit David one last time and then try to pick up the pieces of his life. David had outlived their expectations and Ian had seen him every week since Anne had told him. Not at her home in Dells Lane, but at Ivy

Cottage where she now stayed. It was perfect, rural and remote, so that David, James and Kerris could run free and make the most of their last days, happy and unaware they were any different to others. For that, Ian was grateful.

SIXTY-FOUR

'Have you heard the news?' Beth asked the following morning as she slipped into her office chair.

Matt looked up from his computer screen and frowned questioningly.

'You must have. The raid on the Moller Clinic?'

'Oh yes, I did. You can't miss it. But why are you looking so concerned? Because we weren't part of the action? You know the fraud squad use their own people.'

'That's not the reason,' Beth said. 'You remember Ian Jennings? We interviewed him and his wife after their neighbour reported their baby was missing?'

'Yes.'

'He phoned months ago with concerns about the Moller Clinic. I took his call. He'd found out that his and his wife's parents had used the clinic and they'd both been given the same donor sperm. I didn't do anything. I told him it wasn't a police matter and to contact the adjudication service responsible for the private sector.'

'Oh, I see,' Matt said. 'That was a missed opportunity. Has he filed a complaint?'

'No. But I feel bad I did nothing. In my defence, Ian didn't say that Carstan Moller was their biological father, only that he'd had his and Emma's DNA tested and they shared the same donor.'

'He probably didn't know it was Moller then.'

'Well, he certainly does now!' Beth said. 'It's all over the news. It must have come as a huge shock.'

'Or possibly he was contacted as part of the investigation?' Matt suggested.

'Maybe,' Beth sighed. 'Even so, I feel bad. I should have done more to help him. He thought it could be the reason he and Emma weren't able to have healthy children. He wanted the clinic investigated. I was thinking maybe I should phone him and apologize.'

'I wouldn't,' Matt warned. 'If he does file a complaint, it could be seen as an admission of your guilt.'

'You're probably right,' Beth agreed. 'I'll tell the sergeant, though, just in case there are repercussions. Hopefully Moller's arrest will give Ian and Emma some closure, although I can't see their marriage surviving. That MP was right when she said private clinics need to be better monitored, otherwise it could happen again.'

SIXTY-FIVE

A year later Jan was in the village store in Merryless, buying groceries.

'How are you feeling?' Lillian asked as she scanned the items into the till.

'Good now the morning sickness has stopped. Only it wasn't just in the morning but all day.'

'I know, Chris said. You poor dear. But at least it's passed, and it will have been worth it in the end.'

'Yes,' Jan agreed. 'I've got to have another scan this afternoon. They think I might have my dates wrong, as the baby isn't as big as it should be. They can also determine the sex of the baby from this scan.'

'Do you want to know its sex?' Lillian asked.

'I guess it makes sense,' Jan said, putting the items into her shopping bag. 'It means we can plan ahead and think about names.'

Lillian smiled. 'I'm so pleased you two got together in the end. I always thought you were well suited.'

'I know, you said,' Jan laughed. 'I'm pleased too.'

'You're good for him. Any plans to marry?'

'You sound just like my mother,' Jan said. 'Maybe after

298

the baby is born. There's no rush. We've shown our commitment by living together.'

'Good. Chris is a fine man. He won't let you down.'

'I know,' Jan said, paying. 'You must all come to supper one evening.'

'Thanks. We'd like that, and to see the changes you've made to his house. Even Chris says it's more comfortable now, although I think he needed some persuading at first.'

'Tell me about it!' Jan laughed.

Another customer approached the counter, so, saying goodbye, Jan left the shop and began the walk to what was now her home. Who would have guessed she'd end up living in a village, she mused (not for the first time), surrounded by fields, with a single shop and pub, and where everyone knew each other? She'd always thought of herself as a townie, but then she'd fallen in love with Chris.

A week after she'd returned home, he'd texted as promised. Jan had replied and it had gone from there. They'd started dating and their relationship had flourished. Chris had first suggested she move in with him after they'd been going out for four months, as the travelling was taking its toll. She'd said no to begin with and had then agreed to a trial period. Now, here she was, settled into village life, not missing the town at all, and eighteen weeks pregnant! It had been a heady year – the stuff of romance novels, she thought as she walked. Perhaps she should write one? Her relationship with Chris had all the ingredients of a good romance: attraction at first sight, drama, intrigue, conflict and then the resolution with the couple living happily ever after.

Or so she hoped.

Jan stopped and changed the shopping bag from one hand to the other. Being pregnant was slowing her down. She could have brought the car, but she felt she should walk to keep fit and it gave her the chance to get to know others. Even

Bill Smith recognized her on a good day and had once allowed her to take him home when she'd found him wandering in the wrong direction.

'If you go down there you'll end up in the woods,' she'd told him.

'Oh, mustn't do that,' he said, pulling a face. 'I might get eaten by the dogs there.'

Jan hadn't disagreed. It was now common knowledge in Merryless that Anne Long, the midwife, lived in Ivy Cottage and allowed her dogs to run in the woods when there was no one around. The villagers didn't object, even though they knew she wasn't supposed to let them off their leads and she'd already received a warning from the police. But no one would tell, as their presence helped keep the vandals out of the woods.

Ten minutes later, Jan paused again to swap over the bag and then continued home.

Chris was already in, having taken time off work so he could be with her for the hospital appointment.

'You should have phoned me,' he said, concerned, taking the heavy shopping bag from her. 'I could have collected you.'

'I'm fine. There's no need to fuss.'

'But I want to fuss and look after you,' he said, kissing her.

'I know, and if I'm honest I like it,' Jan laughed.

'Good. Today's the day we find out if it's a boy or a girl,' Chris said, unable to hide his excitement.

'Yes, it is,' Jan replied. She'd played down the other reason for the scan – that the baby wasn't developing properly. Chris was anxious anyway after what had happened to him and Camile. But there was no chance of that happening again, as Chris and she didn't share the same DNA. She'd told him, as she'd told Lillian, that she must have got her dates wrong. This scan would hopefully confirm that, so there was no point in worrying Chris.

SIXTY-SIX

The waiting area in the diagnostic imaging department at Coleshaw Hospital was busy and running late. Jan and Chris had been making conversation, but now he was answering messages on his phone while Jan sipped from the water bottle she'd brought with her, watching the comings and goings of the department. The instruction sheet for the scan had stated to drink two to three glasses of water before the scan. Jan was following these instructions as she'd followed all the antenatal advice. She'd been sipping the water at home, during the car journey here, and was now finishing the second bottle. She hoped she didn't have to wait long as her bladder felt uncomfortably full.

She glanced at Chris and then at the woman sitting opposite, whose partner was also concentrating on his phone. The woman met her gaze and threw her a knowing smile, which Jan returned. She'd found a camaraderie among pregnant women that was reassuring, like joining a support group.

Jan had been very worried when she'd been told she would need another scan, although the nurse had assured her there was nothing to worry about and the baby was fine. The fact that it was very active showed how healthy it was. She had been able to feel it kicking and moving at fourteen weeks, with little bulges appearing in her stomach wall.

A nurse appeared. 'Jan Hamlin, you're next.'

Jan immediately stood, so did Chris. 'This is my partner,' Jan said to the nurse. It was important he felt included.

'This way, please,' the nurse said, with a warm, professional smile. 'How are you both?'

'Fine, thank you,' Jan said.

'And how's the father to be?' she asked, looking at Chris.

'A bit nervous,' he admitted.

'Like all dads are.'

She showed them into one of the scan rooms, closed the door and asked Jan to lie on the couch. Jan knew the routine from the previous scans. Chris helped her onto the couch and then drew up a chair to sit beside her. Jan pulled down the top of her trousers and pants to expose her stomach, now showing a reasonable-sized baby bulge, of which she was proud.

'The gel can feel a bit cold,' the nurse said as she squirted some onto Jan's stomach.

Jan turned her head so she could see the monitor as the nurse began moving the transducer over her stomach. Up and down, and around, pressing on her full bladder. Chris was concentrating on the screen too. He had a better view – sitting, rather than lying as she was. While they had been delighted by the first scan – proof she was pregnant – it hadn't really shown much. A pulsing, indistinct image of a developing foetus with an oversized head, lying on its back in a dark uterus. This scan was far more detailed.

The room was silent except for an irregular click as the nurse took photos of what she was seeing on screen. Jan glanced from the screen to the nurse. Her expression was one of concentration. Jan could see the image of her baby clearly, but had no idea what the nurse was making of it.

'How far gone are you?' she asked.

'Eighteen weeks, I think,' Jan replied.

The nurse moved the transducer to a different position on Jan's stomach. Chris gave her hand a squeeze. He was holding it quite tightly as he too concentrated on the screen.

'Is everything all right?' he asked after a moment.

'It's a boy,' the nurse replied.

'That's great,' Jan said, and could see from Chris's expression how pleased he was.

'I'd just like the doctor to check something,' the nurse said, and put down the transducer. 'It's nothing to worry about.'

'What is it?' Chris asked, immediately anxious.

'Just a precaution. Stay here, please, while I fetch a more senior colleague.' She hurried out of the room.

Jan looked at Chris and saw his fear. 'It can't be much,' she said. 'I can feel him moving and the images looked fine to me.'

'But this didn't happen with your last scan,' Chris said anxiously.

'I know, but it does happen. I joined an online forum for mums-to-be and a lot of the women were worried when second opinions were sought. The nurses do it to cover themselves. I had to have my urine double-checked at the doctor's when I was first pregnant.'

'You didn't tell me that,' Chris said, no less worried.

'There was nothing to tell. I gave another sample and everything was OK. It happens. I'm sure your son is fine.'

Chris's face gave way to a small smile at the mention of his son. 'You're probably right. Sorry. I'm not very good at this, am I?'

'You're doing OK,' Jan said.

But as the minutes ticked by, she began to share Chris's concern. What was taking the nurse so long? Was she

303

discussing what she'd found before coming back into the room? Could it be so bad that it had to be discussed away from them?

The door abruptly opened and the nurse returned with a colleague.

'Hello, I'm Doctor Carter, a consultant radiologist here,' he said. 'Sorry to have kept you waiting, we're very busy today.' He threw them a reassuring smile and then began looking at the recorded images on the screen.

Jan and Chris watched him carefully as he clicked the mouse to move from one image to the next. The nurse pointed to some areas on the photos and Jan assumed that was in relation to what was causing the problem and that it had already been discussed outside of the room. Chris gave her hand another reassuring squeeze and the consultant turned to them.

'You have a son, congratulations,' he said. 'Your baby's heart and lungs are fine. He's a little on the small side but will probably make it up. You're eating well and taking plenty of fluids?'

'Yes,' Jan said.

'He appears to have a slight irregularity in the formation of his feet. But it's nothing to worry about and can be fixed with an operation once he's born.'

'An irregularity? Is it serious?' Chris asked.

'It doesn't appear to be. You've heard of a club foot? It's similar to that.'

'What caused it?' Jan asked.

'We don't really know, but it is correctable. We'll keep an eye on it and scan again in four weeks.'

'Should we be worried?' Jan asked.

'No. It's minor.' He smiled and touched her arm reassuringly. 'I'll leave you with the nurse now.'

With another smile, he left the room.

'Better to be safe than sorry,' the nurse said brightly. 'How many photos would you like?'

'Three, please,' Jan said, while Chris said nothing and looked deep in thought.

SIXTY-SEVEN

The following morning, Chris stopped by Lillian's store on his way to work. He didn't want to buy anything, but he needed to talk to her. He waited as she finished serving a customer and then stepped forward.

'Lovely to see you,' she said. 'Everything OK? Jan was in here yesterday. How did the scan go?'

'It's a boy,' Chris said proudly. 'I've brought a scan photo to show you.' He took the photo from his pocket and handed it to her.

'Wonderful. Congratulations,' Lillian said, genuinely pleased.

'Thank you.'

'What's the matter? You seem worried?'

'Does he look all right to you?' Chris asked. 'I mean, I know the image isn't wonderful, but does he look like a baby should at eighteen weeks? I didn't go with Camile for her scan, so I've got no idea.'

'Yes, of course. Why shouldn't he?'

'The doctor said he isn't as big as he should be so they're going to scan again in four weeks.'

'It happens,' Lillian said stoically. 'When I was expecting

my youngest I was told the same. He was eight pounds when he was born. They catch up.'

'That's what the doctor said, but they also think he may need an operation on his feet. It seems there's an irregularity in the formation of his feet.'

Lillian peered more closely at the photo. 'Well, I suppose they know what they're talking about, but I can't see much wrong.' She looked up.

'Like a club foot,' Chris added.

'Well, that's not serious, is it?'

'I don't think so.'

She held his gaze. 'Chris, the baby looks fine to me. Stop worrying. I know you struggled after what happened to you and Camile, but that won't happen again. Very few pregnancies are completely straightforward. There's always something. I know, I've had four. Blood pressure too high, too much fluid, baby too small, not in the right position, and so on. If there is something wrong, it's correctable, so buck up. Jan needs you.' She handed back the photo.

'Yes, you're probably right, although Jan seems to be taking it better than me.'

'That's understandable. She's a woman.' Lillian smiled.

'Which reminds me,' Chris said. 'Jan has asked if you can come to supper this Saturday.'

'Yes, I'll check with Jim, but I'm sure that's fine.'

The door opened as another customer came in.

'I'll be off then, see you Saturday, around seven?' Chris said.

'Look forward to it. Give my love to Jan.'

SIXTY-EIGHT

Chris returned to his van. He really must get a move on now. He was halfway through rewiring a house in the next village and had finished early yesterday to take Jan for the scan. Now he was late. He texted the couple to say he would be with them soon with apologies. After a restless night, he'd needed the sound voice of reason from Lillian and she'd done her best.

He started the van but didn't drive off. He stared through the windscreen, deep in thought. If Jan was worried, she wasn't showing it, probably for his sake, he decided. Engine still running, he took the scan photo from his pocket. Pity he didn't have a digital copy that he could have enlarged, but that hadn't been offered at the hospital. He supposed he could ask for another, but Jan would want to know the reason, especially as there was already another scan scheduled in four weeks' time.

Returning the photo to his pocket, he drove away.

It wasn't so much his son's low weight that was worrying him. The doctor, nurse, Jan's online friends and now Lillian all agreed that babies usually made up any shortfall in their weight before birth. No. What was really worrying Chris was the malformation of his baby's feet. He told himself he was anxious because their child could be left with a limp or possibly never walk at all. That's what he kept telling himself, but it wasn't true.

A layby appeared and Chris pulled over. Cutting the engine, he took the scan photo and his phone from his pocket. He propped the photo on the steering wheel and then accessed the Internet on his phone. He put *club foot* into a search engine and soon learnt that the term covered a number of conditions. Photos and X-rays appeared alongside articles. He glanced between the images on his phone and the scan photo of his baby, comparing them. There were some similarities, but there were also many differences. The lower leg bones seemed longer in the scan photo of his baby than those of a human child, even allowing for the malformation. Although he couldn't be sure.

He searched again, this time using the more general *leg and foot deformities in an unborn baby*. Pages of links to websites appeared – medical, research and forums. He read the information and compared the images. One research paper said that this type of deformity crossed ethnic groups and could be found in some animals, especially primates, which didn't reassure Chris at all. There were pictures of developing foetuses in the uterus, and in the early stages most species looked very similar. *This is because fish, amphibians, reptiles, birds and humans carry very similar ancient genes*, he read with another stab of fear.

He returned to the information on club feet and possible causes . . . *not caused by the foetus's position in the womb . . . often the cause is unknown . . . genetic factors are believed to be involved . . . specific gene changes have been associated with it . . . can be passed down through families.* He went cold.

But this had nothing to do with the Moller Clinic, he told himself. It couldn't. Jan's parents lived over a hundred miles away and had never used the clinic. Jan and he didn't look alike as he and Camile did, so it couldn't be history repeating itself. It was his paranoia. Simply, it was bad luck that their baby had a malformation of his feet, but it wasn't uncommon and could be easily corrected with surgery, just as the doctor had said.

Returning the scan photo and phone to his pocket, Chris started the van and continued the drive to work, desperately trying to believe that what he was telling himself was true.

SIXTY-NINE

'Ian Jennings?'

'Speaking.'

'It's Chris Giles.'

'Hi, how are you?'

'Fine. And yourself?'

'Not bad. We sold our house, but Emma and I are still in touch.'

'I'm sorry to trouble you but . . .' Chris paused and took a deep breath. God. He hoped he was doing the right thing. 'I need to ask you something, and I'd appreciate it if you kept it to yourself.'

'Sure. What is it? Sounds a bit ominous.' Ian tried a small laugh.

'Hopefully it's nothing. I think you may know that I'm in a relationship with Jan Hamlin, who used to be the tenant at Ivy Cottage.'

'Yes, Anne mentioned it.'

'We're expecting a baby.'

'Congratulations.'

'Thank you.' Chris paused again and steeled himself to ask the question. 'Ian, do you still have the records for the Moller Clinic?'

311

'No, I don't. After I'd emailed all those on the list I deleted all my records. Just in case the police came knocking on my door.'

'I see. But you emailed everyone on the list first?' Chris asked.

'Yes. Some were old email addresses and the email bounced back, so I did my best to trace them. I guess a few of the emails might have gone into junk mail, but there was no way of following that up. Why?'

'Our baby has a slight deformity of his feet that could be genetic. I guess I'm overreacting, but I was going to ask you to check to make sure Jan's parents weren't on the list.'

There! He'd said it, Chris thought. He'd voiced his worst fear.

'If Jan didn't receive an email then you can assume they weren't,' Ian replied.

'That's what I thought. Thank you. Sorry to disturb your evening.'

'No problem. I can understand why you're worried after what happened to us, but I'm sure it's fine.'

'Yes, thanks.'

It was 9.30 p.m. and Jan was already upstairs. She was often tired in the evening now and went up to bed before him. She'd left her laptop on the coffee table, charging. Chris looked away, back again, then picking it up, he lifted the lid. It sprang into life. It wasn't password protected. Jan said she didn't have any secrets from him, so she saw no need for passwords on her laptop or phone. He hesitated and then continued.

Ian had said that some of the emails he'd sent had gone to old email addresses. Chris knew that Jan had an old email account she never used now. How often did she check it? He had no idea. He followed the icon to the old mailbox and his mouth went dry. There were dozens of unopened emails from stores, holiday companies, websites where she was a customer, offering special offers. At least two a week, sometimes more. Chris began scrolling down, last week, last month, last year. Checking each email. He found a couple she might want to keep and left them. Right back to December. He saw it and went cold. The email from Carstan Moller Ian had sent. The subject line: *Confidential and Urgent*. With his heart thumping, Chris forced himself to open the email, hoping against all the odds that it was something else entirely.

All hope vanished as he read.

I am sorry to inform you that there has been a dreadful mistake at the Moller Clinic, resulting in too many patients receiving the same donor sperm. If you are planning to start a family, you should have your DNA tested as a matter of urgency to make sure you don't share the same biological father as your partner.

Regards,
Carstan Moller

A buzzing noise filled Chris's ears and the room swam before him. Jan's parents must have used the clinic and never told her. He felt sick and bile rose in his throat. History *was* repeating itself. First Camile and now Jan. His worst nightmare was coming true. Anne had told him some time ago that while most of those who shared Moller's genes looked very similar, not all did.

What were the odds of this happening to him again! He couldn't believe it. He held his head in his hands. They were half brother and sister, just as he and Camile were. He could cope with anything, but not losing Jan. He loved her and wanted to spend the rest of his life with her. There never could or would be anyone else. Ian and Emma had been able to move on, but he knew he couldn't. He was older than

313

them and had been through this before. Without Jan, he was nothing. He couldn't risk losing her. She believed their baby had a small malformation of his feet and it would stay that way for as long as possible.

Blinking back tears, Chris deleted the email and then, closing the laptop, telephoned Anne.

'I need to talk to you urgently. It's about Jan and our baby.'

SEVENTY

'If you really want a home birth then it's fine with me,' Jan said, kissing Chris's cheek. 'It's not a problem. Although shouldn't I still go for the next scan?'

'No need,' Chris said. 'Anne can do it at home here. She's highly experienced and has all the equipment she needs, including a portable ultrasound scanner. I will feel much happier with Anne taking care of you after what happened to Camile.'

Jan looked at him with compassion. 'But what happened to Camile was very different.'

'I know, but things can still go wrong, and if they do, Anne is the best person to deal with it.'

She saw his sadness and concern. 'Chris, I think you're worrying unnecessarily, unless there's something you're not telling me.'

'Of course there isn't. It's simply that Anne is the best.'

'OK,' Jan agreed.

'You'll like her,' Chris persisted. 'I know you didn't think much of her when you first met her in Coleshaw Woods, but that's because you thought I was seeing her. You haven't really got to know her. She's a fantastic midwife and a good friend of mine.'

315

'So you keep telling me, and I've got nothing against Anne. But what will happen if the birth isn't straightforward and I need to go to hospital?'

'I am sure that won't be necessary, but Anne can advise you. She'll be with you every step of the way until you give birth. I'll be there too, of course,' he added.

'You'd better be!' Jan laughed, lightly tapping his arm. 'I'm not doing this alone.'

'You won't have to. Whatever happens in the future, I'll be there for you.'

'And for our baby,' Jan added. 'You'll be there for our son.'

'Yes, of course.'

SEVENTY-ONE

Three months later, Jan was at home with the back door open, gazing out on another beautiful sunny morning. The chickens Chris kept were in their coop at the very bottom of the garden, clucking. Anne had just left, having given her another routine check-up. She was being very well looked after and Jan felt guilty for ever having thought badly of Anne. She was a fantastic midwife – just as Chris had said. Patient, kind, caring, and with a very reassuring manner. She dispelled any fears Jan had about having the baby at home. She was also a lovely person, who Jan now regarded as a friend.

If she thought Anne was slightly evasive about the 'problem' with the baby's feet, she put it down to her not wanting to worry her. 'We'll cross that bridge when we come to it,' she said in her quiet, confident way, so that Jan found herself reassured.

Anne had taken care of all the arrangements that needed to be made for Jan to have a home birth and had updated the hospital records accordingly. Her manner was always pleasant and empathetic, instilling confidence and a sense of wellbeing. Just what a first-time mother needed. Anne never spoke about her other work – looking after the outsiders, although she knew Jan had been told. Once Jan had asked about them and Anne had replied that she probably wouldn't be needed for much longer as the numbers were falling now the clinic had been exposed. But that was all she'd said and Jan didn't ask again.

Chris didn't speak of the outsiders either, although Jan knew he visited Anne at Ivy Cottage sometimes if she needed help. Jan trusted Chris just as she trusted Anne, now she understood what had created and cemented their friendship. Jan sometimes walked along Wood Lane if the weather was good, but she'd never seen the children again. Their secret remained safe with her, as she'd promised Camile and Chris it would. The Moller Clinic had been closed down and Carstan Moller was in prison. She'd seen it on the news.

Jan was about to go outside into the warm sunshine when a sharp pain shot across her abdomen and lower back. Trying to catch her breath, she grabbed the door to steady herself and waited for it to pass. Whatever was that? Not chronic indigestion, not that bad, and it was too early for labour. She still had another nine weeks to go. Perhaps she should phone Anne for advice?

The pain struck again, tearing through her like a red-hot knife, making her cry out. It was like nothing she'd ever experienced before. She held onto the door and prayed it would pass. A moment later she felt a gush of warm fluid as her waters broke.

Oh no, please, no. Panic gripped her. She was going into labour early. What should she do? She needed Chris. She had to call him now. Where was her phone? She turned and saw it on the sofa. Letting go of the door, she made her way across the room. Another contraction took hold and she froze, paralysed with pain until it had passed. No one had told her it would be this bad, and it wasn't supposed to be happening yet. She'd been told first babies were often late, not early.

She needed to sit down – her legs felt weak – but her jeans were sopping wet. Beyond caring, she lowered herself onto the sofa and then called Chris. It went through to his voicemail. Shit! She tried again. He was at work but checked his phone regularly. She tried one more time with the same result and then, unable to keep the desperation from her voice, left a message. 'Chris! I think I'm in labour! Come quickly, please. I'll call Anne, but I need you here.'

She braced herself as another contraction took hold and tried to remember her deep breathing. It didn't help, but eventually the pain eased. Surely the contractions were coming too regularly for the first stage of labour? Fumbling with her phone, she called Anne.

It rang and rang. Please answer, please. Don't leave me here all alone. I might die.

It continued ringing and then mercifully Anne answered.

'You have to come back straight away,' Jan cried. 'I'm in labour. The contractions are coming every minute.'

'Are you sure? That's too soon. Have you timed them?'

'No. But I don't need a bloody clock to know! I'm in agony and my waters have broken. I'm scared, Anne. Please come. Chris isn't picking up. Please . . . I'm . . .' But the sentence vanished into a cry as another contraction took hold.

'I'm on my way,' Anne said. 'It'll take me about ten minutes. Try to calm down and remember your breathing. It's possible it's a false start. But to be safe, I want you to go upstairs and lie on your bed. Put some towels down first to protect the covers. I'll be there.'

'Should I call an ambulance?' Jan wept.

'No, absolutely not.'

And for the first time since Jan had known Anne, she heard anxiety in her voice.

SEVENTY-TWO

Chris was driving as fast as the country roads would allow and fearing the worst. He'd been up a ladder at the house he was working in when his phone had rung. He'd finished what he was doing before coming down, never dreaming it could be Jan in labour. When he'd listened to her message, he'd immediately phoned her. She hadn't answered and then, when he'd called Anne straight after, neither had she. He now tried them again as he drove, but voicemail cut in on both their phones. God, he was worried, and blamed himself for not checking his phone sooner. He knew that these babies were born earlier than others, but there'd been no sign of labour beginning that morning. Nor when he'd called Jan at 9 a.m. when he'd just arrived at work. Anne was supposed to be visiting her for a check-up and had said she'd phone him straight after, but that hadn't happened. He was sure something had gone badly wrong or Anne would have been in touch.

He accelerated and then had to break hard as a car rounded the bend. The driver sounded his horn angrily as he passed. Calm down, Chris told himself. Only another two miles to go.

Usually the birth of these babies was straightforward, Anne had reassured him. But not always, he thought, as he and Camile had found out. Supposing Jan needed to go to hospital, possibly for a caesarean? It was the only procedure Anne couldn't carry out at home. It had never happened before when Anne had been the midwife, but there was a first time for everything. What if Owen – as they'd named him – couldn't be born naturally? He was larger than most of these babies.

Chris's heart clenched as he remembered the look of horror on the faces of the nurses when Camile had given birth. And now it was happening again, only much later in the pregnancy, which made it a whole lot worse. Questions were sure to be asked at the hospital and their secret exposed. Anne would be struck off and Owen, and the others like him, would be taken away to a life of hell. The very thing they'd strived and managed to avoid for so long was about to happen. Chris was devastated.

He made a sharp right turn into his road and his heart stopped. An ambulance was parked outside his house. So was Anne's car. Jan was being taken to hospital! His worst fear had come true. Anne would never have called for an ambulance unless it was serious – life-threatening. Jan's life was in danger. He could lose her.

Coming to an abrupt halt in front of the ambulance, Chris jumped out. As he passed the ambulance, he saw the rear doors were open but there was no one inside. The front door to his house was wide open and he ran in. 'Jan!' he shouted at the top of his voice.

'Up here!' Anne returned.

He took the stairs two at a time and went into their bedroom. The room seemed full. Jan was being helped into a wheelchair by one of the paramedics while the other held a bundle in his arms.

'Jan, my love,' he cried, going to her. 'I'm so sorry.' He didn't dare look at the baby.

'She's all right,' Anne said.

He took Jan's hand and she gave a weak smile. 'I'm exhausted,' she said.

'We're going to the hospital now,' Anne said. 'I was going to ride with them in the ambulance but now you're here you can, and I'll follow in my car.'

She seemed very calm, Chris thought, and looked from her to the paramedics, not really understanding what was going on. There was no sign of horror on their faces and Jan looked worn out but not distraught.

'We need to get going now,' the paramedic holding the baby said.

'Go on, Chris,' Anne told him. 'Go with Jan.'

He went to speak, but Anne said, 'It'll be fine. Your son was early, but the problem with his feet is no worse than expected. I'll explain at the hospital.' She held his gaze.

Chris nodded dumbly and followed the paramedics out of the room. They paused on the landing.

'If you could hold your baby,' the paramedic said, turning to Chris. 'I can help carry the chair with your partner in downstairs.'

He placed the bundle into Chris's arms, but it was a moment before Chris dared look. The little face was slightly wrinkled from the birth and his eyes were tightly closed, premature, but there was no excessive hair or unusual features.

'It's going to be OK,' Anne said, quietly joining him. 'Just keep going.'

SEVENTY-THREE

The journey in the ambulance to hospital seemed to take forever, Chris thought, although they were on a blue light. He sat on one of the seats opposite Jan, who was lying on the couch. He had Owen cradled in his arms, but he was concentrating on Jan. She was dozing, exhausted from the birth and from the pethidine Anne had given her.

Chris sat in a trance, unable to take in what was happening. It's going to be OK, Anne had said. She was now in her car, following the ambulance. Did that mean his baby was going to be able to live a normal life? He dared to hope.

'It can be a bit overwhelming to begin with,' the paramedic riding with them said, seeing his expression. 'Is this your first child?'

'Yes,' Chris said quietly.

'Don't worry. Your partner and baby are fine. He will probably go in an incubator for a while. It's usual with prems.'

Chris nodded. The paramedic had checked Jan's and Owen's vital signs and was now entering her observations on a chart.

The siren sounded to clear traffic and then finally they were pulling into the ambulance park at Coleshaw Hospital.

The rear doors opened and the paramedic who'd been driving appeared. Chris stayed where he was as they wheeled Jan out first. Then Anne appeared. 'Come with me,' she told him.

Chris stood and, carrying his baby, went carefully down the rear steps of the ambulance, then followed the paramedics and Anne into the hospital. It was busy.

'I can take the baby through if you could register your partner and child at reception,' the paramedic said to Chris.

He looked back, unsure.

'Yes, of course,' Anne replied, and touched his arm. 'This way.'

Still in a daze, Chris handed over his baby and went with Anne to reception.

'Jan Hamlin and baby Owen,' Anne said to the receptionist, then gave their details. Anne had taken charge and Chris was grateful.

'Thank you,' the receptionist said once the registration was complete. 'You can go to see them now. Straight down that corridor.' She pointed in the direction they were to go, although Anne knew the way.

They took a few steps away from reception and Anne drew Chris to one side. 'Before you see Jan, I need to tell you something.'

Chris stared back, petrified. 'Why? What's wrong?'

'The baby is all right. Normal,' Anne said, her voice low. 'I've checked him over, so be careful what you say to the staff here.'

'You mean he doesn't have the condition?' Chris asked in disbelief.

'That's right. He's premature, but you've been lucky this time. He will need corrective surgery on his feet, but as far as I can tell that's all that's wrong.'

'I can't believe it,' Chris said, his eyes filling. 'I really can't. Did you know while Jan was pregnant?'

'I dared to hope. I thought we were in with a chance, but I couldn't be certain until he was born. Which is why I didn't say anything to you in case I was wrong. And of course Jan never knew about any of it.'

'Thank goodness she was saved from all these months of worry,' Chris sighed with relief.

'But she needs to know about the email,' Anne said, her face serious. 'I kept quiet as you asked, but it's not right, Chris. You may not be so lucky next time. Apart from that, there's the moral issue of you two being related. You can't ignore it. Technically you are half brother and sister. Most couples parted once they knew. Ian and Emma did. Jan needs to be told.'

'But I couldn't bear to lose her,' Chris said. 'That's why I haven't told her. She's my life. It feels so right being with her. I can't tell her now and risk losing her. We have a child.'

'You must,' Anne said. 'She has to know. It's not right to keep it from her. Supposing you have another child and it has the condition?'

'We won't have any more children.'

'Chris, I won't be part of your deception any longer. If you don't tell Jan, I will.'

SEVENTY-FOUR

Chris gazed lovingly at Owen, now awake in his crib. He was happy and contented, even though both his legs were in plaster. Jan was sitting on the sofa, talking to him as he grinned and gurgled. At eight weeks old, he was steadily putting on weight and meeting all the developmental milestones. The consultant paediatrician had said that surgery probably wouldn't be necessary and Owen's legs could be straightened using manipulation and plaster casts, which was a huge relief.

Chris knew how lucky they'd been, but Anne's words were constantly in his thoughts. He hadn't told Jan yet and he needed to. Anne had given him an ultimatum: tell Jan by the end of the weekend or I will. It was Sunday evening now and he was running out of time.

He didn't blame Anne. She was doing what she thought was right. If Jan wasn't told and they had another baby, as she wanted, it could have the condition. But he dreaded losing her, which he feared would happen when she found out they were related.

Aware that he couldn't put it off any longer, Chris steeled himself and went over and sat on the sofa beside Jan. She turned to look at him and smiled.

326

Chris took her hand. 'You know how much you both mean to me? How much I love you?'

'Yes, of course,' she laughed. 'I love you too.'

He hesitated and took a deep breath, summoning his courage. 'Jan, there's something I have to tell you, something that I should have told you much sooner.'

Her face immediately grew serious. 'What is it, Chris?' She took her hand away. 'You're not having an affair?'

'No, of course not. Nothing like that.' He hesitated again. 'You remember I told you about Ian Jennings, in connection with the Moller Clinic? He emailed all those on Moller's list to warn them they could be affected, and tell them to get their DNA checked.'

'Yes, vaguely, but what's that got to do with us?'

'You were on that list, Jan. You received an email, but it went to your old email address.'

'What! How do you know?'

'I looked on your laptop. I'm sorry, but I needed to check. Your parents must have used the Moller Clinic. I've been worried sick all these months. Owen is going to be OK, but any future children we have could be affected. Also – and this is the most difficult part – it means that biologically we are half brother and sister. I'm so sorry, Jan. I should have told you sooner, but I couldn't risk losing you.' He looked at her with pain and misery, expecting the worst – tears, cries of anguish and utter rejection.

Yet she remained calm, composed and cool, which seemed even worse. What was she thinking? What would she say and do?

'That's a lot to take in,' she finally said. 'Did Anne know all this time? I guess she did.'

'Yes. I'm sorry. She wanted me to tell you straight away. I made her promise not to. But she says she can't live with the

327

lie any longer and you must know. I'm scared of losing you, Jan. I love you so much. I couldn't face life without you.'

He tried to read her expression, but it was impossible.

'It was very wrong of you not to tell me,' she said at last.

'Yes, I know. I'm so sorry.'

'It was also wrong of you to look at my emails without me knowing. I trusted you.'

'Yes. But you can see why I did it, can't you?' he asked in desperation.

'A little, I suppose. Even so . . .'

'You won't leave me, will you?' he cried. He took her hand again. 'Not all couples like us have separated. We can stay together, but we won't have any more children. I know we share the same biological father, but it's not like we were brought up as brother and sister, so it's not immoral. You won't leave me, will you?' he said again.

'No,' Jan said. 'I won't leave you.'

He hardly dared to believe. 'Thank you. Thank you so much. I'll make it up to you, I promise. I won't ever hide anything from you again.'

'Good. But if you and Anne had told me sooner, I could have saved you both a lot of worry. There is something you don't know.'

'What do you mean?' he asked apprehensively.

'That email was only partially correct. My parents *did* use the Moller Clinic. But I've checked, and it was definitely to conceive my older brother, not me. Mum miscarried that baby at sixteen weeks and then they had me naturally. Moller must have assumed I was his, or Ian made a mistake. We're not related, Chris.'

He stared at her, astounded. 'Are you sure?'

'Yes.'

'Why didn't you tell me?'

'I didn't want to worry you unnecessarily with talk of the

328

clinic after all you've been through. So we can stay together and have another child. But if you snoop in my emails again, I won't forgive you.' She kissed his cheek. 'Now you'd better tell Anne and put her out of her misery.'

'I will.'

Although this book is fiction, atavism exists and this story was inspired by true events. A number of clinics offering donor insemination have been discovered to be using only one donor – that of the founder of the clinic.

Suggested topics
for reading-group discussion

Describe Ivy Cottage and the village of Merryless.

The author builds suspense from different viewpoints. As a writing technique, what advantage does this have?

How does Tinder add to the atmosphere and suspense of the plot?

Which characters in the book do you have most sympathy with, and why?

All the main characters are faced with moral dilemmas – for example, should Ian tell Emma that David survived? Discuss these dilemmas. Are their decisions correct given the circumstances?

Why might parents not tell their child they were conceived by donor sperm? Would you?

Ian and Emma, Chelsea and Grant, Chris and Camile and other couples are biologically half brother and sister. Should they separate? What would you do?

Secrecy is maintained to protect the outsiders. What would be the likely outcome if their existence became known?

Could DC Beth Mayes and DC Matt Davis have done more to investigate the concerns raised by Mrs Slater and Ian? If so, how might their actions have changed the course of the novel?

HE SAYS HE WANTS TO SAVE YOU...

BUT DOES HE?

How much do you know about the couple next door?

When Emily and Ben move in next door to Dr Burman and his wife Alisha, they are keen to get to know their new neighbours. Outgoing and sociable, Emily tries to befriend the doctor's wife, but Alisha is strangely subdued, barely leaving the house, and terrified of answering the phone.

When Emily goes missing a few weeks later, Ben is plunged into a panic. His wife has left him a note, but can she really have abandoned him for another man? Or has Emily's curiosity about the couple next door led her straight into danger?

AVAILABLE NOW

One moment she's there

The next she's gone...

Have you seen Leila?

8-year-old Leila Smith has seen and heard
things that no child should ever have to.
On the Hawthorn Estate, where she lives,
she often stays out after dark to avoid going home.

But what Leila doesn't know is that someone
has been watching her in the playground.
One day, she disappears without a trace...

The police start a nationwide search
but it's as if Leila has vanished into thin air.
Who kidnapped her? What do they want?
**Will she return home safely
or is she lost forever?**

AVAILABLE NOW

Lisa Stone also writes under the name of

CATHY GLASS

Don't miss her latest book...

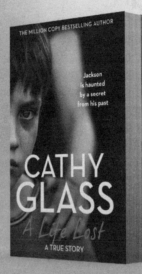

THE MILLION COPY BESTSELLING AUTHOR

Jackson is haunted by a secret from his past

CATHY GLASS

A Life Lost

A TRUE STORY

Jackson is aggressive, confrontational and often volatile.
His mother, Kayla, is crippled with grief after
tragically losing her husband and eldest son.
Struggling to cope, she puts Jackson into foster care.

Cathy, his carer, encourages Jackson to talk about
what has happened to his family, but he just won't engage.
His actions continue to test and worry everyone.

Then, in a dramatic turn of events, the true
reason for Jackson's behaviour comes to light ...

AVAILABLE NOW